Militiamen, Rangers, and Redcoats

The Military in Georgia,
1754—1776

The publication of this book
is made possible through a generous grant from
the Watson-Brown Foundation, Inc.,
Thomson, Georgia.

Militiamen, Rangers, and Redcoats

The Military in Georgia, 1754—1776

James M. Johnson

Mercer University Press
Macon, Georgia

ISBN 0-86554-379-8

Militiamen, Rangers, and Redcoats
The Military in Georgia, 1754–1776

by James Michael Johnson

copyright © 1992
Mercer University Press, Macon, Georgia 31207 USA

Library of Congress Cataloging-in-Publication Data

Johnson, James Michael.
Militiamen, rangers, and redcoats : the military in Georgia,
1754–1776 / James Michael Johnson.
xviii+208pp.   6x9" (15x23 cm.)
Includes bibliographical references and index.
ISBN 0-88886554-379-8 (alk. paper)
1. Georgia—History, Military. 2. Georgia—Military—History—
18th century. 3. Georgia—History—Colonial period, ca. 1600–1775.
I. Title.
F289.J683 1992
975.8'02—dc20   91-27412
                                                    CIP

Contents

To

LOIS,

KRISTIN,

and

ADAM

Acknowledgments

A project such as this book spans many years and depends upon the assistance, guidance, and support of many people. I thank I. B. Holley, Jr. of Duke University for his help with both argumentation and style. Theodore Ropp, Peter H. Wood, and Robert F. Durden, also of Duke, likewise provided insight into the topic. As heads of the Department of History of the United States Military Academy, Brigadier Generals Thomas E. Griess and Roy K. Flint and Colonel Robert A. Doughty in turn provided time during breaks in the academic schedule for me to work on the project and encouraged and supported me in my efforts. Without them I would never have had the opportunity to be both a soldier and a historian.

The following people provided assistance and information during the course of my original research: Pat Bryant, Marion R. Hemperley, and Janice Gayle Blake of the Georgia Surveyor General Department; Ruth Corry, Edwin Bridges, Gail Miller, and Len Cleveland of the Georgia Department of Archives and History; Robert M. Willingham, Jr., and J. Larry Gulley of the University of Georgia Libraries; Anthony Dees, Lilla Mills Hawes, Connie Stephenson, and Gordon B. Smith of the Georgia Historical Society; Ken Thomas and Robert B. Davis, Jr. of the Historic Preservation Section of the Georgia Department of Natural Resources; Robert E. Schnare, Alan C. Aimone, and Marie Capps of the United States Military Academy Library Special Collections. I am indebted to Jean Schucker for the two original sketches of the ranger and the militiamen of Georgia. I appreciate the support and patience of Marvin Bergman and Edd Rowell of Mercer University Press. I thank also the USMA Faculty Development and Research Fund for the grant that helped to make this book possible. Finally, I could never have sustained my efforts without the love and support of my wife, Lois, and my children, Kristin and Adam. I thank them for being content at times to see only the back of my head as I sat at the computer keyboard.

I acknowledge my indebtedness to each of these people, the institutions that they represent, and the others whose contributions and encouragement made this endeavor possible. Mistakes of fact or interpretation that remain are entirely my own. The views expressed herein are those of the author and do not purport to reflect the position of the United States Military Academy, the Department of the Army, or the Department of Defense.

List of Illustrations

Introduction

Although the United States Army traces its lineage from the formation of the Continental Army in 1775, the roots of the army and the American heritage of the citizen-soldier are firmly grounded in the colonial military establishments that predated its official birth. In several colonies, including Georgia, militiamen, full-time provincial troops (primarily the rangers), and British regulars performed their respective military functions side by side throughout the early years of American history. These forces faced the timeless challenges of war and peace, lauded or damned, neglected or supported, as the times and the dangers dictated.

Contemporary debates about the relative capabilities of professional or citizen soldiers surfaced first in America in the colonial context and raised, from that point on, the question of the proper relationship and mixture of regulars and militia (or reservists). Answers to the questions raised in these debates are particularly relevant today as soldiers of the United States Army Reserve and the Army National Guard outnumber their Active Army counterparts and already fill the majority of the combat service support units.[1]

Despite the occasional presence of British regulars and full-time colonial soldiers, the militia—the focus of this study—was the force upon which the early settlers generally had to rely for local protection and even survival during the years before the American Revolution. The degree of need and thus the emphasis given to the maintenance of strong militia forces depended upon the period of time, the individual colony involved, the immediacy of external or internal threats, and the number of British troops actually in the colony. While generically the same as an English institution, the militia varied, therefore, to some degree from province to province in terms of organization and preparedness.[2]

---

[1]Don Higginbotham, *The War of American Independence: Military Attitudes, Policies, and Practice, 1763–1789* (New York: Macmillan, 1971) 16; John Shy, *Toward Lexington: The Role of the British Army in the Coming of the American Revolution* (Princeton University Press, 1965); Kenneth J. Hagan and William R. Roberts, eds., *Against All Enemies: Interpretations of American Military History from Colonial Times to the Present* (New York: Greenwood Press, 1986) 363.

[2]John W. Shy, "A New Look at Colonial Militia," *William and Mary Quarterly* 20 (April 1963): 175-76. Recent studies include Lawrence Delbert Cress, *Citizens in Arms:*

Although early Americans generally recognized, exaggerated, or perhaps even took for granted the importance of the militia, later historians, publicists, and soldiers have made its worth the subject of intense debate. Until relatively recently this attention had been directed in most cases to the poor performances by militiamen when in combat against regulars during the periodic colonial wars and, more to the point, during the American Revolution. Brevet Major General Emory Upton's historical arguments against the militia and for regulars, published in 1904 as *The Military Policy of the United States*, made such a lasting impression that they became the standard with which all later critiques and proposals would have to contend. As late as 1942, Colonel William Ganoe recounted in his *History of the United States Army* that the militia under General Sullivan at Brandywine "gave way like sheep."[3]

Major General John McAuley Palmer, building upon the ideas of General George Washington, Major General John A. Logan (a citizen-soldier during the Civil War), and Major General Leonard Wood (army chief of staff from 1910 to 1914), presented arguments to counter the Uptonian strand of thought.[4] A professional soldier himself, Palmer none-theless acknowledged that the modern nation in arms would have to depend upon trained citizen-soldiers in time of war. Within the American experience, World War I had been proof enough. Drawing on George Washington's "Sentiments on a Peace Establishment" of 1783 (which Palmer had rediscovered) as a warrant for his own ideas, Palmer, in both *Washington, Lincoln, Wilson: Three War Statesmen* and *America in Arms*, advocated an organized citizen army sustained by universal

---

The Army and the Militia in American Society to the War of 1812 (Chapel Hill: University of North Carolina Press, 1982); John K. Mahon, *History of the Militia and the National Guard* (New York: Macmillan, 1983); T. Harry Williams, *The History of American Wars from 1745 to 1918* (New York: Alfred A. Knopf, 1981); and Fred Anderson, *A People's Army: Massachusetts Soldiers and Society in the Seven Years' War* (Chapel Hill: University of North Carolina Press, 1984). None of these gives the Georgia militia its due.

[3]Brevet Major General Emory Upton, *The Military Policy of the United States* (Washington: U.S. Government Printing Office, 1904) xiii-xiv, 15, 67; William Addleman Ganoe, *The History of the United States Army* (New York: D. Appleton-Century, 1942; rpt., Ashton, MD: Eric Lunberg, 1964) 43.

[4]See Russell Weigley, *Towards an American Army: Military Thought from Washington to Marshall* (New York: Columbia University Press, 1962) chaps. 2, 8, 12.

military training.[5] Although such training never advanced beyond the service requirements of the colonial militia, the incorporation of the concept of a citizen army into the National Defense Act of 1920 represented a dramatic challenge to the Uptonian school of the regular long espoused by the army general staff. In the process of strengthening the policy of defense of the country, Palmer did much to rehabilitate the militia by noting that "during the American Revolution, the American militia, when properly trained and organized, had given a good account of itself."[6] Palmer had planted the seeds.

Walter Millis, with the publication in 1956 of his book *Arms and Men*, continued the efforts begun by Palmer and added another dimension to the contributions of the militiamen in the Revolution. Without diminishing the role of the Continentals, he provided an alternative to the negative image of the militiamen so long held by soldiers and others of the Uptonian school. In evaluating the performance of the militia in the War of Independence, he found that "while the Regular armies marched and fought more or less ineffectually, it was the militia which presented the greatest single impediment to Britain's only practicable weapon, that of counter-revolution."[7]

Walter Millis's reinterpretation of the part played by the militia in the American Revolution and John Shy's call for additional study have both borne fruit as an increasing number of scholars have devoted their efforts to this colonial and Revolutionary military institution. Several generalizations about the colonial militia have emerged.

First, because the king generally did not provide troops to protect the early colonists against the Indians, the French, and the Spanish, they had to protect themselves. This they did as militiamen, using a system transplanted to the New World from England. Although the specifics of the militia laws differed from colony to colony, able-bodied men of

---

[5]John McAuley Palmer, *Washington, Lincoln, Wilson: Three War Statesmen* (Garden City, NY: Doubleday, Doran, 1930); idem, *America in Arms: The Experience of the United States with Military Organization* (New Haven: Yale University Press, 1941) 165-90. Also, see Weigley, *Towards an American Army*, chap. 13; and I. B. Holley, Jr., *General John M. Palmer, Citizen Soldiers, and the Army of a Democracy* (Westport, CT: Greenwood Press, 1982) 555-56.

[6]Palmer, *America in Arms*, 21-22.

[7]Walter Millis, *Arms and Men: A Study in American Military History* (New York: Capricorn Books, 1956) 34.

military age—generally sixteen to sixty—bore the obligation of service. Under the command of officers holding commissions from the colonial governors, these men in most cases armed themselves and trained for local defense at musters held at prescribed intervals throughout the year. Custom, term of service (usually three months), and legal and economic considerations dictated that the militia would generally be a local defensive force. As might be expected, those colonies most threatened, such as Virginia and Massachusetts in the seventeenth century, South Carolina until the founding of Georgia, and then Georgia itself, depended most upon a healthy militia.[8]

Second, by the mid-eighteenth century, as settlers moved westward and the direct threats by Indians against the coastal centers of population diminished, the colonists increasingly came to depend on provincial and regular soldiers to police the backcountry. In these cases, the militia served as a general training base and as a manpower pool from which to draw volunteers and conscripts for punitive expeditions and at times for frontier defense.[9] Third, as full-time soldiers and "expeditionary" soldiers assumed a greater responsibility for external defense, the standing militia companies served as a defensive reserve, provided internal security, and fulfilled ceremonial or social functions. In the South, for example, the fear of insurrection by Negro slaves led colonial assemblies to provide for slave patrols manned by militiamen. Finally, as John Mahon has aptly pointed out, the militia always "remained the mechanism for large-scale mobilization in case of an attack serious enough to threaten the life of the colonies."[10]

---

[8]Cress, *Citizens in Arms*, 4; Mahon, *History*, 19, 22, 32; Williams, *History of American Wars*, 8-9; Douglas Edward Leach, *Arms for Empire: A Military History of the British Colonies in North America, 1607–1763* (New York: Macmillan, 1973) 9-38.

[9]Mahon, *History*, 33; Cress, *Citizens in Arms*, 3-5, 41; Anderson, *A People's Army*, 26-27; Theodore Henry Jabbs, "The South Carolina Colonial Militia, 1663–1733" (Ph.D. diss., University of North Carolina, 1973) 13-14, 310-11; Frederick Stokes Aldridge, "Organization and Administration of the Militia System of Colonial Virginia" (Ph.D. diss., American University, 1964) 230-31.

[10]Mahon, *History*, 22; David William Cole, "The Organization and Administration of the South Carolina Militia System, 1670–1783" (Ph.D. diss., University of South Carolina, 1953) iii-iv; Jabbs, "South Carolina Colonial Militia," 454; James Kirby Martin and Mark Edward Lender, *A Respectable Army: The Military Origins of the Republic, 1763–1789* (Arlington Heights, IL: Harlan Davidson, 1982) 16-20.

Many of the roles of the colonial militia carried over into the American Revolution. Militia companies provided essential reserves of manpower for the Continental Army, harassed British units that ventured beyond their protected enclaves, stymied British attempts to use Loyalist forces as a mechanism for counterrevolution, and, perhaps most important, acted as the ultimate instruments of political coercion or internal security.[11] Thus it is obvious that the militia played a significant role in the colonial period and in the American Revolution, particularly when it is viewed in a larger context than just that of fighting British regulars. (Under the right leadership and conditions, militiamen even acquitted themselves well in pitched battles such as Bunker Hill, Cowpens, and Guilford Court House).

Although the structures of the militias of some colonies have been examined in considerable detail, the militia of Georgia has to date been neglected.[12] This is surprising for several reasons. First, the relatively short duration of the colonial experience—forty-three years—has made Georgia an attractive subject for important political, social, and economic

---

[11]Millis, *Arms and Men*, 34-35; John Shy, *A People Numerous and Armed: Reflections on the Military Struggle for American Independence* (New York: Oxford University Press, 1976) 217-24; Higginbotham, *War*, 7-18, 273-75; idem, "Militia in the War of Independence: A Traditional Institution with Revolutionary Responsibilities" (Paper delivered at the United States Military Academy Symposium on the American Revolutionary War, West Point, NY, 1976); Roy K. Flint, "The Web of Victory: Revolutionary Warfare in Eighteenth Century America," Department of History, United States Military Academy, West Point, NY, 1977; Clyde R. Ferguson, "Carolina and Georgia Patriot and Loyalist Militia in Action, 1778–1783," in *The Southern Experience in the American Revolution*, ed. Jeffrey J. Crowe and Larry E. Tise (Chapel Hill: University of North Carolina Press, 1978) 175, 182, 184, 194; Allan R. Millett, "Whatever Became of the Militia in the History of the American Revolution?" (Paper delivered to the Society of the Cincinnati, Washington DC, 24 October 1986) 8, 11-12; John Morgan Dederer, *Making Bricks without Straw: Nathanael Greene's Southern Campaign and Mao Tse-Tung's Mobile War* (Manhattan, KS: Sunflower University Press, 1983) 45-46; Williams, *History of American Wars*, 41; Mahon, *History*, 38, 44-45.

[12]For a summary of studies of the colonial militia in general and those of the individual colonies, see Robin Higham, ed., *A Guide to the Sources of United States Military History* (Hamden, CT: Archon Books, 1975) 72-73; for the legal aspects, see Arthur Vollmer, *Background of Selected Service*, mon. no. 1, vol. 2, *Military Obligation: The American Tradition: A Compilation of the Enactments of Compulsion from the Earliest Settlements of the Original Colonies in 1607 through the Articles of Confederation 1789* (Washington: U.S. Government printing Office, 1947).

studies; this appealing compactness applies equally to a military study.[13] Second, the British government founded Georgia as a military buffer colony, although this fact is generally obscured by the better-known philanthropic motivation of giving a number of the "worthy poor" of England a second chance in the New World.[14] In this role Georgia had to react to pressures faced earlier in the colonial period by other colonies bordered by Indian lands or territories garrisoned by forces of other European powers. Third, these elements of a hostile wilderness environment and the influence of neighboring colonies—particularly South Carolina—spawned a military tradition that carried over to the first skirmishes of the American Revolution. At the heart of this military tradition was reliance on a healthy militia. Next, the presence of both provincial and regular troops in the colony during long stretches of time provides an interesting basis for the comparison of their respective functions and capabilities with those of the militia. Finally, the political divisions within the colony until very late in the Revolutionary crisis had military as well as purely political implications. As a consequence, each of the military forces, but particularly the militia, was caught in the escalating struggle between the colonies and Great Britain during the years from 1763 to 1776.

This book examines the role of the military establishment of Georgia during the crucial period from 1754 to 1776 and devotes particular attention to the militia. It addresses three questions. First, what were the military institutions in Georgia in the colonial period, and how did they develop? Second, what were their respective roles in both colonial and early Revolutionary society, and did these roles differ from those performed by similar forces in neighboring colonies? Finally, of the

---

[13]Kenneth Coleman, *Colonial Georgia: A History* (New York: Charles Scribner's Sons, 1976) xvi; William A. Abbot, *The Royal Governors of Georgia, 1754–1775* (Chapel Hill: University of North Carolina Press, 1976) 33; Harold E. Davis, *The Fledgling Province: Social and Cultural Life in Colonial Georgia, 1733–1776* (Chapel Hill: University of North Carolina Press, 1976) 3.

[14]For the latest treatment, see Coleman, *Colonial Georgia*, 17, and Davis, *Fledgling Province*, 4, 8-9; see also Clarence L. Ver Steeg, *Origins of a Southern Mosaic: Studies of Early Carolina and Georgia*, Mercer University Lamar Memorial Lectures, no. 17 (Athens: University of Georgia Press, 1975) 74; Phinizy Spalding, "Colonial Period," in *A History of Georgia*, gen. ed. Kenneth Coleman (Athens: University of Georgia Press, 1977) 16-17.

forces present, was the militia a pivotal element in the beginnings of the American Revolution in Georgia? The results of this quest should contribute to a greater understanding of the early militiamen of Georgia, the citizen-soldiers of the other colonies, and their descendants who have made contributions in war and peace.

Chapter 1

The Buffer Colony: Roots of a Military Heritage

James Wright, royal governor of the English colony of Georgia, "attended by a number of gentlemen" and the militia Troop of Horse, set out from Savannah on 20 October 1763 bound for Augusta, about 140 miles to the north on the Savannah River.[1] Upon arriving at his destination, Wright was to meet with three other southern governors, the superintendent of Indian Affairs, and the headmen of the neighboring Indian tribes to discuss colonial-Indian relations in the aftermath of the British victory in the Seven Years' War (or, as it was referred to in America, the French and Indian War).[2] With the elimination of the French and the Spanish from the Southeast, successful reconciliation with these Indian tribes held out the promise of a future of peace that was particularly attractive to Georgia.

As a buffer colony on the southern frontier of the British empire in North America, Georgia, since its founding thirty years before, had been the point of contact between the major European powers and their Indian allies. As a result of these encounters, survival itself had been threatened

---

[1]*Georgia Gazette*, Savannah, 20 October 1763, 3; the *Gazette* was the only colonial newspaper. See Francis Harper, ed., "Diary of a Journey through the Carolinas, Georgia, and Florida from July 1, 1765, to April 10, 1766," *Transactions of the American Philosophical Society* 33, pt. 1 (December 1942): 28, for John Bartram's estimate of the distance, and, for that of Governor Wright, "Report of Governor Sir James Wright to Lord Dartmouth on the Condition of the Colony, September 20, 1773," in *Collections of the Georgia Historical Society* (Savannah: Georgia Historical Society, 1873) 3: 161, hereinafter cited as *Collections*.

[2]John Richard Alden, *John Stuart and the Southern Colonial Frontier* (Ann Arbor: University of Michigan Press, 1944) 182-85.

upon several occasions. In these years of uncertainty, concern for defense had been paramount. The dawning of a new era in British-American-Indian affairs had significant implications for a colony in which prosperity, philanthropic experimentation, and growth had been subordinated to military necessity.

The military escort accompanying the governor on his diplomatic mission to Augusta, aside from its ceremonial function, reflected both the military roots of the past and the continuing awareness of the potential hazards present within a frontier colony, even during a time of relative peace. The Troop of Horse, commanded by Captain Lachlan McGillivray, had an authorized strength of 200 men of "substance." By law it served as the personal escort of the governor and therefore would remain with him throughout his entire journey.[3] During the march, at planned intervals, additional militia units drawn from the localities along the way would augment these mounted soldiers of the official party until they reached the relative protection of the garrison of about thirty provincial rangers and thirty-five Independents, or British regulars, at Augusta.

The militia companies joining the party as it passed through their respective districts were drawn from the First Regiment of Foot, located in the parishes of Christ Church and St. Matthew, and were under the command of Colonel Noble Jones. The first of these companies, Captain William Ewen's Third, greeted the party about five miles outside of Savannah and remained with it as far as the village of Abercorn, the end of the day's journey of some fourteen to seventeen miles. The next day the Fifth Company of the town of Ebenezer, commanded by Captain Theobald Kieffer, and then the Ninth Company of the Bethany District, commanded by Captain Conrade Rahn, in turn marched with the governor. At Barton's Branch, north of Mount Pleasant, the militiamen of the latter company turned over their charges to a detachment of provincial rangers who had preceded them from Savannah a day earlier.[4]

---

[3]*Gazette*, 27 October 1763, 3; "Governors' Commissions," vol. B-1 (1754–1778), Georgia Department of Archives and History, Atlanta, 133; Allen D. Candler et al., eds., *The Colonial Records of the State of Georgia*, 32 vols. to date (Atlanta and Athens: Printers and publishers vary, 1904–1916, 1978–1979, 1982, 1985, 1986, 1989) 18:14-16, hereinafter cited as *CRG*.

[4]The locations of the militia companies and the officers of all of the militia and the provincial units are based upon an analysis of "Governors' Commissions" (see 61, 87, 101,

About fifty rangers—almost one-third of the total force in the colony—were present at the rendezvous for the journey through the sparsely populated parishes of St. George and St. Paul. Led by Second Lieutenant Moses Nunez Rivers of the First Troop and Third Lieutenant Mungo Graham of the Second Troop, these mounted, colonial troops of the English Crown in all likelihood would be with the governor until he returned to Savannah. Although lacking the polish and splendor of British regulars on parade, the militiamen and rangers with Governor Wright nonetheless must have been an impressive sight as they passed among their fellow provincials.

Despite the relative peacefulness of the colony as Governor Wright rode toward Augusta, strong government and reasonable self-sufficiency had been possible in Georgia only with the advent of Crown control. Prior to 1754 Georgia had been administered from London by a group of twenty-one trustees to whom King George II had granted a proprietary charter in 1732.[5] Trustees had hoped to emphasize the philanthropic and mercantilistic purposes enumerated in this charter; however, these hopes were soon overshadowed by the third element of the document.[6] Rather than serving primarily as a refuge for the worthy poor of England or as

---

120, 121, 132); see also *Gazette*, 20 October 1763, 3; 27 October 1763, 3; Allen D. Candler, ed., "The Colonial Records of the State of Georgia," 13 vols. (Atlanta: Georgia Department of Archives and History, 1937, typescript) 28, pt. 2B:428, hereinafter cited as *CRG, TS*. These volumes of typescripts begin with vol. 27 of the 39 vols. of "Colonial Records." Kenneth Coleman and Milton Ready have edited and published through vol. 32 as *CRG*. Citations will refer to the applicable vol. Distances are based on a photostat of a map by Lieutenant Colonel Archibald Campbell, "Sketch of the Northern Frontiers of Georgia, extending from the Mouth of the River Savannah to the Town of Augusta," 1780, Surveyor General Department, Office of the Secretary of State, Atlanta; also see Robert Scott Davis, Jr., ed., *Encounters on a March through Georgia in 1779: The Maps and Memorandums of John Wilson, Engineer, 71st Highland Regiment* (Sylvania GA: Partridge Pond Press, 1986) 49.

[5]Sarah B. Gober Temple and Kenneth Coleman, *Georgia Journeys: Being an Account of the Lives of Georgia's Original Settlers and Many Other Early Settlers from the Founding of the Colony in 1732 until the Institution of Royal Government in 1754* (Athens: University of Georgia Press, 1961) xi; for a copy of the charter, see George White, *Historical Collections of Georgia* (New York: Pudney & Russell, 1855) 1.

[6]Temple and Coleman, *Georgia Journeys*, x; Albert Berry Says, *A Constitutional History of Georgia, 1732-1968* (Athens: University of Georgia Press, 1948; rev. ed., 1970) 4-5.

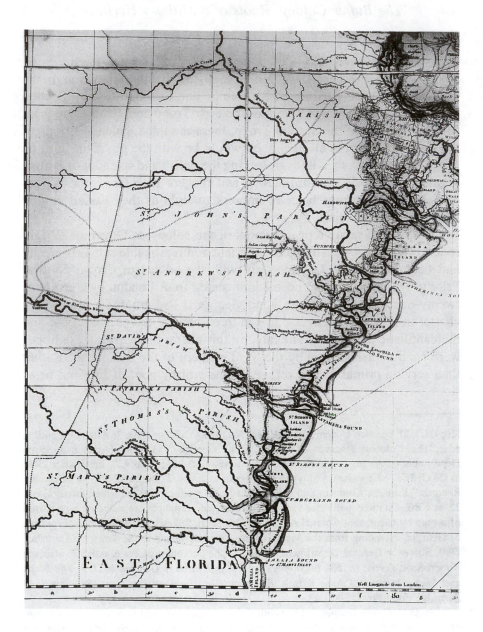

Fig. 1: A Map of Georgia and Florida. Courtesy of the Hargrett Rare Book and Manuscript Library, University of Georgia.

a source of raw materials for the industries of the mother country, Georgia, after the first colonists landed there in February 1733, became a buffer colony to protect British southern interests.[7] The military escort accompanying Governor Wright in his ride to Augusta indicated the major impact that military affairs had had on the development of the colony.

The creation of a colony as a buffer in the disputed zone between South Carolina and the Spanish Floridas, the French territories to the west, and Indian tribal lands predetermined that defensive concerns would dominate the affairs of the early settlers—a condition still familiar to Governor Wright as late as 1763.[8] As the two ward against the Spanish—the War of Jenkins' Ear and King George's War—interrupted agricultural and other economic pursuits, this domination became so complete that, at least through 1749, the military was almost the principal industry of the colony; of the £135,200 granted by Parliament to Georgia during these years, £100,000 went for defense between 1738 and 1743 alone.[9]

Realizing that the first priority must be survival, in the decade from 1733 to 1743 James Oglethorpe, a trustee and the first de facto chief executive, built up and employed a three-part military establishment.[10]

---

[7]For the definitive treatment of this aspect of proprietary history, see Larry Ivers, *British Drums on the Southern Frontier: The Military Colonization of Georgia, 1733–1749* (Chapel Hill: University of North Carolina Press, 1974) 10; also see the dated yet comprehensive study of other aspects of this period in James Ross McCain, *Georgia as a Proprietary Province* (Boston: Richard G. Badger, 1917) 21. For the most recent accounts, see Davis, *Fledgling Province*, 8-9; Coleman, *Colonial Georgia*; idem, History.

[8]White, *Historical Collections*, 1, General James Oglethorpe to Trustees, 26 July 1736, "Letters from General Oglethorpe to the Trustees of the Colony and Others, from October 1735 to August 1744," *Collections* 3:41; Daniel J. Boorstin, *The Americans: The Colonial Experience* (New York: Random House, 1958) 94; Coleman, *Colonial Georgia*, chap. 6.

[9]Ivers, *British Drums*, 214; Evarts B. Greene and Virginia D. Harrington, *American Population before the Federal Census of 1790* (New York: Columbia University Press, 1932) 180; Oglethorpe to Sir Jos. Jekyll, 19 September 1738; to Trustees, 19 September and 7 October 1738, *Collections* 3:49-50, 53; U.S. Department of Commerce, Bureau of the Census, *Historical Statistics of the United States, Colonial Times to 1957* (Washington: U.S. Government Printing Office, 1960) 757, hereinafter cited as *Historical Statistics*; Coleman, *Colonial Georgia*, 74, 90, 118; Ver Steeg, *Origins*, 89; Davis, *Fledgling Province*, 11-14.

[10]Coleman, *Colonial Georgia*, xv.

The three types of forces providing protection for Governor Wright and the colony in 1763 traced their roots from the local militia, provincial forces, and British regulars formed and nurtured by General Oglethorpe. Although his personal faith as a soldier rested with the regulars, Oglethorpe's own description of the individual soldier with a spade in one hand and a sword in the other depicted the colony's ultimate dependence upon the settlers themselves for the performance of military duties. The settlers, of course, composed the manpower pool for the militia, the only organic and relatively numerous force available for the first few years.[11]

Following long-standing colonial precedent, the charter of the colony had prescribed that the final burden of defense would rest upon the local militia. Circumstances would dictate that the militia would remain so encumbered throughout the colonial period.[12] The trustees delegated to Oglethorpe the power "to appoint such Commander, or other Officer or Officers, as he shall think fit, to train and Exercise the Militia in Georgia," but it failed to appoint him the overall commander. The governor of South Carolina was the official commander of the Georgia militia until 1738.[13] Fortunately for Oglethorpe, the first settlers had at least some familiarity with the militia, and the system itself was not tested during this period of greatest vulnerability.

Although the militia in England had begun to lose its vitality as early as 1690, it had remained a traditional feature of English life, despite its relative ineffectiveness, and had proven particularly adaptable when transplanted to the colonies in the New World.[14] To those colonists recently

---

[11]Oglethorpe to Trustees, 28 May 1742, *Collections* 3:122. Charles Wesley described the garrisons scattered throughout the colony as early as 1736; see Robert G. McPherson, ed., *The Journal of the Earl of Egmont: Abstract of the Trustees Proceedings for Establishing the Colony of Georgia, 1732–1738* (Athens: University of Georgia Press, 1962) 217-18.

[12]White, *Historical Collections*, 12; Albert B. Saye, ed., *Georgia's Charter of 1732* (Athens: University of Georgia Press, 1942) 59-61.

[13]*CRG* 1:87, 228; McPherson, *Journal*, 9, 105, 122; Ivers, *British Drums*, 29; White, *Historical Collections*, 12.

[14]J.R. Western, *The English Militia in the Eighteenth Century: The Story of a Political Issue, 1660–1802* (London: Routledge & Kegan Paul, 1965) 73; Correlli Barnett, *Britain and Her Army, 1509–1970: A Military, Political, and Social Survey* (New York: William Morrow, 1970) 36, 171; Shy, *Toward Lexington*, 3.

Fig. 2: General James Oglethorpe. Courtesy of Hargrett Rare Book and Manuscript Library, University of Georgia.

arrived from the mother country, the militia most familiar to them was that defined in 1706 by an English editor as " a certain Number of the Inhabitants of the City and Country formed into Regular Bodies, and train'd up in the Art of War, for the Defence and Security of the Kingdom."[15] Oglethorpe built upon this familiarity by organizing and drilling the first settlers both before they left England and when they were aboard ship. Peter Gordon, an upholsterer by trade and the commander of a tithing, or detachment of ten men, described the watch system instituted by Oglethorpe soon after the arrival of the settlers in the New World. He reported in his journal that

> I mounted the first guard at eight oclock at night, received orders from Mr. Oglethorpe to fix two Centinells at the extream parts of the town [Savannah] who were to be relieved ever'y two hours. . . . The next night at eight oclock I was relieved by Mr. Causton, who march'd to the guard house with his Tything under arms where I received him with my Tything drawn up before the guard with their arms rested.

Because of their background, necessity, and training, the men in Georgia were able to adjust to the military routine required of an active militia in a potentially hostile land.[16]

Oglethorpe soon realized after arriving in Georgia, if he had not realized it before, that the militia available in Georgia was not adequate to protect the colonists against the potential threats from the French, Spanish, and Indians. There were just too few militiamen. By 1735 the total force mustered only 397 men and boys; this had increased to no more than 700 men by 1737. In the event of foreign invasion, Georgia would have had to depend upon assistance from the 3,000 or so militiamen of South Carolina—had they been willing to respond.[17] The small number of settlers not only jeopardized the defenses of the new colony

---

[15]Definition in the *Oxford English Dictionary* (1933), s.v. "Militia"; also see Capt. George Smith, *An Universal Military Dictionary* (London: J. Millan, 1779; rpt., Ottawa: Museum Restoration Service, 1969) 175.

[16]For descriptions of Oglethorpe's actions, see the *Gentlemen's Magazine*, London, October 1732, 1029; E. Merton Coulter, ed., *The Journal of Peter Gordon, 1732–1735* (Athens: University of Georgia Press, 1963) 32, 35, 43; Coleman, *Colonial Georgia*, 24.

[17]Ivers, *British Drums*, 28-29; McPherson, *Journal*, 248; Oglethorpe to Jekyll, 19 September 1738, *Collections* 3:48-49.

but affected its economy as well. The militiamen complained that they had to spend too much time performing military duties to "the neglect of their own affairs."[18]

During the Yamasee War several decades earlier, South Carolinians had faced a similar challenge. Because the militia took too many men away from the fields, the leaders of South Carolina replaced it in the campaigns against the Indians with a "paid army." The militia then served "as a kind of recruiting depot for the local volunteer defensive forces."[19] The militia of Georgia developed similarly throughout the period of the War of Jenkins' Ear and King George's War. From 1739 to 1748, this force, despite its small size, formed the final line of defense and constituted the only manpower pool from which provincial companies could be recruited.

Heightened tensions between the Spanish and the English continued to give impetus to musters and training.[20] Although it might have been unreasonable to expect that "the Discipline of the Militia can be perfect in the manner tis expected in Regular Troops," the militiamen nonetheless had to be prepared, should a last-ditch fight for survival ever have proved to be necessary.[21] In Georgia, as in South Carolina earlier, the battles generally would be fought not by the militia but by soldiers recruited for combat.

As a result of the weaknesses in the militia system, General Oglethorpe established a full-time military force in the colony of Georgia soon after he arrived in the New World. He developed this provincial force from the existing manpower, as small as it was, patterning these soldiers after the sixteen rangers and a contingent of Southern Scouts— who manned a scout boat—sent by South Carolina to provide security for its infant neighbor.[22] South Carolina's and then Georgia's reliance upon paid scouts and rangers for the frontier was consistent with the experience of Virginia as well. Each of these neighboring colonies built

---

[18]McPherson, *Journal*, 232.

[19]Jabbs, "South Carolina Colonial Militia," 303, 310-11.

[20]These musters, training, and guard duty are described in some detail in E. Merton Coulter, ed., *The Journal of William Stevens, 1741–1745*, 2 vols. (Athens: University of Georgia Press, 1958–1959) 1:101, 143-44, 217-18; 2:98, 103-104, 117, 130.

[21]Ibid. 1:163-64.

[22]*CRG* 3:90; Ivers, *British Drums*, 11-16, 28, 53, 61; McPherson, *Journal*, 95.

forts along the frontier and then employed scouts or rangers recruited from the militia to cover the gaps between the garrisons.[23]

The provincial military establishment of Georgia eventually included the Highland Company of Foot, scout boats, a few ships, and the small and mobile ranger organizations, the first of which was formed in 1734. These types of units would take part in Oglethorpe's raid into Florida in 1739, his invasion of Florida in 1740, and his defensive victory over the invading Spanish in the Battle of Bloody Marsh in 1742.[24] Although their strength peaked at 15 officers and 122 men in 1746, the rangers proved particularly adaptable to the conditions of the frontier and would consequently appear time and again throughout Georgia's early history.[25] Oglethorpe personally described the rangers as special troops who are acquainted

> with woods mounted on horseback, they not only carry advices through these vast Forests & swim Rivers, but in Action, by taking an Enemy in Flank or Rear, do great Service. . . . They also are of great Service in watching the Sea Coasts, since they can swiftly move from one Place to another, and engage to advantage Men with wet arms & Accoutrements, before they can be able to form themselves after landing. . . . [With garrisons] upon the passes of the River and the Roads to the Indian Countrey. . . . having horses [they] patroll about the Countrey, and thereby give alarms of Indian Enemies, intercept Spies & ca.[26]

---

[23]Jabbs, "South Carolina Colonial Militia," 311, 370, 392; William L. Shea, *The Virginia Militia in the Seventeenth Century* (Baton Rouge: Louisiana State University Press, 1983) 65-66, 126.

[24]Ivers, *British Drums*, 91-95, 105-106, 108, 163-68; Douglas Edward Leach, *Roots of Conflict: British Armed Forces and Colonial Americans, 1677–1763* (Chapel Hill: University of North Carolina Press, 1986) 42-49; Coleman, *Colonial Georgia*, chap. 4.

[25]Coleman, *Colonial Georgia*, 35, 51-52, 185; Oglethorpe to Trustees, 13 February 1735/36, 5 March 1735/36, 16 March 1736, 26 July 1736, *Collections* 3:13, 18-20, 41, 134; "An Account of Extraordinary Services . . . May 1741 . . .," James Edward Oglethorpe Papers, William R. Perkins Library, Duke University, Durham NC, hereinafter cited as Oglethorpe MSS; for the authorization as of 9 September 1746, see "Establishment of Our Troops of Rangers, Highland Company Boatmen, and Officers & Men for Half Gallys or Schooners in Georgia. . . ," Georgia Miscellaneous Papers, 1727–1905, William R. Perkins Library, Duke University, hereinafter cited as GA Misc. MSS.

[26]Oglethorpe to Duke of Newcastle, January 1742/43, *CRG*, TS 36:67-68.

Drummer Field-Grade Officer Grenadier Private, Battalion Company
  Private

Creek Scout

Fig. 3: The Forty-second Regiment on Foot
Courtesy of the Company of Military Historians

Despite the rangers' specialized talents and their distinguished service in encounters with the Spanish forces from Florida, the king ordered them disbanded as the war was drawing to a close because such forces seemed to be excessively costly and unnecessary in peacetime. The marines, who had manned oared vessels, and all other specialized troops suffered a similar fate. As a result, after June 1747 as peace returned, only one boat—the *Prince George*—with a crew of eight to ten men remained in the provincial establishment.[27]

The disbanding of the provincial forces was not nearly as great a loss to the colonists as was the disbanding of the regiment of British regulars that the king had ordered to Georgia in 1737 to augment its meager defenses. As the possibility of war with Spain had become more real, Oglethorpe had convinced King George II that his namesake colony needed British soldiers for protection if it was to survive. The king directed an Independent company to move from South Carolina to St. Simons Island off the coast of Georgia.[28] Oglethorpe was not satisfied, however, with this small body of regulars, and so, while in England, he argued in a personal audience with the king that a full regiment was essential. The sovereign agreed and appointed him general and commander in chief of the forces in South Carolina and Georgia and the colonel of the regiment as well.[29]

---

[27]Oglethorpe wrote many times of the value of the rangers; for example, see *Collections* 3:75-76. See also Ivers, *British Drums*, 202; Henry Fox, secretary of state, 1747, quoted in Trevor Richard Reese, *Colonial Georgia: A Study in British Imperial Policy in the Eighteenth Century* (Athens: University of Georgia Press, 1963) 83-84. Recognizing the worth of the rangers, the trustees proposed to the British secretary at war that they be retained (letter, 4 April 1748, *CRG* 1:514). The number of scout boats peaked at ten (Ivers, *British Drums*, 53-54, 101); for the *Prince George,* see *CRG* 26:87, 204-206, 269.

[28]For a discussion of the Independent companies, see William Alfred Foote, "The American Independent Companies of the British Army, 1664-1764" (Ph.D. diss., University of California, Los Angeles, 1966) 97, 100; Barnett, *Britain and Her* Army, 196; McPherson, *Journal*, 145; Oglethorpe to Trustees, 16 March and 18 May 1736, and Oglethorpe to Lieutenant Governor of South Carolina, 28 March 1736, *Collections* 3:19, 30, 34; Ivers, *British Drums*, 61.

[29]Ivers, *British Drums*, 78-79; McPherson, *Journal*, 232, 243, 303, 310; *CRG* 2:213.

The Forty-second Regiment of Foot, as constituted in Georgia, consisted of the Independent Company, 250 men drafted from the Twenty-fifth Regiment of Foot at Gibraltar, and a number of men recruited by Oglethorpe in England. The last of these soldiers arrived in Georgia with General Oglethorpe in September 1738; the regiment then mustered 629 officers and men present for duty out of an authorized strength of 684 officers and men.[30] The Forty-second Regiment emerged as perhaps the decisive element during the course of the Spanish wars. The Redcoats figured prominently in the incursions into Florida and the Battle of Bloody Marsh. Despite this critical wartime role, an economy-minded British government disbanded the regiment on 29 May 1749, now that the danger had passed. Three Independent Companies of Foot formed from soldiers of the old regiment for garrison duty took its place to defend both South Carolina and Georgia.[31]

In the absence of rangers and a substantial number of regulars, the standing militia, beginning a pattern to be repeated later, assumed the primary military role in Georgia. Only two small contingents from the three Independent companies, supplied by the scout boat *Prince George,* augmented the militia companies along the seacoast and the frontier. Sixty Independents guarded Jekyll and Cumberland islands and Frederica

---

[30]Ivers, *British Drums*, 82; McPherson, *Journal*, 303, 316, 371; the regiment would stay at less than authorized strength ("A Return of the Strength of Brigr. General Oglethorpe's Reg't of Foot the 23d of Febry 1742/3," Papers Relating to Georgia, PRO, CO 5/5, Special Collections, University of Georgia Libraries, Athens GA, hereinafter cited as GA, MSS, UGA); see also T. Smith to Henry Dolham (?), 10 May 1746, Telamon Cuyler Collection, Special Collections, University of Georgia Libraries, hereinafter cited as Cuyler MSS.

[31]For a discussion of the wars, see Ivers, *British Drums*, 90-183; also see "The Case of His Majesty's Regiment of Foot Now in Georgia Commanded by Lieutenant General Oglethorps," Oglethorpe MSS; "Order & Instructns for forming 3 indept Companies out of Lt. Genl. Oglethorpe's Regt and disbanding the other Four companies," PRO, WO 26/21, Margaret Davis Cate Collection, Georgia Historical Society, Savannah GA, hereinafter cited as Cate MSS; some of the soldiers from the Forty-second joined these companies (Ivers, *British Drums*, 214); see also *CRG* 1:520, 525; Vice President & Assistants to Trustees, 8 May 1751, ibid. 26:207; Shy, *Toward Lexington,* 33, 38; Leach, *Roots*, 42-47; W. Stitt Robinson, *The Southern Colonial Frontier, 1607–1763* (Albuquerque: University of New Mexico Press, 1979) 189, 198-200.

Courtesy Peachtree Garden Club, Atlanta, and the Georgia Society of the Colonial Dames of America

Captain Noble Jones, the first owner of Wormsloe, from a painting owned by Mr. Noble Jones of Savannah

Fig. 4: Noble Jones. Courtesy of the Hargrett Rare Book and Manuscript Library, University of Georgia.

on St. Simons Island, and twenty-four garrisoned Fort Augusta.[32] Behind this thin screen of regulars, William Stephens, formerly the secretary and now the president of the colony, provisionally organized the militia in 1749 under Captain Noble Jones.

Captain Jones was no novice in military affairs and was typical of the early officers of the militia. One of the original settlers, he—by trade initially a carpenter—had been the colony's surveyor as well and had accepted a commission into the Marine Boat Company. He served throughout the wars against the Spanish as a lieutenant and commander of two scout boats, and by 1746, now a captain, he directed the company of Northern Marines. He would eventually command in turn the Troop of Horse Militia and the First Regiment of Foot Militia.

As Jones's military responsibilities increased, his personal wealth, prestige, and political power grew as well. The king appointed him to the original colonial council after Georgia became a royal colony. Jones also served as the treasurer, a church warden for Christ Church, and an assistant judge of the Court of General Sessions. Despite the burdens of public office and a medical practice, Noble Jones found time to manage his 5,405 acres and ten lots, which included his estate at Wormsloe near Savannah. While these honors lay in the future, in 1747 Captain Jones was already a citizen and a soldier of the first order.[33]

The existence of Captain Jones's militia companies soon proved to be fortuitous. In August 1747 the Troop of Horse, led by Jones, escorted

---

[32]Fitzhugh McMaster, *Soldiers and Uniforms: South Carolina Military Affairs, 1670–1775*, Tricentennial Booklet, no. 10 (Columbia: University of South Carolina Press, 1971) 52; *CRG* 1:574, 3:354; 6:324-25; 26:208-11; Lilla Mills Hawes, ed., "Proceedings of the President and Assistants in Council of Georgia, 1749–1751," *Georgia Historical Quarterly* 36 (March 1952): 47, 67.

[33]In August 1749 the militia numbered about 170 men, both foot and members of a "small Body of Horse" (*CRG* 6:261-62); see also Ivers, *British Drums*, 66, 146-47, 195; "Commissions," 55, 80, 139; Leonard Woods Labaree, *Royal Instructions to British Colonial Governors, 1670–1776*. 2 vols. (New York: D. Appleton-Century, 1935) 1:24; James Wright, "Answers to the Queries Sent by the Right Honorable the Lords of Trade and Received by Me the First of October 1761," Wymberley Jones DeRenne Collection, Special Collections, University of Georgia Libraries, hereinafter cited as DeRenne MSS; *Gazette*, 6 April 1774, 2; 24 December 1766, 2; Silas Emmett Lucas, Jr., *Index to the Headright and Bounty Grants of Georgia, 1756–1909* (Vidalia GA: Georgia Genealogical Reprints, 1970) 349; *The Jones Family Papers*, ed. John Eddins Simpson, vol. 17 of *Collections* (Savannah GA: Georgia Historical Society, 1976) 3.

visiting Indians to the president's house in Savannah for a series of conferences. The rest of the militiamen, drawn up on the parade, received them and fired a fifteen-gun salute with cannons. These citizen-soldiers subsequently responded to a disturbance by the visitors on 12 August and remained on duty as guards until the meetings terminated on 19 August.[34] Despite the militia's obvious utility, President Parker, Stephens's successor and the last proprietary chief executive, did not place the institution on a firm legal footing until 1751.

President Parker and his assistants commissioned officers in April 1751 for companies in the areas surrounding Savannah.[35] Captain Noble Jones paraded these three foot companies and one troop of horse on 11 June as a part of the annual celebration of King George's accession to the throne. According to the provincial leadership, these 220 men were "well armed and accoutered; they behaved well, and made a pretty appearance."[36] Four days earlier, the colonial leaders had authorized a company of foot and a troop of horse for Augusta.

Military procedures and routines had now been established that would continue through the remainder of the colonial period. An unforgiving frontier and too many impractical ideas combined by 1752 to thwart the hopes and the plans of the trustees. In exasperation they surrendered their charter on 5 June and, after a transition period of two years, returned a "sickly charge" to the king. The revitalization of the militia had been a positive step and would help to bridge the changeover from proprietary to royal government.[37]

---

[34]*CRG* 6:262-65.

[35]Lilla Mills Hawes, ed., "Proceedings of the President and Assistants in Council of Georgia, 1749–1751," *Georgia Historical Quarterly* 34 (December 1951): 329, 347; Francis Harris, who commanded the Company of Foot from Savannah, eventually succeeded Jones as the colonel of the First Regiment. He too became a prominent landholder and merchant ("Commissions," 139).

[36]Hawes, "Proceedings," 36 (March 1952): 51, 55; the captains of the militia even ordered a standard and two sets of colors to be made of silk cultivated in Georgia ("Extract from a Journal of Mr. Habersham Mercht at Savannah in Georgia with some remarks on the Same," 3, Habersham Family Papers, William R. Perkins Library, Duke University, hereinafter cited as Habersham MSS); also see Charles C. Jones, Jr., *The History of Georgia*, 2 vols. (Boston: Houghton, Mifflin, 1883) 1:439.

[37]Hawes, "Proceedings," 36 (March 1952): 55; Anthony Stokes, *A View of the Constitution of the British Colonies, in North-America and the West Indies, at the Time*

As Governor Wright rode through the long stretches of wilderness, he had an opportunity to reflect upon the nature of the colony, its people, and the government over which he presided in 1763. His contingent moved by stages from Savannah to Augusta following a route alongside the Savannah River and passed through a representative cross section of a colony that had expanded considerably in both territorial extent and population since its inception thirty years before. The colony itself now consisted of about 3,560,800 acres of land as compared to the 1,152,000 acres held between 1739 and 1763. From the St. Marys River on the south to the Ogeechee River on the north, the new Indian boundary line of 1763 paralleled the seacoast some thirty or forty miles inland and broadened to some sixty-five miles between the sea and the Savannah River. Then with the Ogeechee as the left boundary and the Savannah as the right, the claimed territory formed a rough V that spread to a width of about sixty miles above Augusta at the Little River, its northern limit.[38]

In March 1758 the provincial assembly divided the province into eight parishes; these parishes would later include those lands not formally ceded by the Indians until 1763 and later.[39] Originally intended to define Anglican congregational limits, these parishes more practically served as administrative and legal units for provincial officials and, in some cases, militia companies.[40] With the addition of four southern parishes in 1765,

---

the Civil War Broke Out on the Continent of America (London: B. White, 1783) 115; Abbot, *Royal Governors*, 6-7; Saye, *Constitutional History*, 46.

[38]The description is based on that of Kenneth Coleman, *The American Revolution in Georgia, 1763–1789* (Athens: University of Georgia Press, 1958) 2; Saye, *Constitutional History*, 70; and of Governor Wright himself in *Collections* 3:159-60; each was compared with a photostat of the 1763 Yonge and De Brahm map of Georgia, Georgia Surveyor General Department; a version of this map is also contained in Louis De Vorsey, Jr., *The Indian Boundary in the Southern Colonies, 1763–1775* (Chapel Hill: University of North Carolina Press, 1966) 142. For guides to Georgia maps, see William P. Cumming, *The Southeast in Early Maps*, 2d ed. (Chapel Hill: University of North Carolina Press, 1962), and Janice Gayle Blake, comp., *Pre-Nineteenth Century Maps in the Collection of the Georgia Surveyor General Department* (Atlanta: State Printing Office, 1975).

[39]"An Act for Constituting and Dividing the Several Districts and Divisions of This Province into Parishes. . . ," in *Acts Passed by the General Assembly of Georgia, 1755–1770*, DeRenne MSS.

[40]For examples, see *CRG* 13:472, *Gazette*, 24 February 1768, 2; 6 April 1768, 3. For militia companies, see "Commissions," 211-12; Davis, *Fledgling Province*, 212, 231.

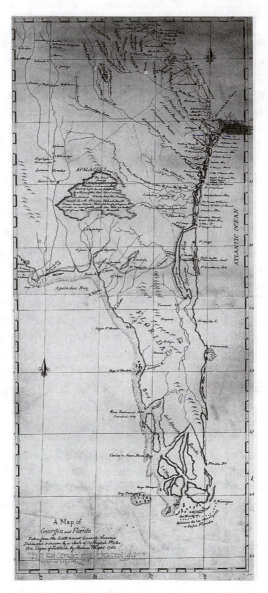

Fig. 5: A Map of Georgia and Florida. Taken from the latest and most Accurate Surveys. Thomas Wright. 1763. CO 700/Georgia No 13, Public Record Office. Crown copyright material published with the permission of the Controller of Her Majesty's Stationary Office.

Georgia would remain within these legally defined boundaries until 1773.[41]

Settlement had not kept pace with this expanding territorial base. As a matter of fact, in the course of his journey Governor Wright actually passed through a number of the largest centers of population in the colony. Although some settlers ventured farther inland, the majority stayed close to the coast and the principal rivers, particularly the Savannah.[42] Many of those who chose to congregate in villages and towns had religious and cultural ties, especially during the early years of the colony. For example, Lutheran Salzburgers and other Germans generally lived and worshiped together in and around Old and New Ebenezer, while Congregationalists predominated around Midway and Sunbury in the Parish of St. John. Highland Scots could be found in Darien on the Altamaha River, and settlers of Scotch-Irish extraction around Augusta and Queensborough on the Great Ogeechee River. Beginning in 1767, Quakers populated the settlement of Wrightsborough, some thirty miles from Augusta. The seaport of Savannah in the parish of Christ Church, while fairly cosmopolitan by contrast—the dwellers included Jews and Germans, for example—more nearly reflected the overall English character of the colony.[43] None of these towns was large; even Savannah contained only about 200 houses in 1762.[44] This is not surprising, as the total population of Georgia at the time numbered only 6,800 whites and

---

[41]These new parishes were St. David, St. Patrick, St. Thomas, and St. Mary; see Coleman, *Colonial Georgia*, 231.

[42]Herman R. Friis, *A Series of Population Maps of the Colonies and the United States, 1625–1790*, American Geographical Society Mimeographed Publications, no. 13 (New York: American Geographical Society, 1940; rev. ed., 1968) 12, 13; Lester J. Cappon, ed., *Atlas of Early American History: The Revolutionary Era, 1760–1790* (Princeton: Princeton University Press, 1976) 22-23.

[43]Coleman, *Revolution*, 9; idem, *Colonial Georgia*, 224; Davis, *Fledgling Province*, 14-26; Cappon, *Atlas*, 24, 36.

[44]Quoted in Mills Lane, ed., *Savannah Revisited: A Pictorial History* (Savannah: Beehive Press, 1973) 37. For detailed descriptions of the town of Savannah at different times, see *CRG* 27:69; Francis Harper, ed., "Diary of a Journey through the Carolinas, Georgia, and Florida from July 1, 1765, to April 10, 1766," *Transactions of the American Philosophical Society* 33, part 1 (December 1942): 29, 31; Henry R. Howland, ed., "A British Privateer in the American Revolution," *American Historical Review* 7 (1902): 294; James Bain, Jr., ed., "The Siege of Charleston: Journal of Captain Peter Russell, December 25, 1779, to May 2, 1780," ibid. 4 (1899): 482.

4,500 blacks, a sizable increase nonetheless from the 114 men, women, and children who first landed in Georgia in 1733.[45]

The increase in population indicated that the colony through which James Wright rode in 1763 was now firmly rooted. The governor himself could claim no small role in the present growth and stability. Although two chief executives, John Reynolds and Henry Ellis, had preceded him after Georgia officially became a royal colony in 1754, James Wright raised the royal powers to their full potential after he assumed office in October 1760.[46] By conscientious and concerned leadership, he furthered the development of the province. Following closely upon the Treaty of Paris, ending the Seven Years' War, the success of the Indian Congress in Augusta inspired a new confidence among the inhabitants. This was an important development for which the governor received a large measure of the credit.[47] John Bartram, the famous traveling naturalist from Pennsylvania, observed as late as September 1765 that Wright was "universaly respected by all ye inhabitants thay can hardly say enough in his praise which all such good Governours is worthy of."[48]

Building on the respect and loyalty normally shown to the chief executive, Governor Wright was enjoying a personal popularity that had developed steadily since his arrival. This was due not only to the recently restored peace, which the very mission he was embarked upon in 1763 signified, but to his personal background as well. Although he had been born in England in 1716, he had lived in South Carolina from 1731 to 1739 while his father served as chief justice. After being schooled in England, he returned to the colony to be the attorney general in an acting and then

---

[45]Coleman, *Colonial Georgia,* 23; James Wright, "Answers to the Queries Sent by the Right Honorable the Lords of Trade and Received by Me the First of October 1761," DeRenne MSS; Cappon, *Atlas,* 25.

[46]For the latest treatment of the first two governors, see Coleman, *Colonial Georgia,* 175-93; also see Abbot, *Royal Governors,* 27, 56, 82; *CRG* 6:461; *South Carolina Gazette,* Charleston, 7 November 1754, 1, on microfilm at the William R. Perkins Library, Duke University. For contemporary reactions to Ellis and his governorship, see *The Letter Book of Thomas Rasberry, 1758–1761,* ed. Lilla Mills Hawes, vol. 13 of *Collections* (Savannah: Georgia Historical Society, 1959) 18; *CRG* 28, pt. 1:104.

[47]Abbot, *Royal Governors,* 13-14; Alden, *John Stuart,* 224.

[48]Harper, "Diary," 29; Governor Ellis also made a favorable assessment of his successor in Ellis to Board of Trade, 20 October 1760, *CRG* 28, pt. 1:289; Saye, *Constitutional History,* 68-69.

a full capacity for fifteen years. At the time of his appointment as lieutenant governor of Georgia, he was in the mother country as the colonial agent for his adopted home.[49]Additionally, Wright became one of the principal landowners in Georgia, giving him a personal stake in its economy. He owned about 2,332 acres in 1763, and by 1774 these holdings, which included eleven rice plantations worked by some 523 slaves, would grow to around 17,639 acres.[50]

Governor Wright's personal financial success was an indicator of the overall economic development in a colony that was very much dependent upon trade. Rice was the major money crop and accounted for almost one-third of the value of Georgia's exports. Other staples included indigo, lumber, and wood products.[51] The advent of peace, with its favorable impact on trade, and the governor's firm guidance finally seemed to have brought the opportunity for prosperity to the king's youngest colony.

The state of foreign affairs and the economy shaped the system of government over which James Wright presided in Georgia. The lengthy instructions given to the first governor by the king had introduced political institutions to Georgia modeled after those developed during the long colonial experience of the Crown colonies. They sought to ensure that the governor would possess broad powers and notable prestige in political and military affairs.[52] As chief executive, with the advice and consent of a council originally established with twelve gentlemen appointed by the king, he acted as viceroy, or representative, of the sovereign and executed the royal will in a host of administrative duties. These ranged from controlling patronage among lesser official, including

---

[49]*Dictionary of National Biography*, 1921–1922 ed., s.v. "Wright, Sir James." Also see Coleman, *Colonial Georgia*, 193.

[50]Lucas, *Index*, 731; also see Pat Bryant and Marion R. Hemperley, comps., *English Crown Grants* series (one for each parish)(Atlanta: State Printing Office, 1972–1974). For plantations, see Coleman, *Colonial Georgia*, 213; an inventory made by the Whig government in January 1777 indicated that eight plantations with 375 slaves still nominally belonged to Wright (see "Inventory of Slaves Rice & c.," Cuyler MSS).

[51]For a summary of the major exports and the general economy of Georgia, see Davis, *Fledgling Province*, 123-24; *Historical Statistics,* 767-68; Wright, "Answers," 1761, DeRenne MSS; *Collections* 3:164-65.

[52]Albert B. Saye, ed., "Commission and Instructions of Governor John Reynolds, August 6, 1754," *Georgia Historical Quarterly* 30 (June 1946): 125; Labaree, *Royal Instructions* 1:24, 95-96, 392-93, 397, 404, 426.

Fig. 6: Governor Sir James Wright. Courtesy
of the Georgia Department of Archives and History.

officers in both the militia and the provincial forces, to issuing grants for land, an important symbol of wealth in colonial society. Of critical importance militarily, as captain general and vice admiral, the governor commanded the militia and provincial forces of the colony and, under certain conditions, could request assistance from components of both the British Army and Royal Navy.[53] In essence, the governor was the dominant colonial official in the formulation and execution of political and military policies.[54]

Aside from executive or administrative functions, the governor was a part of the legislative process and strongly influenced the actions of the assembly, which consisted of the Upper House (the Council) and the elected Commons House of Assembly.[55] The assembly passed laws and appropriated funds necessary for the routine affairs of the colony, including those required for the support of the militia. In Georgia, however, as with three other of the newest and poorest Crown colonies, the governor was not totally dependent upon the legislature to finance his government: appropriations by Parliament supported the civil establishment of the colony, including the salaries of the governor and all other Crown officials.[56] Insofar as he appointed the lesser judges and court officials and presided himself over a number of specialized courts, the chief executive held sway over the judicial process as well.[57] Royal administration in Georgia had thus brought centralized control, with the governor as the focal point of power in every aspect of the government.

---

[53]Labaree, *Royal Instructions* 1:5, 24; Abbot, *Royal Governors,* 9; Percy Scott Flippin, "The Royal Government in Georgia, 1752–1776," *Georgia Historical Quarterly* 8 (March 1924): 15-24; Coleman, *Colonial Georgia,* 175-79; William Bacon Stevens, *A History of Georgia,* 2 vols. (New York: D. Appleton, 1847; Philadelphia: E. H. Butler, 1859) 1:386-87; Davis, *Fledgling Province,* 156; "Commissions"; the governor was subordinate to the commander in chief of British forces in North America (Saye, *Constitutional History,* 52-57).

[54]Abbot, *Royal Governors,* 8-9; Jack P. Greene, *The Quest for Power: The Lower Houses of Assembly in the Southern Royal Colonies, 1689–1776* (Chapel Hill: University of North Carolina Press, 1963) 46.

[55]Coleman, *Colonial Georgia,* 177-78; Flippin, "Royal Government," 8:15-24.

[56]Abbot, *Royal Governors,* 12, 38; Saye, *Constitutional History,* 72; the other three colonies were Nova Scotia and East and West Florida (Coleman, *Colonial Georgia,* 179).

[57]Coleman, *Colonial Georgia,* 178-79; Saye, "Commission," 129; Flippin, "Royal Government," *Georgia Historical Quarterly* 10 (December 1926): 251; Saye, *Constitutional History,* 63-65.

Despite what must be considered lesser economic and philanthropic failures in the long run, Georgia had survived the challenges of the proprietary era and the transition to royal control and had successfully served as a buffer for the southern frontier. Philanthropy and mercantilism had suffered in hostile surroundings, which made military affairs a major preoccupation of the settlers for at least the first two decades; in order to survive, the colonists had been forced to channel their efforts from internal development to defense.[58] As a result, these men nurtured an English military tradition of reliance upon the militia, shaped by the nature of the colony itself as a buffer and reinforced by the ever-present threats posed by hostile Indian tribes and European nations and the disbanding of the provincial troops and the Forty-second Regiment. With relatively few members and in its infancy organizationally, the militia, behind a thin screen of fewer than 100 Independents, emerged from the proprietary era and entered the early royal period as the dominant military force. While the militia's presence in Governor Wright's escort underscored its vitality and importance in 1763, Georgia's military establishment had experienced growing pains since 1754.

---

[58]For an evaluation of the proprietary experience, see Abbot, *Royal Governors*, 6-7; Coleman, *Colonial Georgia*, xv-xvi; Trevor R. Reese, ed., *The Glamorous Malcontents: Criticisms and Defenses of the Colony of Georgia, 1741–1743* (Savannah: Beehive Press, 1973) xv; Saye, Constitutional History, 69; Ivers, *British Drums*, 214.

Chapter 2

The Militia, the Rangers, and Early Royal Government

Treaty settlements after the wars of the 1740s brought only temporary respites to the colonists of Georgia. Despite the presence in the colony by 1754 of a royal governor, John Reynolds, and the British power and institutions that he represented, the basic threats to existence remained. The Spanish to the south and the French to the southwest were checked for a time, but their territorial ambitions continued to burn brightly. Contacts with the Indians, particularly the Creeks, became more frequent as the colony grew, and this potential menace exacerbated the fears of the inhabitants still further. Georgia remained a defensive barrier, and as a result, military affairs remained central to Georgia's way of life as they had in the proprietary era.

The royal governors and both houses of the assembly continually pointed out the weak state of Georgia's defenses, but their efforts generally elicited few constructive responses from the British government. For example, in 1762 the Committee of Correspondence from the assembly wrote William Knox, the colonial agent in London, "that we are in fact in so weak and defenseless a state, that any attempt of our enemy must prove fatal to our existence as a Province and it is really surprising that our surrounding enemies . . . have not availed themselves of it."[1] As the Seven Years' War intensified long-held fears,

---

[1]Reynolds to Lord Commissioners of Trade and Plantations, 5 December 1754, CRG, TS 27:70; Ellis to Earl of Halifax and Board of Trade, 5 October 1756, ibid. 27:283, 286; *CRG* 13:149-50, 232-33, 436, Ellis to Pitt, 12 February 1759, in *Correspondence of William Pitt*, ed. Gertrude Selwyn Kimball, 2 vols. (New York: Macmillan, 1906) 2:40; Committee of Correspondence to William Knox, 1 July 1762, in "Letters to the Georgia Colonial Agent, July, 1762, to January, 1771," ed. Lilla Mills Hawes, *Georgia Historical Quarterly* 36 (September 1952): 252-53.

provincial leaders discovered that the development of defenses and hence the very survival of the colony rested primarily in their hands alone.

Although a handful of British Independent soldiers remained from the proprietary era and, after 1756, the rangers gradually began to reappear, for all practical purposes the militia constituted the only force of any magnitude to which the royal governors could turn in times of crisis. Consequently, the governors and colonial legislators, faced with multiple threats, took steps to develop the militia into a viable military force, all the while clamoring "for a small body of Troops"—British troops—to be stationed in Georgia.[2]

The first step in the revitalization of the militia was the creation of a sound, legal foundation upon which it could rest. The instructions originally given to Governor Reynolds had directed him "to Levy, Arm, Muster, Command and employ all persons" in the colony for its defense.[3] The parallels were obvious from the proprietary charter and reflected the experiences of other colonies in North America as clearly as did the provisions relating to political institutions. Reynolds continued the existing militia organizations and reaffirmed the positions of the current officers until he could formalize the status of both.[4] Although the governor's instructions contained sufficient authority for this procedure, the assembly spelled out the details and completed the process by passing the militia act for Georgia on 24 January 1755.

The assembly entitled the militia law of Georgia an "Act For Regulating the Militia of this province and for the security and better Defence of the same." This act codified into forty-five provisions the existing concepts relating to the militia and delineated the powers of the governor as commander in chief and those of his officers who commanded the individual units. The law, as it was drafted, owed its form, almost word for word, and general substance to a similar act passed by the South Carolina General Assembly on 13 June 1747. The Georgia law varied from that of its sister colony only in particulars that related to fines, distances specified for musters, political and geographic divisions to which militia organizations were tied, and some legal requirements.

---

[2]Ellis to Board of Trade, 25 May 1757, *CRG* 28, pt. 1:30; Hawes, "Letters," 253.
[3]Saye, "Commission," 130, 156.
[4]Reynolds to Lords Commissioners of Trade and Plantations, 5 December 1754, CRG, TS 27:69-70.

South Carolina, the older and more prosperous of the two, levied higher fines for violations of the law and established requirements for the inspection and manning of fortifications. Although these provisions illustrate that there were some minor differences, Georgia's law had clearly been modeled after that of its closest neighbor.

The first provision of the militia act of Georgia specified that the rank-and-file members of the militia were to be "all Male persons in this province" from sixteen to sixty years of age. This provision relating to service was consistent with the other colonies, except Pennsylvania (which had a volunteer militia only), which generally made men of this age group liable for military duty. The second provision established the militia as a flexible organization that could be enlarged as the colony grew; it comprised one or more regiments in every district, subdivided into one or more companies in every political division. The governor was to determine the strengths of the individual companies and to grant commissions to their officers.

Company commanders were to conduct regular musters no more often than six times a year, and the colonels commanding the regiments could also assemble at a general muster individual companies that were not more than ten miles apart. Each individual militiaman was to have the following items of equipment in his possession: a gun, a cartridge box with nine cartridges filled with "good powder" and ball, a horn or flask containing one-quarter of a pound of powder, a girdle or belt, a worm (for extracting the charge), a picker (for cleaning the vent hole), four spare flints, and a bayonet, sword, or hatchet. Officers had the authority to levy fines for incompleteness of equipment at a muster or upon inspection at an individual's home.

Recognizing the limitations of communications, the law authorized militia captains to call out their companies to "suppress pirates, sea rovers, Indians, and fugitive slaves." When faced with an invasion that would require service outside of the local division, the company leaders had to fill quotas by drawing lots or by accepting volunteers or substitutes. At the same time, they had to leave behind one-fourth of their men to guard against slave insurrections.

For mounted service, "inhabitants of sufficient substance," not to exceed 200 men, were to form a troop of horse, equipped "as the majority of officers shall decide," to attend the governor "whenever service may be required as it was in October 1763 for the trip to

Augusta. In a practice similar to that of South Carolina, militia captains were to enlist slaves "recommended as faithful" in the event of an invasion or other emergency. The colony would provide compensation to their owners for their use or disability and rewards to individual slaves for their bravery in battle. The remaining provisions addressed fines, penalties, exemptions from service for key officials, and other administrative details.[5]

The militia act of 1755 effectively defined the practices of the colonial militia in Georgia. The provisions ranging from organizations to exemptions were generally consistent with those of the laws of the other English colonies, although each colony's law reflected its own uniqueness. For example, in New England for a time the men of each company elected their own officers rather than having them appointed by the governor; the use and control of slaves in Georgia followed the practices common in the other slave-holding colonies. Succeeding assemblies and governors reaffirmed this original act without major change, with one lapse from 1770 to 1773, until it was revised in the latter year. The comprehensive nature of the law, periods of relative peace, and other priorities may have contributed to this longevity.[6]

In addition to traditional practices, the militia in the southern colonies, including Georgia, also performed a further duty reflecting a unique community concern: slave patrols.[7] The General Assembly of South Carolina had passed a patrol law in 1690 and had legally tied these patrols to the militia in 1721; by the 1720s, the militia "was increasingly regarded as an institution for controlling the resident negroes." Virginia as well had placed increased emphasis in this period on the militia's role

---

[5]The militia act is summarized from *CRG* 18:7-47 and Vollmer, *Georgia Enactments*, vol. 2, pt. 4 of *Military Obligation* (Washington: U.S. Government Printing Office, 1947) 2-56. This law was compared to South Carolina's in 1747 (Vollmer, *South Carolina Enactments*, vol. 2, pt. 1, ibid. 38-56). To make a comparison with the laws of Virginia, see Vollmer, *Virginia Enactments*, vol. 2, pt. 14, ibid.; for North Carolina, see Vollmer, *North Carolina Enactments*, vol. 2, pt. 10, ibid. For a more general discussion of the militia of the colonies, see Williams, *History of American Wars*, 8-10.

[6]To trace the life of the militia law through the early years, see *CRG* 18:251, 620; *Gazette*, 28 March 1765, 2; "An Act for Continuing Several Laws . . . ," *Acts*, 227, 263, DeRenne MSS; Mahon, *History*, 14-22.

[7]Shy, *Toward Lexington*, 12, 40; Mahon, *History*, 22.

of internal security.[8] The trustees of Georgia had made the ownership of slaves illegal until the very end of the proprietary period; however, under the royal regimes the number of blacks increased to about 3,000 out of a total population of fewer than 10,000 people by 1758.

The burgeoning black population created problems of control for the planters and the colony as a whole.[9] "An Act For Establishing and Regulating of Patrols," which the assembly passed on 28 July 1757, made internal slave patrols a responsibility of the militia.[10] This was a sound administrative decision, as the existing organization of the militia could be readily adapted to this new need. The militia continued to perform this duty of internal security, with varying degrees of attention, throughout the colonial period as it grew in size and responsibility.

With the militia resting on the legal foundation of a royal colony, the governors in their turn began to initiate and to oversee organizational growth. Beyond securing the passage of the militia law, Governor Reynolds accomplished very little substantively to improve the obvious weaknesses in the overall defenses and the militia still existing from the proprietary period.[11] Although he clearly recognized "the Defenseless State of this Frontier Province," as he put it, he chose to prepare unrealistically elaborate defensive plans rather than to improve the situation aggressively with the resources at hand. One of his plans, for example, called for 3,200 regulars, militia, Indians, and rangers in garrisons with 172 cannons and mortars of various calibers at an estimated cost of £28,750.[12] Such plans never bore fruit, and Reynolds consequently passed on to Henry Ellis, his successor, a militia force of

---

[8]Jabbs, "South Carolina Colonial Militia," 256, 454; Allan R. Millett and Peter Maslowski, *For the Common Defense: A Military History of the United States* (New York: Free Press, 1984) 7; Cole, "South Carolina Militia System," iii-iv, 34, 59; Aldridge, "Colonial Virgina," 115.

[9]Greene, *Population*, 181.

[10]*CRG* 18:225; the life of the patrol law paralleled that of the militia law; also see Oliver H. Prince, *A Digest of the Laws of the State of Georgia* (Milledgeville GA: Grantland & Orme, 1822) 441-45; *Acts*, 103, DeRenne MSS.

[11]Coleman, *Colonial Georgia*, 185; Abbot, *Royal Governors*, 13.

[12]Reynolds to Board of Trade, 31 May 1755, CRG, TS 27: 151; for the plan, see ibid., 244-53.

about 756 whites who were organized into eight companies but who were "badly Armed . . . [and] very remotely situated from each other."[13]

Unlike Reynolds, Governor Ellis was both genuinely concerned and, more important, highly practical about improving the shortcomings in defense. He began working to alleviate one problem of the militia—the availability of weapons—before he left England. In October 1756 he requested that the secretary of state approve the shipment of 500 "stands of Arms" for use by the militiamen, and after his own arrival in Georgia, he had the satisfaction of receiving the arms he had asked for the year before.[14] Ellis's positive attitude was reflected in an otherwise pessimistic report on the state of the forts of the colony made to the Board of Trade in 1757. Having noted the decay of the forts at Augusta, Argyle, and Frederica, he observed, "Poor as we are we are not without hands & I will endeavor to direct them to the execution of a plan that I have formed of raising a little fort here out of the wretched materials we have."[15] Ellis's general approach to the myriad problems of defense and politics reflected this overriding personal spirit of self-reliance and thus his recognition of the relative indifference of a distant British ministry to the local defensive needs of Georgia.

With the goal of improving the existing forces, Governor Ellis devoted his energies to reorganizing the independent companies of militia that he found to be "without connection, without subordination & without discipline."[16] To rectify these ills, he consolidated the companies into two regiments, allowing each company three officers (a captain, a lieutenant, and an ensign) and a varying number of enlisted men: the First Regiment of Foot (seven companies of foot and one troop of horse) for the Savannah Division, and the Second Regiment (five companies of foot) for the Augusta Division. He commissioned the officers for an additional company for the Second Regiment in 1758 and formed a Third Regiment (three companies of foot) for the Southern Division in 1759.[17] By this

---

[13]Reynolds to Board of Trade, 5 January 1756, CRG, TS 27:239.

[14]Abbot, *Royal Governors*, 69; Ellis to Earl of Halifax and Board of Trade, 5 October 1756, CRG, TS 27:284, 599. He was, however, disappointed with the quality of the arms (Ellis to Board of Trade, 25 May 1757, *CRG* 28, pt. 1 :28-29).

[15]Ellis to Board of Trade, 11 March 1757, *CRG* 28, pt. 1:178.

[16]Ellis to Board of Trade, 5 May 1757, ibid., 25-26.

[17]"Commissions," 57, 63, 67-68, 82.

time the militia strength, according to the governor, had reached 1,264 men enrolled from a total population of 7,000 whites and 2,100 blacks.[18]

Upon his succession, Governor Wright continued the work of Henry Ellis, but for a time, the number of militiamen on the rolls appeared to decline. By Wright's count, the strength of the militia was only 895 officers and men in December 1760, with the regiments having respectively 582, 120, and 193 men. The strength of this force increased to 1,100 men a year later and in organized units constituted a total of nineteen companies of foot and at least one troop of horse by 1763.[19] Significantly, although he fostered the development of the militia, Governor Wright viewed the effectiveness of these militiamen with a jaundiced eye, perhaps as a result of his long colonial affiliation. Very soon after arriving in Georgia, he reported to the Board of Trade that "perhaps not half, or I may rather say a Quarter Part of these to be in any Sort depended on in time of Real Danger, but would run away into the next Province out of Danger."[20]

Despite such reservations, as the militia companies increased in number and strength, the royal governors in Georgia called upon them to participate in a wide range of activities. The most important responsibility continued to be that of external defense; in times of crisis the royal government called upon the militia officers to meet requirements with men from their own militia companies. Surprisingly, the Spanish and the French failed to exploit the weakness of the colony directly during the Seven Years' War, although the potential for intervention by either or both powers certainly weighed on the minds of the Georgians. Several French privateers in 1757 and a French schooner in 1762 harassed the plantations along the seacoast; the latter vessel actually landed men, who made off with slaves valued at, £1,000. Such scares served to awaken previously dormant fears, and the militiamen in the threatened areas were "constantly under Arms."[21]

---

[18]Ellis to Board of Trade, 28 January 1759, *CRG* 28, pt. 1:178.

[19]Wright, "Answers," 11th Query, DeRenne MSS; "Commissions," 68, 82, 94, 96, 101, 120.

[20]Wright to Board of Trade, 23 December 1760, CRG, TS 28, pt. 1B:293-94.

[21]Wright to Board of Trade, 20 February 1762, *CRG* 28, pt. 1:355; Ellis to Pitt, 1 August 1757, in Kimball, *Correspondence* 1:92.

Such actions were nuisances, but the Indians, particularly the Creeks and the Cherokees, posed the greatest immediate threat to the colony. The common militia companies responded on several occasions to conflicts as they arose. In 1756, in a disturbance with the Creeks on the Ogeechee River, settlers killed three Indians, and a number of whites and one Indian were wounded. The inhabitants of the region were "justly alarmed," and to lessen the dangers of retaliation by the Creeks, magistrates and officers of the militia of Augusta "sent out a Party in Pursuit of the White People who were first engaged in this unhappy Fray." The militiamen apprehended seven persons and turned them over to a constable. This reliance on the militia structure differed from the more general practice in other colonies of calling upon volunteer expeditionary forces (outside the militia) to handle external threats, a practice even General Oglethorpe had used earlier.[22]

A more ominous series of events took place during the early months of 1760 as first the Cherokees and then the Creeks threatened to ravage the backcountry. The affair started as a squabble between the Cherokees and the settlers of South Carolina over trade, protection, and treatment.[23] After an apparent settlement, the Indians once again "broke out into an open War." Uncertain as to "how long we are to be spared," Governor Ellis took preventive actions that received the support of the assembly. He immediately drafted 200 militiamen from the three regiments for "constant duty until assistance [regulars] can arrive."[24] Having been provided subsistence by the assembly, militiamen from the designated

---

[22]Lieutenant White Outerbridge to Governor Lyttelton, 11 and 23 September 1756, in *Documents Relating to Indian Affairs, 1754–1756*, ed. William L. McDowell, Jr., vol. 2 of *Colonial Records of South Carolina* (Columbia: University of South Carolina Press, 1970) 185, 188-89, hereinafter cited as *CRSC*; Lieutenant Outerbridge commanded the Independents at Fort Augusta; some Independents may have participated, but it seems unlikely (Cress, *Citizens in Arms*, 3, 5, 7, 13). Cress, who claims that "by the last quarter of the seventeenth century, the militia had ceased to be the principal military arm of the colonies," failed to consider the military experience of Georgia; "Georgia" is not even an entry in the index.

[23]For background, see Shy, *Toward Lexington*, 103-104; Abbot, *Royal Governors*, 79-80; Rasberry to William Thomson, 3 March 1760, *Collections* 13:104.

[24]Ellis to Pitt, 16 February 1760, in Kimball, *Correspondence* 2:255-56.

companies, 200 strong, formed a defensive screen along the Indian boundary and the Savannah River.[25]

For a time the intensity of the crisis diminished somewhat as no attacks occurred, but by June the Creeks seemed ready to join the Cherokees. As a result, the Council directed that militiamen rotate weekly so that one-third of the "whole Militia" would always be on "actual Duty." Fears ran so high that the Council considered using "trusted" blacks to augment the companies. Some blacks may have actually been impressed into service.[26] The danger passed, and on 1 July the Council directed that the militiamen "be excused . . . until further Orders." Although untested recently in combat, the militia companies, reflecting Governor Ellis's efforts, had reacted to a threat with commendable responsiveness. The necessity to rely on the standing militia as its principal military force, particularly for external defense, set Georgia apart from other more secure colonies, in which the role of the militia had largely shifted by this time to internal security and social functions.[27]

In addition to the traditional defensive role, the militia companies of the three regiments performed a variety of ceremonial and law-enforcement tasks as well. First, they looked for slaves violating the provisions of the patrol law. Although the law required that a patrol be mounted one night in every fourteen, the frequency with which this duty was actually performed is difficult to document. Patrols may have been so routine as not to have warranted particular notice or may have been carried out only when militiamen were directed to respond to a specific instance of lawlessness. On at least one occasion, for example, Governor Wright ordered the First Regiment to patrol the road to the Ogeechee ferry because of robberies committed there by a number of runaway blacks.[28]

Joined by either the few regulars or rangers, militiamen also participated in a number of important ceremonies, including those

---

[25]*CRG* 8:250-51; Ellis to Pitt, 16 February 1760, ibid. 28, pt. 1:229; Hawes, "Letters," 253-54.

[26]*CRG* 8:266, 324; Rasberry to Thomson, 2 June 1760, *Collections* 13:112.

[27]Rasberry to Thomson, 5 September 1760, *Collections* 13:119-20; *CRG* 8:338; Cress, *Citizens in Arms*, 5; Mahon, *History*, 22; Shy, *Toward Lexington*, 40; Millett and Maslowski, *For the Common Defense*, 4.

[28]*Gazette*, 4 August 1763, 3; Prince, *Digest*, 443.

announcing the accession of King George III to the throne in February 1761, marking the birthday of the new king on 4 June 1763, declaring war against Spain in May 1762, and ending the Seven Years' War in September 1763.[29] In at least two other instances the militia formed ceremonial ranks through which parties of Indians passed to greet the governor.[30] Finally, the colonial leadership used militia muster formations to disseminate proclamations and notifications of the provisions of new laws.[31]

The militiamen apparently mustered and trained as the law prescribed when not otherwise occupied. Many of the activities in which the militia participated took place in conjunction with musters. The commander of the First Regiment called the general (or annual) muster with consistent regularity on the king's birthday. A typical notice of the First Company, for example, as it appeared in the *Georgia Gazette*, proclaimed: "Notice is hereby given, to all gentlemen of the first company of foot militia, commanded by Capt. James Deveaux, that they are to appear at the usual place of parade, completely accoetred, on Saturday the 4th of June, it being a general muster."[32] Company captains also seem to have had regular musters as well, but the evidence is sketchy. Governors Reynolds and Wright both reported that musters were held according to the provisions of the militia law, which called for six each year.[33] During the musters the company officers and sergeants in all likelihood had the men practice formation drills and firing exercises modeled after those of British regulars.[34]

All of these factors taken together—organizational growth, the militia's numerous activities, and its ready response to the Cherokee-

---

[29]*CRG* 8:493-94, 687-88; *Gazette*, 9 June 1763, 3; *CRG* 9:38, 86.

[30]*CRG* 7:644-45; 8:284.

[31]Ibid. 7:909; *Gazette*, 8 September 1763, 2; *Acts*, 46, 199, 403, DeRenne MSS.

[32]*Gazette*, 26 May 1763, 2; 18 August 1763, 3.

[33]For an example, see ibid. Only two companies regularly used the *Gazette*, the only paper in the colony, to advertise. See Reynolds to Board of Trade, 5 January 1756, CRG, TS 27:239; 28, pt. 2B:427-28.

[34]For a typical New England muster, see Leach, *Arms for Empire*, 24-36; officers may have consulted such manuals as Nicholas Boone, *Military Discipline: The Newest Way and Method of Exercising Horse and Foot* (Boston: n.p., 1718), and Colonel Martin, *A Plan for Establishing and Disciplining a National Militia in Great Britain, Ireland and in All the British Dominions of America* (London: for A. Millan, 1745).

Creek crises—indicated that the militia companies, such as greeted the governor in October 1763, were reasonably sound military organizations. Although untried in actual combat, they represented a substantial force in being within the community and at the ready disposal of the royal governor.

In the wars against the Spanish, the provincial soldiers, particularly the rangers, had proven themselves uniquely suited to the conditions and demands of a frontier colony. As Indian troubles flared first in 1756 and then intensified in the succeeding years, the colonists and their leaders called upon them again. A group of backcountrymen petitioned Governor Reynolds very soon after the disturbances between the whites and the Creeks in September 1756 to provide for the defense of the frontier.

The governor decided, with the advice and consent of the Council, to act upon this request by forming a troop of rangers with six officers (a captain, two lieutenants, a cornet, two quartermasters) and seventy men. Only after approving the proposed action did Reynolds attempt to find a means to support them. His solution was to petition John Campbell, the earl of Loudoun, commander in chief of British forces in North America, to accept the rangers into the British regular establishment and, in the meantime, to draw upon "his Lordship for Money to defray the Expence." As the Seven Years' War intensified, the assembly asked the governor to authorize an additional scout boat and two more troops of rangers. Additionally, a company of about 100 provincial troops from Virginia, the "Blues," bolstered the ranger force in Savannah for several months in 1757.[35] Frugality soon overtook the initial excitement, and only one additional troop eventually materialized, almost three years later.

With the departure of John Reynolds, Governor Ellis inherited the administrative nightmare that followed the rebirth of the rangers. Recognizing the worth of these soldiers, however, he subsequently wrote no fewer than thirteen letters to Lord Loudoun, to Major General James Abercromby, Loudoun's successor as commander in chief, to the Board of Trade, and to William Pitt, the prime minister, attempting to gain

---

[35]This paragraph is based on Henry Ellis to Board of Trade, 11 March 1757, *CRG* 28, pt. 1:7; 7:400, 413; Reynolds to Lords Commissioners of Trade, 29 September 1756, *CRG*, TS 27:592-93; for the Virginia Blues, see Ellis to Board of Trade, 20 September 1757, *CRG*, 28, pt. 1:69; Ellis to Board of Trade, 1 January 1758, ibid., 103.

sanction for the rangers.[36] Lord Loudoun advanced Ellis a credit "on the Pay Master" of £850 as a temporary measure while he himself sought approval from the prime minister. His justification was "that it would be much less Expence to the Government to support it [the province], than to retake it when lost."[37]

Rather than disband the troop altogether after exhausting the original £850, Governor Ellis reduced its strength by half from forty to twenty men and maintained them on his own personal "Credit & risque" while attempting to draw on the deputy paymaster general of British forces in New York for an additional £600.[38] Finally, as of 18 May 1759, on the orders of the prime minister, the First Troop of Rangers officially joined the British military establishment in North America, and the deputy paymaster acquired responsibility for handling the pay and expenses of the troops. The Second Troop of Rangers followed its sister unit into service on 1 January 1760.[39] Governor Ellis had fought a long, successful battle to have the rangers established.

Governor Ellis had been willing to go to such great lengths to gain the continuance of the rangers because he believed that they were essential to the defensive capability of a colony threatened, he felt, from

---

[36]Ellis to Board of Trade, 11 March, 1 August, and 20 September 1757; 1 January, 20 May, and 25 October 1758; 28 January 1759, CRG 28, pt. 1:8-9, 41, 69, 102-103, 157, 166, 177; Ellis to William Pitt, 31 October 1758, ibid., 168-69; Ellis to William Pitt, 10 December 1757, Kimball, Correspondence 1:131; Wm. Sloper, James Oswald, Richard Rigby, and W. G. Hamilton to William Pitt, 22 November 1758, CRG, TS 39:229.

[37]Lord Loudoun to Pitt, 17 June 1757, in Kimball, Correspondence 1:79.

[38]Ellis to Board of Trade, 20 May and 25 October 1758; 28 January 1759, CRG 28, pt. 1:157, 166, 177; for a sample of Ellis's handling of the finances, see his certificate to John Milledge, 31 January 1758, Keith Read Papers, Special Collections, University of Georgia Libraries, hereinafter cited as Read MSS; for the legislative side, see CRG 7:503, 842, 845; 13:233.

[39]To see how the credit was handled prior to 18 May 1759, consult Rasberry to New Grace, Carr . . ., 13 September 1758, and Rasberry to Thomson, 20 February, 29 June, and 7 September 1759; 1 February, 2 June, and 14 July 1760, Collections 13:13, 38, 62, 80, 95, 111, 115; Rasberry to Cornelius Cook, 20 March 1760, and to Josiah Smith, 2 June 1760, ibid., 105-106, 111; for establishment dates, see muster roll, 28 January 1762, PRO, Ranger Pay Bills, T 64/20, on microfilm, Georgia Historical Society, Savannah GA. Major General Jeffrey Amherst transmitted the orders from Pitt in Amherst to Ellis, 1 June 1759, GA MSS, UGA.

"every quarter."[40] In words reminiscent of those of General Oglethorpe, he summed up the worth of the rangers: soldiers "well calculated for this Country service especially in case of Indian disturbances as they can shoot on horseback & ride full speed thro' the Woods."[41]

In a far-sighted and realistic analysis, Governor Ellis continued by writing that such a "military force [was necessary] in this province not only to preserve its inward tranquility but to defend itself & the other provinces to which it must be considered as a barrier against such powerful neighbors as the French, Spaniards, & two of the most formidable of the Indian Nations."[42] Consequently, because of Ellis's dogged determination, Governor Wright controlled 2 ranger troops with 70 men and 5 officers authorized in each. By 1763 he actually had a total of 14 officers and cadets and 140 rangers upon whom he could call if an emergency arose.[43]

Although the duties performed by the rangers did not vary greatly at first from those assigned to the militia companies, one major distinction set them apart: the rangers were full-time soldiers. As such, their primary concern was external defense, and in order to fulfill this role, they manned, with a number of Independents, a series of forts around the outer perimeter of the colony. By 1761 this network included the forts and garrisons in Table 1.[44]

---

[40]Ellis to Board of Trade, 11 March 1757, *CRG* 28, pt. 1:8-9.

[41]Ellis to Board of Trade, 1 January 1758, ibid., 102-103.

[42]Ellis to Board of Trade, 11 March 1757, ibid., 8-9.

[43]The initial authorization had been for four officers and forty men (Amherst to Ellis, 1 June 1759, GA MSS, CO 5/55, UGA); see also Wright to Board of Trade, 23 December 1760, CRG, TS 28, pt. 1B:410; Committee of Correspondence to Wm. Knox, 16 March 1763, Hawes, "Letters," 256; paybills, Gage Warrants, Thomas Gage Papers, William L. Clements Library, University of Michigan, Ann Arbor, hereinafter cited as Gage MSS.

[44]For description of the forts and garrisons, see Wright, 12th Query, DeRenne MSS; Ellis to Board of Trade, 20 May 1758, 25 August 1760, *CRG* 28, pt. 1:155, 285; Captain John Gray to War Office, 5 October 1762, Cate MSS; for the fortifications around Savannah, see "Plan of the City of Savannah and Fortifications," John Gerar William DeBrahm, 1757, Georgia Surveyor General Department; for the location of Fort Halifax, see map of Savannah, 1765, in John Ettwein Papers, Georgia Historical Society, Savannah GA; other garrisons included St. John's Fort, with a corporal and nine rangers, abandoned in July 1761, and the "Great Indian Pass" on the Ogeechee River. (*CRG* 8:541 and Ellis to Board of Trade, 20 September 1757, ibid. 28, pt. 1:69).

Table 1. Georgia Full-Time Military, 1761

Outpost	Rangers	Independents
Savannah (included Fort Halifax)	30	16
Fort Augusta	30	35
Fort Argyle (19 miles from Savannah on the Great Ogeechee River)	36	—
Fort Barrington (on the Altamaha River)	25	—
Fort William (on Cumberland Island)	—	4
Fort Frederica (on St. Simons Island)	—	40

Within a year Fort George dominated the mouth of the Savannah River from Cockspur Island; eventually about twenty rangers would compose its garrison.[45] These forts, substantial structures in the cases of Forts Barrington and George, would all require continuous maintenance because of the nature of the materials used in their construction, mostly wood; unfortunately, the emphasis given to their upkeep varied according to the immediacy of perceived threats.[46]

Although several of the forts, including Frederica, George, and William, protected the seacoast, the remainder, with relatively large garrisons, served as a barrier against the Indians. In the Cherokee-Creek crisis of 1760, Governor Ellis ordered rangers from the forts near the

---

[45]For the law authorizing the construction of Fort George, see "An Act Raising and Granting to His Majesty the Sum of Four Hundred and Forty Pounds Sterling, for Erecting a Fort and Battery on the Island of Cockspur . . . ," in *Acts*, 123, DeRenne MSS; for background, see *CRG* 8:541; 28, pt. 1:354-55; it was completed by the fall of 1762 (ibid. 13:704-706); for the garrison, see Wright to Earl of Shelburne, 18 November 1766, CRG, TS 37:142; for a sketch of the fort and its exact location, see Jones, *History* 2, pt. I:opposite page 22, in Charles Colcock Jones, Jr. Collection, Special Collections, University of Georgia Libraries, hereinafter cited as C. C. Jones MSS.

[46]For the attempts to maintain the forts and their states of disrepair at various times, see Reynolds to Board of Trade, 5 January 1756, CRG, TS 27:238-39; *CRG* 28, pt. 1:168; 13:442-43, 450, 452-53, 458-59, 604-606, 645, 705-706, 715-17, 723.

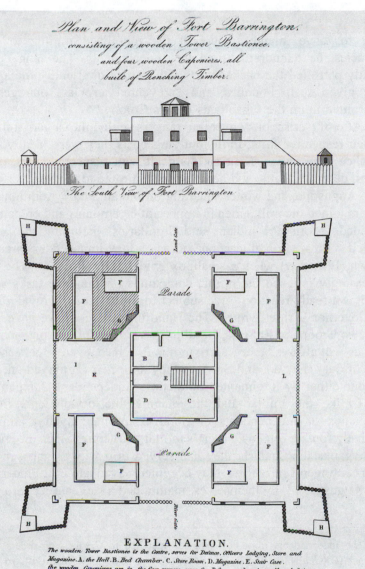

Plan and View of Fort Barrington,
consisting of a wooden Tower Bastionee,
and four wooden Caponieres, all
built of Renching Timber.

The South View of Fort Barrington

EXPLANATION.

The wooden Tower Bastionee is the Centre, serves for Deïnce, Officers Lodging, Store and
Magazine. A. the Hall. B. Bed Chamber. C. Store Room. D. Magazine. E. Stair Case.
the wooden Caponieres are in the four corners serve for Defence and private Mens Lodging.
F. are Beds for 12 Men in each Caponiere. G. Fire Places. the 4 Centry Boxes H. are joined
to the Caponierres with faces and flanks formed of Pallisadoes. I. the Well. K. Baking Oven
L. Necessary Houses.

Fig. 7: *Plan of View of Fort Barrington. John Gerar William DeBrahm,* History of the Province of Georgia *(Wormsloe GA, 1849). Courtesy of the Hargrett Rare Book and Manuscript Library, University of Georgia.*

coast to move inland to support the mobilized militia; to fill the vacancies, he temporarily used the Independents. The rangers subsequently patrolled the backcountry with parties of friendly Indians, who were given scalp bounties, and "prevented any late outrages being Committed upon the Inhabitants of this Colony."[47]

After the crisis blew over, the rangers settled into a garrison routine in their respective forts. In the outlying posts they were ideally situated to police the frontier. Their patrols dealt with suspected spies, runaway slaves, deserters, cattle and horse traders en route to the Spanish garrison at St. Augustine, and whites squatting on Indian land.[48] Additionally, the rangers joined the militiamen in important ceremonies and on patrols and provided escorts for Indians and dignitaries, including the governor himself.[49] Finally, on at least one occasion they imposed a quarantine on a town (Ebenezer) when a smallpox epidemic broke out.[50] The rangers increasingly relieved the militia companies of mundane tasks and also acted as a ready reaction force subject to the will of the royal governor. As Governor Wright wrote, "The Handfull of Troops we have, I mean our Two Troops of Rangers, I find to be very usefull People, and indeed such as will always be necessary in this Province, even on a Peace as the kind of duty they do, and Services they are often Employed on, Cannot be done either by Regimented Soldiers, or independant Companys."[51]

Unlike the militia and the rangers, the detachments from the companies of Independents of South Carolina played a minor and relatively routine role in Georgia's military structure. Since the end of the wars against the Spanish, they had served primarily as garrison troops. With contingents of rangers, they occupied Savannah, Fort Frederica, and Fort Augusta and, by themselves, maintained a sergeant's guard at Fort

---

[47]The Independents from Fort Augusta marched to Carolina on orders from the governor (*CRG* 8:160, 191-92, 228, 248); see also Ellis to William Pitt, 16 February 1760, ibid. 28, pt. 1:229-30; Ellis to Board of Trade, 15 May 1760, ibid. 250; Rasberry to Josiah Smith, 11 February 1760, *Collections* 13:103.

[48]*CRG* 8: 594, 688, 703; CRG, TS 37:171; Ellis to Board of Trade, 28 January 1759, *CRG* 28,pt. 1:176.

[49]Wright to Board of Trade, 20 February 1761, *CRG* 28, pt. 1:302; *Gazette*, 4 August 1763, 3; 20 October 1763, 3; *CRG* 7:643-44, 826; Edmund Atkin to Henry Ellis, 25 January 1760, Cuyler MSS.

[50]*CRG* 7:780, 824.

[51]Wright to Board of Trade, 15 April 1761, ibid. 28, pt. 1:309.

VIEW of COCKSPUR FORT at the Entrance of SAVANNA River in GEORGIA. Dec.r 1764.

Fig. 8: *View of Cockspur Fort. Courtesy of the Hargrett
Rare Book and Manuscript Library, University of Georgia.*

William on Cumberland Island. Their total strength generally remained somewhere between eighty and ninety officers and men during most of their existence.[52] Additionally, the scout boat *Prince George*, retained from the proprietary era and manned by a crew of a coxswain and ten men, carried provisions to the garrisons.[53]

The governor of South Carolina technically still retained control over the regular troops in Georgia as well as those in his own colony. This hazy relationship, which was detrimental to the defense of Georgia, was finally sorted out in late 1763 and early 1764, when the king ordered the three Independent companies disbanded and replaced by three companies from the First Battalion of the Sixtieth Regiment of Foot—the Royal Americans.[54] Despite the small size of this detachment (sixteen officers and men in early 1764), taken as a whole, the military establishment, made up of the militia, rangers, and regulars, represented a sizable percentage of the total white male population of the colony and constituted a diversified force with which the governor in 1763 could theoretically influence internal and external matters.[55] By the time of his trip to Augusta in 1763, Governor Wright had apparently decided to

---

[52]Ibid. 7:300, 324, 425; 13:497, 515; Reynolds to Board of Trade, 28 February 1755, CRG, TS 27:127; Ellis to Earl of Halifax and Board of Trade, 5 October 1756, ibid. 284; Ellis to Pitt, 10 December 1757, 1 March 1759, in Kimball, *Correspondence* 1:131; 2:45; Ellis to Pitt, 31 October 1758, *CRG* 28, pt. 1:168-69; Thomas Goldsmith to Ellis, ibid. 192; Wright, "Answers," 12th Query, DeRenne MSS; "A Muster Roll of One of His Majestys Independent Companys Doing Duty in South Carolina and Georgia," folder Ph-54, Cate MSS; Lieutenant Outerbridge to Governor Lyttelton, 23 September 1756, *CRSC* 2:189.

[53]Pay bill, 28 May to 27 November 1759, Read MSS; pay bill, 20 November 1759–27 May 1760, Edwin Parsons Collection, Georgia Historical Society, Savannah GA; *CRG* 8:540-41; 13:140; Rasberry to William Thomson, 3 March and 25 October 1760, *Collections* 13:104, 131.

[54]For a discussion of the dispute over this relationship, see Wright to Earl of Egremont, 4 May 1762, CRG, TS 37:7, 9-10; for the arrival of the Royal Americans, see General Jeffrey Amherst to General Thomas Gage, 17 November 1763, *The Correspondence of General Thomas Gage with the Secretaries of State, 1763–1775*, ed. Clarence E. Carter, 2 vols. (New Haven: Yale University Press, 1931, 1933) 2:210; *Gazette*, 8 December 1763, 2; 15 March 1764, 2; some Independents were drafted into the Royal Americans (McMaster, *Soldiers and Uniforms*, 55); see also Governor Thomas Boone [South Carolina] to Secretary at War, 16 July 1763, folder Ph-68, Cate MSS.

[55]Wright to Board of Trade, 27 March and 26 May 1764, CRG, TS 28, pt. 2A:42-43, 66.

place his faith in the rangers, despite the presence of militia and regulars.

The year 1763 marked a watershed in the history of colonial America as a whole and Georgia in particular. As a colony, Georgia had until then been largely oriented toward defensive matters. Two major wars against the French and the Spanish and skirmishes with the Indians combined to make mere survival seem at times a tenuous proposition. The Treaty of Paris and the Treaty of Augusta seemed to promise an end to these threats. The colony had apparently turned the corner in terms of potential growth and prosperity after Governor Wright concluded his business in Augusta in 1763. Politically, under his able tutelage, royal government appeared to be planted firmly after the failure of the proprietary scheme of the trustees and its own slow start. Perhaps at no other time before or after were Georgians as a whole so content with English rule and with their perception of themselves as English citizens.

As members of a buffer colony during the thirty years between 1733 and 1763, Georgians had nurtured a strong military tradition. In the proprietary period the military had been, to a large extent, the "principal industry." As a result, three distinctive forces took root and developed side by side for a time, shaped by the demands of a frontier colony and the changing priorities caused by the transition from war to peace. The *militia* emerged from the proprietary years as the dominant military alternative. During the French and Indian War, the royal government relied on the local militia companies rather than volunteer expeditionary forces to react to crises. With the revitalization of the *rangers* and the advent of peace, the militia slipped temporarily into the background as these full-time, provincial soldiers began to play an increasingly important role. *British regulars*, first Independents and then Royal Americans, filled garrisons; however, because of their small numbers, they remained relatively insignificant and generally beyond the orders of the governor. After 1763 the traditional orientation of both the full-time and the part-time soldiers to the dangers presented by European powers and, to a degree, the Indians would gradually change as internal groups rather than these external forces threatened the stability of the colony and as the colonists' perception of themselves changed from that of English citizens to Americans. Despite the solidarity in the colony at the time that Governor Wright arrived in Augusta on 25 October 1763, the first test, the Stamp Act crisis, was to come all too quickly.

Chapter 3

The Military and the Stamp Act Crisis

The promises of peace and prosperity were fulfilled for a time after Governor Wright and the other southern governors concluded negotiations and signed the treaty with the Indians at Augusta in the fall of 1763. The colonies of East and West Florida were now in English rather than Spanish hands as a result of the Treaty of Paris. Optimism swept the colony to such a degree that James Habersham wrote to a friend in 1764: "I think the Inhabitants of this Province are in general in a thriving situation, and we seem to be in no more apprehension of Danger from the Savages, than you are in London. . . . I now begin to think the Time is come, when we shall no more be harrassed and, alarmed by them."[1]

Sensing a general lessening of tensions, although the Indians still remained, the colonists changed their general orientation and hence the immediate priorities of society from defense against external threats to internal affairs. This shift in emphasis from mere survival to the possibilities of progress and growth soon brought the Georgians into conflict with economic policies of the British government that threatened to disrupt the equilibrium and trade upon which plans for the future rested. As a result of this confrontation of interests, by late 1765 the first tremors of opposition to Crown authority would shake Georgia, as well as her sister colonies, and would, of course, involve her military forces.

The transition to peace did not outwardly affect the military institutions of Georgia. Despite the precedent established by the reduction of forces after the wars against Spain, the rangers and the regulars survived after 1763 alongside the militia. With these two full-time forces present and manning the first line of defense along the frontier and the

---

[1]James Habersham to William Russell, 10 October 1764, *The Letters of the Hon. James Habersham, 1756–1775*, vol. 6 of *Collections* (Savannah GA: Georgia Historical Society, 1904) 27; J. Leitch Wright, Jr., *Florida in the American Revolution* (Gainesville: University Presses of Florida, 1975) 2, 12.

seacoast, the militiamen could pursue their private interests, no longer burdened by the frequent calls to arms experienced during the Seven Years' War and before. They could be citizens first and soldiers second. As a consequence, the military burdens shifted perceptibly from the militiamen, the part-time soldiers, to the full-time soldiers—the rangers and, to a more limited extent, the regulars.

Even as a shift of responsibilities was taking place, delegating to the rangers and to the regulars the routine duties of garrison life, the militia retained considerable vitality and continued to increase and to muster as prescribed by law. Although by 1765 the militia as a whole increased by only one company, the newly formed Seventh Company of the Second Regiment, the total force now numbered twenty companies of foot and at least one troop of horse. The number of men involved had grown from 1,100 to 1,350. The First Regiment continued to have the greatest number of companies with nine, while the Southern Regiment, the third, had only four.[2] Consequently, the growth of the militia roughly kept pace with, and reflected, the overall expansion of the colony.

With few exceptions the officers' positions in the militia at regimental level and below were almost totally filled during these years. While, as Governor Wright pointed out, the ranks were composed of men who had relatively little or perhaps no property, the officers were in many cases well-to-do men with both extensive landholdings and influence. Out of sixty-four officers in the three regiments in 1765, the governor had granted to forty-three more than 100 acres of land each, and of these, he had granted to twenty-seven more than 500 acres; in all but two cases, both majors, the regimental staff officers and commanders fell within the latter category. For example, Francis Harris, who succeeded Noble Jones as the commander of the First Regiment, was a prominent merchant in the firm of Harris and Habersham as well as a planter who, by the time of his death in 1771, owned some 5,850 acres of land, tilled, as of 1765, with the help of at least eighty-six slaves. The officers who had been granted fewer than 100 acres of land generally increased their holdings after 1765; those who did not were usually merchants, lawyers, or not listed in the grants. The most affluent officers were in the Third Regiment, which was located in the Southern Division

---

[2]Commissions," 127, 132, 148; Answers to Board of Trade, CRG, TS 28, pt. 2B:427-28; Wright to Board of Trade, 20 February 1762, ibid. 37:5.

to the south of Savannah; here these officers, as planters, grew most of Georgia's rice.[3]

The influence that the militia officers wielded also extended to politics. Two of them served as members of the royal council and nine as delegates to the Commons House of Assembly. In addition, many acted as tax collectors, judges, justices of the peace, and church officials. In sum, the officers of the militia constituted an influential segment of society and government.[4] Despite some organizational growth, the companies of militia declined in military usefulness as the full-time soldiers assumed the defensive burden, and the opportunity for actual field service virtually disappeared for a time. The militia remained no more than a potential force, as were the organizations of such other colonies as South Carolina and Virginia. The colonial government still had cause to maintain the companies because of the uncertain intentions of the Indians, despite the treaty of 1763, and because of the growing number of slaves in the colony.[5] Nonetheless, the militiamen did not perform the wide range of duties they had in earlier times. In fact, training musters were the only documented activity in which they participated between 1763 and 1765, although, in all likelihood, militiamen routinely continued to perform slave-patrol duty.

The musters themselves seemed to slip from center stage, even when held in conjunction with ceremonial events. The First Regiment, for example, held a general muster on 4 June 1764, but unlike the year before, the *Georgia Gazette* made no mention of the militia's taking part in the ceremony marking the king's birthday.[6] In the past, in 1763 for instance, the militiamen had fired the ceremonial volleys, and ostensibly

---

[3]No muster rolls for the militia seem to be extant; this data for the officers was extracted from the following sources: "Commissions"; Lucas, *Index*; Bryant and Hemperley, *English Crown Grants; CRG*, vols. 8-9; for Harris, in addition, see Atlanta Town Committee, *Abstracts of Colonial Wills of the State of Georgia, 1733-1777* (Hapeville GA: Atlanta Town Committee for the Department of Archives and History, 1962) 66.

[4]Greene, *Quest*, 493-95; *Gazette*, 21 February 1770, 3; 21 January 1767, 3; 21 December 1768, 2; 11 April 1770, 6; *CRG* 19:37, 107.

[5]Alden, John Stuart, 191; Aldridge, "Colonial Virginia," 245-46; Cole, "South Carolina Militia System," 139; Robert M. Weir, *Colonial South Carolina: A History* (Millwood NY: KTO Press, 1983) 196; Mahon, *History*, 33.

[6]*Gazette*, 16 February 1764, 3; 24 May 1764, 4.

the entire First Regiment of Foot was available in 1764 to continue the tradition. The militia's role during the celebration of the king's birthday the next year went unreported as well.[7] This change in the official importance of the musters, however, in no way diminished their social significance, as they continued to provide an occasion for settlers to congregate and to socialize. The officers, for example, generally attended the governor's reception after completing the formalities associated with the royal birthday. Such practices were common throughout the colonies.[8]

Contributing to the general reliance upon the full-time soldiers rather than militiamen was Governor Wright's distrust of the effectiveness and loyalty of the latter. His initial impression in 1760 that these citizen-soldiers would run away when confronted with danger apparently had not changed, for he continued to write of them in the same vein.[9] For example, in a letter to the Board of Trade written in 1762 he lamented, "Your Lordship will easily see & judge, what such an hand full of People can do against an Enemy, especially when scattered over a Vast Extent of Country, and many of them being men of no Property, and who on an alarm either from Indians or other Enemies, would move away to the next Province."[10] Since such impressions emerged during a time of war and of potential danger, it is not likely that Governor Wright had changed his mind a great deal by 1765, in time of peace. To carry this one step further, in a political confrontation within the community itself, this doubt would be compounded still more by the question of loyalties; Governor Wright had no way of knowing the militiamen upon whom he could rely. In all likelihood, in the event of internal disorder, a large number of these men, if not the actual participants, would at least be sympathetic to the goals of the protestors and would be reluctant or unwilling to act against them.[11]

---

[7]Ibid., 7 June 1764, 4; 6 June 1765, 2; 9 June 1763, 3.

[8]The social aspects of musters seem self-evident, but it is difficult to find evidence that describes the activities accompanying the training exercises. The officers, however, generally attended the governor's reception after completing the formalities of the king's birthday (*Gazette*, 9 June 1763, 3); for general references, see Donna J. Spindel, "The Stamp Act Riots" (Ph.D. diss., Duke University, 1975) 283; Leach, *Arms for Empire*, 34.

[9]Wright to the Board of Trade, 23 December 1760, CRG, TS 28, pt. 1B:479.

[10]Wright to Board of Trade, 20 February 1762, ibid. 37:5.

[11]Spindel, "Stamp Act Riots," 25, 28.

With the peace in Georgia unbroken, the militia an unknown quantity, and other forces available, Governor Wright seems to have relegated the militia to secondary importance as a military force. Of the full time soldiers, the British regulars played a relatively inconsequential role. By mid-1764 detachments from the Royal Americans (the Sixtieth Regiment of Foot) had replaced those of the Independent Companies as the token force of regulars in the colony. Few in number and scattered as well, these men constituted no more than a symbol of British authority as they helped to enforce the Proclamation of 1763, which limited the encroachments of whites beyond the Indian boundaries to the west. The contingent comprised between thirty-two and forty-three officers and men: an ensign, a surgeon's mate, and twenty to thirty-one men at Fort Augusta and a sergeant or corporal and nine men at Fort Frederica on St. Simons Island.[12] Formally serving the commander in chief of British forces in North America, these regulars occupied forts, some of which were at least 150 miles from Savannah, previously manned by the Independents. The headquarters and six companies of the battalion were even more distantly deployed in Quebec, Canada.[13]

Captain James Marquis Prevost, the commander of the three companies of the Sixtieth Regiment in Georgia and South Carolina, was less than pleased with the conditions of the forts his men occupied.[14] Because the twenty-foot-square Fort Augusta was constructed of wood, it was virtually in need of replacement only five years after it had been built. Although Fort Frederica, a square fort with each side sixty feet long, had some walls made of tabby (a mixture of lime and sea shells), it was also in need of repair. Furthermore, the ten Royal Americans there could not possibly hope to defend such a fort designed for some four officers and one hundred men.[15] Isolated from the major centers of

---

[12]Wright to Henry Seymour Conway, 31 January 1766, CRG, TS 37:109; 28, pt. 2B:428; see the map, "Cantonment of His Majesty's Forces in N. America," 29 March 1766, file 34, Cate MSS; Jack P. Greene, ed., *Colonies to Nation, 1763–1789* (New York: W. W. Norton, 1975) 16-18.

[13]Board of Trade to Wright, 4 May 1762, CRG, TS 37:8; Shy, *Toward Lexington*, 158, 163.

[14]*Gazette*, 14 June 1764, 3; Carter, *Correspondence* 1:23. As a lieutenant colonel, Prevost led an expedition into Georgia in late 1778 (Coleman, *Revolution*, 119).

[15]"General State of the Monies in the hands of the Treasurer. . . ," 4 July 1772, Noble Wimberly Jones Collection, William R. Perkins Library, Duke University, hereinafter

population and subjected to harsh discipline, these soldiers, who were generally recruited for life (typically serving about twenty years) from the nonproductive segments of society, suffered through their terms of service facing both general boredom and brief bursts of excitement in much the same way as their fellow soldiers stationed elsewhere in the colonies and the rest of the empire.[16]

Even under ideal conditions, the red-coated Royal Americans, now no more than garrison troops, were most unsuited for dealing with threats from Creeks, Cherokees, or whites, for that matter. Ironically, the regiment had been raised in America during the Seven Years' War to fight as a light infantry unit, using tactics adapted to the frontier. Many of the original 4,000 American recruits were Germans from Pennsylvania. As late as 1767, forty-four German recruits became a part of the three companies that were stationed in South Carolina and Georgia.[17] Small numbers, long distances, and an unworkable structure of command had combined to place the regulars beyond the call of the governor. Stuck at the extremities of the colony's defenses now, as had been the case since the end of the wars against the Spanish, the Redcoats served only as a symbolic force of little military consequence. As the militia returned to its traditional role as a defensive force and the regulars served only to show the British flag and to augment the garrisons, the rangers, or provincial soldiers, as early as 1764 began to emerge as the dominant military force upon which Governor Wright could rely in the event of an immediate crisis of any kind. Divided between two troops with about 120 effective men out of a total authorized strength of 14 officers and cadets and 137 enlisted men, the rangers continued to occupy almost the same

---

cited as N. W. Jones MSS; *Collections* 3:168-69; Harper, "Diary," 31-32; *Gazette*, 29 November 1764, 1; Captain John Gray to the War Office, 5 October 1762, file Ph-63, Cate MSS; "An Act for Building a Fort. . . ," 25 March 1765, *Acts*, 236, DeRenne MSS.

[16]Lieutenant Winter killed a "private man" on 5 June 1766 (*Gazette*, 18 June 1766, 2); another soldier died when a cannon burst on the king's birthday (ibid., 22 June 1768, 3); also see ibid., 26 August 1767, 2; R. Arthur Bowler, *Logistics and the Failure of the British Army in America, 1775–1783* (Princeton: Princeton University Press, 1975) 12; Shy, *Toward Lexington*, 118, 173-75, 358-63; Barnett, *Britain and Her Army*, 169.

[17]Barnett, *Britain and Her Army*, 96-98; J. F. C. Fuller, *British Light Infantry in the Eighteenth Century* (London: Hutchinson, 1925) 97-110; Gage to Barrington, 22 February 1767, Carter, *Correspondence* 2:409; Shy, *Toward Lexington*, 173; McMaster, *Soldiers and Uniforms*, 59.

Private, Bn. Co.   Officer, Grenadier Co.   Private, Bn. Co.   Sergeant, Bn. Co.

British 60th Foot (Royal-American Regiment), 1756-1760

Fig. 9: British 60th Regiment of Foot (Royal Americans).
Courtesy of the Company of Military Historians

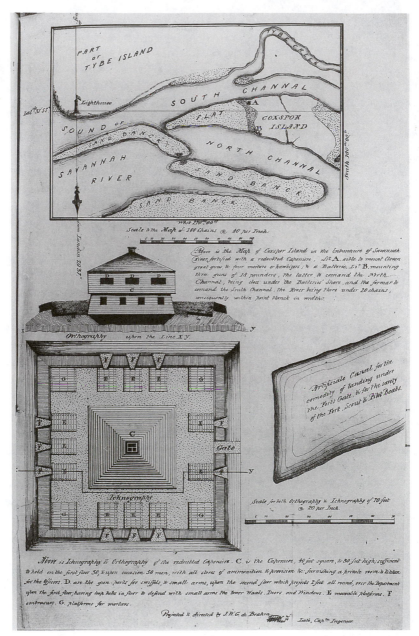

Fig. 10: Fort George on Cockspur Island. Courtesy of the Hargrett Rare Book and Manuscript Library, University of Georgia.

forts and garrisons as before: Savannah (20 men), Fort Frederica (50), Fort Argyle (35), Fort Barrington (25), and Fort George (20).[18] Of these forts, Fort George, constructed of "mud walls faced with Palmettoe Trees" with a caponier, or raised barracks (blockhouse), in the interior and located on Cockspur Island near the mouth of the Savannah River, would become increasingly important with the passage of time.[19] The garrison here and the one in Savannah (about 35 to 40 rangers), because of their proximity, were the forces most responsive to the governor.

The social composition of the troops of rangers seems to have resembled that of the militia companies. The officers, whose ranks were captain, first, second, and third lieutenant, and quartermaster, were for the most part prominent landholders or merchants; this was particularly true of the captains. John Milledge of the First Troop, one of the original settlers, had received, by grants, almost 3,000 acres of land by 1765. He worked them with at least twenty-three slaves. He was also a representative in the Commons House of Assembly during most of the decade of the 1760s. With landholdings of almost 2,000 acres, James Edward Powell of the Second Troop was, after a short stint in the assembly, a member of the provincial council for the remainder of the royal era. Of the eight other officers, four had more than 500 acres; two, of whom one was a merchant, would eventually have more than 3,000 acres; First Lieutenant Noble Wimberly Jones, the son of Colonel Noble Jones, was also a physician; he, unlike his father, in the not-too-distant future would be a prominent Whig, or patriot.[20]

---

[18]For the British garrisons and forts in North America, see Cappon, *Atlas*, 41; Answers to Board of Trade, 29 November 1766, CRG, TS 28; pt. 2B:428; Wright to Board of Trade, 15 January 1766, ibid., pt. 2A:303-304; Wright to Conway, 31 January 1766, CRG, TS 37:109; "Georgia Pay Bill[s]," 18 May to 18 August 1764 and 1 April to 1 July 1764 (Second Troop of Rangers), Gage MSS; Wright to Gage, 2 April 1767, CRG, TS 37:245. The number of rangers at each location was determined by deduction; although Governor Wright placed the number of soldiers at Frederica at sixty (presumably fifty rangers and ten regulars), this figure seems too high. There is no evidence that directly specifies from which of the two troops each of the detachments came. On the basis of internal evidence in letters and minutes, the men of the Second Troop occupied Fort George during this period (*CRG* 9:342); a detachment of the First Troop was at Fort Barrington (ibid. 437).

[19]*Collections* 3:168.

[20]This analysis was compiled and tabulated from Lucas, *Index*; the *CRG*;

The enlisted men—corporals, drummers, and privates—were probably from about the same cross section of society as their contemporaries in the militia companies. They stand out today as no more than names on aging pay bills. Few owned land. As of 18 August 1764, for example, apparently only ten men had any land at all, and their holdings averaged about 200 acres. Beyond this, it is difficult to establish the identities of the rangers. Some of them were quite possibly adventurers, vagrants, or even criminals. Others may have been newcomers to the colony or migrant settlers in need of a regular job.

Analysis of the pay records supports a tentative conclusion that a number of the men may have viewed honorable service in the rangers, at £2 a month, either as steady employment or as a means for individual advancement. Turnover among the soldiers in both troops from one three-month pay period (quite likely the term of enlistment as well) to the next ranged from a low of 3 percent to a high of 17 percent. Over a two-year period, this rate of turnover could even reach 57 percent, as it did in the Second Troop from 1 April 1764 to 1 July 1766, when thirty-eight men enlisted to fill that same number of vacancies.

Despite the steady changes in the ranks, reenlistments kept pace. From 1762 to 1764 the officers remained much the same, while the number of privates averaged sixty-two for the First Troop and sixty-five for the Second. The men generally served a reasonable time after enlistment, although they had to provide their own rations after 1763. For example, twenty-four of the thirty-eight men mustered out of the Second Troop by 1 July 1766 had been in the troop from four and one-half to six and one-half years. Moreover, in the five years between 1762 and 1767, apparently only five rangers served a minimum term of three months or less. Finally, as many as twenty-six of the provincial soldiers on duty in 1764 may have owned land by 1775. For these men tours of duty in the troops had provided employment, adventure, and perhaps even social advancement.[21]

<hr />

"Commissions"; Bryant and Hemperley, *English Crown Grants*; Greene, *Quest*, 493-95; Labaree, *Royal Instructions* 1:24; pay bills for the rangers from the Gage MSS and folder Ph-64, T 64/20, Cate MSS; *Collections* 17:68.

[21]This analysis was made in much the same way as that for the officers. The task of correlation is much more difficult, since the privates among the rangers left few records. There is very little definitely known about the rank and file of either the militia or the

Regardless of their individual backgrounds or aspirations, the rangers received a diversity of responsibilities, which was an apparent measure of their growing prominence. One, in particular, assumed importance: the rangers increasingly represented the military at official ceremonies. For example, on the king's birthday in both 1764 and 1765, the rangers (but not the militia) took part in the festivities and fired the ceremonial volleys. Since ceremonial events placed the military participants on public display as an extension of the political power of the governor and hence the king, the military actors involved in a particular ceremony seem to give a clue as to their relative importance.

In addition to the ceremonial role, the rangers, as they had done in the past, enforced the colonial laws along the frontier. Lieutenant Robert Baillie of the First Troop received orders from the Council on 12 November 1765 to search for a "Nest of Villains" near the Canoochee River. In December 1765 the troopers from Fort Barrington pursued and captured three runaway slaves who had killed a Creek near the Satilla River; after trying the slaves, the colony hanged them for the murder.[22] Patrolling through the backcountry, the rangers thus continued to perform the types of missions for which they were uniquely suited because of their mobility, location, and organization.

Between the two extremes represented by the regulars and the militiamen, the rangers in 1765 became potentially the most reliable and the most responsive troops available to the governor, regardless of the threat. Relatively few in number and scattered though their garrisons

---

rangers. Separations and enlistments were calculated for each of the pay periods where records existed. The periods of greatest turnover, 1762 to 1763 and 1764 to 1766, were also the ends of the Seven Years' War and the Stamp Act crisis respectively. See Lucas, *Index*; the pay bills for the rangers from the Gage MSS; folder Ph-64, Cate MSS; Amherst to Ellis, 1 June 1759, GA MSS, UGA. There are some glimpses: at least two rangers, Mordecai Maddox and William Coombs, had wives and children (*CRG* 9:243, 306). One ranger was discharged because he was a deserter. "Georgia Pay Bill of his Majesty's second Troop of Rangers. . . , 1 April to 1 July 1764," Gage MSS). Also see CRG, TS pt. 2A:431.

[22]Although the First Regiment of Foot held general muster on both occasions, its presence was not mentioned in the newspaper accounts. In the past, the militia companies had performed the military honors, and the *Gazette* had duly reported their involvement. See *Gazette*, 7 June 1764; 6 June 1765, 2. *CRG* 9:437, "Talk" by James Wright and John Stuart, 27 December 1765, CRG, TS 37:154, 168.

were, the rangers were indisputably Crown soldiers. The governor commissioned the officers from prominent men whom he apparently trusted, and the Crown supported and paid them and the rank and file. The rangers owed their ultimate loyalty to the governor and, through him, to the king. At least three garrisons, those of Savannah, Fort George, and Fort Argyle, were close enough to respond fairly quickly to the orders of the chief executive. So, it was with these military options, basically intact in spite of peace, limited in numbers, and traditionally oriented to outside threats, that Governor Wright unknowingly stood on the brink of domestic disorder early in 1765. The Stamp Act crisis would soon test both the authority of the Crown and the military forces upon which it rested.

The Stamp Act crisis, which began to unfold in the spring of 1765, marked the first major confrontation between elements within the society of Georgia and Crown authorities during the royal period. Earlier parliamentary measures before the Stamp Act, such as the Sugar and Currency acts of 1764, and ministerial decisions, such as the Proclamation of 1763 and the order to reform the Customs Service, while having an effect, had not caused widespread public reactions in Georgia. The ministry and Parliament had designed each measure to tighten the reins on the empire after years of benign neglect, to recoup some of the costs of the Seven Years' War, or to support military forces and Crown officials in the colonies. The Stamp Act, on the other hand, affected a wide cross section of the inhabitants throughout the colonies and therefore sparked direct resistance.[23]

Parliament passed the Stamp Act on 22 March 1765 and declared that it was to defray costs involved in defending the thirteen colonies. Politically, the colonists objected because they had not been consulted and because the Parliament rather than their own legislatures had passed the law; economically, the tax covered a wide variety of important items and

---

[23]For the general background, see John R. Alden, *A History of the American Revolution* (New York: Alfred A. Knopf, 1972) 45-65; Greene, *Colonies*, 12-26; Georgia's lumber trade with the West Indies was most affected by the Sugar Act (Coleman, *Revolution*, 17); see also Edmund S. Morgan and Helen M. Morgan, *The Stamp Act Crisis: Prologue to Revolution* (Chapel Hill: University of North Carolina Press, 1953).

activities. Stamp duties were required on "legal papers, commercial papers, liquor licenses, land instruments, indentures, cards, dice, pamphlets, newspapers, advertisements, almanacs, academic degrees, and appointments to office." In one way or another, then, the measure, when enforced in the colonies, imposed a tax on almost every social group in the colonies. In response, colonists, calling themselves Sons of Liberty, "enforced the nonimportation agreements, forced stamp collectors to resign, and mobilized mobs to ransack the homes of unpopular Crown officials."[24]

In Georgia, aside from the obvious consequences for the merchants and legal transactions, the Stamp Act directly impinged upon the large rice planters and masters of ships; ships loaded with rice could not clear port until cargo invoices were properly authenticated on stamped paper.[25] As rice by 1765 was one of the major money crops, the Stamp Act made itself felt throughout the economy of the colony.[26] The governor and the customs officials had to enforce the measure after 1 November. As this date approached, tension within the colony began to build.

Public demonstrations against the measure did not start in Savannah until October, although news of the Stamp Act had reached there in the spring. On the night of 25 October, a muster day and the fourth anniversary of the king's accession to the throne, a group of the inhabitants of Savannah publicly expressed their disapproval of the Stamp Act. "About seven o'clock that night, the effigy of a stamp-officer was carried through the streets, and afterwards hanged and burnt, amidst the acclamations of a great concourse of people of all ranks and denominations assembled together on the occasion."[27]

Another protest took place on 5 November, Guy Fawkes Day, the anniversary of the Gunpowder Plot against Parliament.[28] In the meantime, the first of November had come and gone, and neither stamped papers

---

[24]Greene, *Colonies*, 42-43.

[25]Abbot, *Royal Governors*, 113.

[26]*Historical Statistics*, 767-68; Davis, *Fledgling Province*, 53-54.

[27]*Gazette*, 17 October 1765, 4; 31 October 1765, 1; Wright to Conway, 31 January 1766, CRG, TS 37:104. For an overview of the crisis, see Coleman, *Colonial Georgia*, 245-50; Abbot, *Royal Governors*, chap. 5. Also see Spindel, "Stamp Act Riots," 25, 28.

[28]*Gazette*, 7 November 1765, 2; the Gunpowder Plot took place in 1604; see William L. Langer, ed., *An Encyclopedia of World History*, 5th ed. (Boston: Houghton Mifflin, 1968) 400-401.

nor a stamp collector had arrived. On the night of 4 November the Sons of Liberty, opponents of the stamping fee and a growing faction, met in Machenry's Tavern to discuss possible actions to be taken once the stamp official reached Savannah.[29] Then overt resistance ceased for a time as the colonists watched and waited for the ship bearing the stamps to anchor.

The governor and his council, in the meantime, were making plans of their own. In the session of 12 November they decided that Wright should have the paper placed in the guardhouse in Wright's Square "and there protected by such a Guard as in his Excellency['s] Power to place for that Purpose."[30] The governor also took precautions of a military nature sometime during this period. "On the first appearance of Faction & Sedition [he] ordered in some of the Rangers from each Post, & made up the Number here at Savannah 56 Privates & 8 officers."[31] Finally, in preparation for the implementation of the provisions of the law, he closed the port of Savannah on 4 December.[32] The governor could now do no more than the Sons of Liberty, and so he too waited.

The actual arrival of the stamped papers was almost anticlimatic. His Majesty's Ship *Speedwell* anchored in the Savannah River on 5 December. After receiving assurances from "several of the Principal Inhabitants . . . that there was then no intention or design to attempt to seize upon or destroy the Papers," the governor had them immediately landed "without and [sic] appearance of Tumult." He then had the commissary deposit them in the King's Store, just east of the town at Fort Halifax—a square fort completed in 1760 and made of planks with a caponiere at each corner—where the Indian trade presents were normally kept.

The month of December passed without incident, although Governor Wright reported that "Cabals were frequently held & Inflamatory letters &c sent from Charles Town." (Governor Bull of South Carolina, faced with pressure from mobs, failed to distribute his stamps and stood by as

---

[29]*Gazette*, 7 November 1765, 2.
[30]*CRG* 9:438.
[31]Wright to Conway, 31 January 1766, CRG, TS 37:109.
[32]Habersham to Knox, 4 December 1765, *Collections* 6:50; *CRG* 454-58; Coleman, *Colonial Georgia*, 247.

they forced the two stamp collectors to resign.)[33] With the papers out of view and the lifeline of the colony, the port, closed, a surface calm prevailed—for a time.

Beneath the surface, tensions were building as the Sons of Liberty, encouraged by their counterparts in South Carolina, made plans to destroy the hated stamped papers.[34] Opposition to the Stamp Act reached a climax in Georgia on 2 January 1766. After a muster of the militia, a crowd of people gathered, obviously including some "off-duty" militiamen, and, "having provided themselves with drums and colours," marched to the gate at the governor's house at the northwestern edge of St. James Square.[35] Before the Liberty Boys had arrived, Wright had received notice from his ranger captains that 200 of them intended to seize and to destroy the stamped papers stored at Fort Halifax. He ordered Captain James Edward Powell, Second Troop of Rangers, and John Milledge, First Troop of Rangers, to assemble their available men at the guardhouse. He grabbed his own musket and went to Wright's Square, where fifty-four rangers had gathered. From there he noticed that people were gathering at his house. With musket in hand, he walked back there and into the middle of the crowd. Asked if he intended to appoint a distributor of stamps, he dismissed the question by telling the members

---

[33]*CRG* 9:453-54; *Collections* 3:168; Wright to Conway, 31 January 1766, CRG, TS 37: 105-109.

[34]CRG, TS 37:105-109; Weir, *Colonial South Carolina*, 295-96; also see Francis Harrold, "Colonial Siblings: Georgia's Relationship with South Carolina during the Pre-Revolutionary Period," *Georgia Historical Quarterly* 77 (Winter 1989): 729-32.

[35]Three firsthand accounts are available for the actions that took place on 2 January; these accounts, the first and second by Wright and the third by a Son of Liberty, are similar and are summarized, CRG, TS 37:105-109. Wright to Board of Trade, 15 January 1766, ibid. 28, pt. 2A:304; letter in the *Pennsylvania Gazette*, 13 February 1766; quotations are from the latter; see also Shy, *Toward Lexington*, 214-15. For a capsule summmary, see John Richard Alden, *The South in the Revolution, 1763-1789*, vol. 3 of *A History of the South* (Baton Rouge: Louisiana State University Press, 1957) 95-97; *CRG* 9:453-54. On the basis of the available evidence, it is impossible to document direct participation by militiamen as such in this demonstration; it is reasonable, however, to speculate that individual militiamen, as members of the community, took part. Since musters presented opportunities for citizens to congregate and discuss political issues and news, demonstrations could develop with relative ease under favorable conditions, particularly when the issue was important.

of the group, among other things, that such gatherings were "not a manner to wait upon the governor of a province."

After Wright's personal intervention, the crowd dispersed with the intention of gathering again later when they learned that an official had been appointed. Then Governor Wright marched with the rangers to the store at Fort Halifax, where they loaded the stamps on a cart and moved them to the guardhouse. Forty men remained on duty there overnight and for the next two weeks as well. Governor Wright patrolled the streets the night of 2 January with about forty merchants, their clerks, and some captains of ships, all armed, until between eight and nine o'clock. The next day, 3 January, an officer and a party of rangers in the scout boat *Prince George* rowed down the river, picked up Mr. George Angus, the distributor of stamps, at Tybee Island and escorted him back on Saturday to the governor's house. Wright administered the "State Oath of Office" to him and then—the lone governor to do so—had some of the papers distributed to the shipping offices, thereby opening the port. (Ships sailed from the Charles Town harbor in January as well; the ships' masters may have used stamped paper from Georgia.)[36]

Mr. Angus—the only colonial distributor to offer stamps for sale— stayed with the governor for two weeks and then "went into the country to avoid the resentment of the People for awhile." Governor Wright in the meantime managed to quiet the unrest for a time by not issuing the remaining papers, since "the People in general have agreed not to apply for any other Papers till His Majesties Pleasure is known on the petitions sent from the Colonies" protesting the Stamp Act. He also sent "Expresses with Letters to many of the most Prudent People, I had the satisfaction to find that my weight & ceredit [sic] was sufficient to check all commotions & disturbances in the country at that time." The "spirit of faction & sedition" quieted for a short while.[37]

The storm of political crisis moved in again almost as quickly as it had dissipated. "Incendiaries," according to Wright, from Charles Town came and "inflamed the People to such a degree that they were again assembling together in all Parts of the Province." Forewarned that some 600 people planned to destroy the papers on 30 January and to "commit

---

[36]Habersharm to Rev. Mr. George Whitefield, 27 January 1766, *Collections* 6:55-56; Weir, *Colonial South Carolina*, 296.

[37]Wright to Conway, 31 January 1766. CRG. TS 37:105-109.

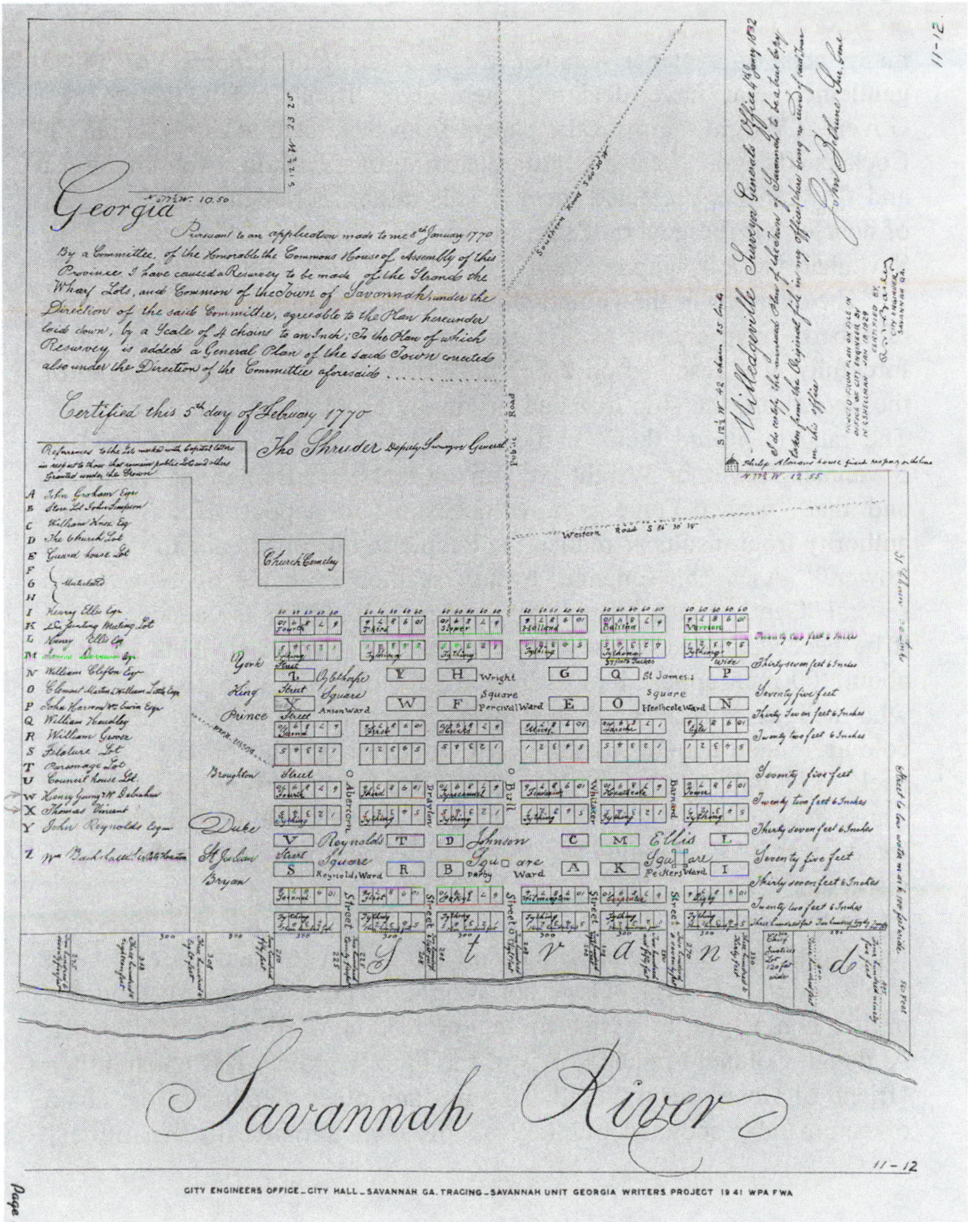

Fig. 11: Town of Savannah. Tho. Shruder. 1770.
Courtesy, Georgia Department of Archives and History.

many acts of violence against the Persons and Property of those gentlemen that have declared themselves friends of Government," Governor Wright removed the papers from Savannah to Fort George on Cockspur Island, where a guard consisting of a captain, two subalterns, and fifty rangers protected them.[38] This desire to safeguard the stamps, of course, left the governor himself and the "friends of Government" in Savannah virtually unprotected.

The dilemma of the vulnerability of the government, should the Sons of Liberty have chosen at this time to contest its control in Savannah forcefully, was resolved on 2 February by the arrival at Tybee Island of the *Speedwell*, the ship that had originally brought the stamped papers. The rangers placed them on board ship and immediately returned to Savannah. Governor Wright recognized that a confrontation was likely and that "further Force is now necessary to support His Majesties authority from insults & reduce the People to due obedience to the Civil Power."[39] As a consequence, twenty seamen from the *Speedwell* and several "Gentlemen & others" who had promised their assistance, should it be needed, joined the seventy rangers two days later. This force of about 100 men opposed an estimated gathering of 240 Sons of Liberty who had assembled near the town common "with their arms and colours," intent upon demanding that Governor Wright "order the Papers back, to be delivered up to them & if I did not they were to shoot me." Three hours later, when it once again became obvious that the royal forces were too strong, the mob, differing "amongst themselves," dispersed.[40]

In the confrontations of the Stamp Act crisis, the colonial governors found that they could not depend on the militia to maintain or restore public order. In Georgia, Governor Wright did not even try to call out the militia companies to assist in the protection of the stamped paper. Although Colonel Francis Harris of the First Regiment was apparently a "friend of Government," neither he nor any other member of the chain of command responded publicly on his own initiative to the military

---

[38]Ibid.
[39]Ibid.
[40]Wright to Conway, 7 February 1766, ibid., 110-11.

challenge.[41] The potential actions of the militia, had the rangers not been available or a larger force been necessary, are conjectural.

Governor Wright decided that he had sufficient reasons for not putting the militiamen unnecessarily to the test, reasons he had elaborated in the past but even more precisely set down in a letter to Henry Seymour Conway in the midst of the crisis. "Possibly your Excellency may be surprised that I have not mentioned calling out the Militia but I have too much Reason to think that I should have armed more against me than for me, & that Volunteers were the only People I could have any Confidence in or dependence upon." Governor Wright obviously understood the difficulties inherent in the use of citizen-soldiers in a crisis in which many of them sympathized with, or actually were, members of the opposition. Although a potential source of support that might very well have responded to the authority of the Crown if they had been called, the militia companies played no official or direct role in the defense of the royal prerogatives by Governor Wright.[42]

The Sons of Liberty, on the other hand, did not utilize the militia companies as units against the governor. They were, however, able to exploit two aspects of the militia system. Legal musters on 25 October and 2 January provided the opportunity for protest because they afforded one of the few occasions for assembly in a colony with a widely dispersed population. After the training day was over, militiamen, as private citizens, could join the protesting crowds. The military trappings of the companies—the weapons, the drums, and the colors—indicated their presence and lent a sense of legitimacy to the protests held after the musters. The fact that these items were present, particularly the colors, normally carried in the British army by the ensigns, seems to indicate that junior officers as well may have been involved in the protests. Nonetheless, the militia as yet remained untested as an organization, since militia companies had played no role at all in the crisis.

In March 1766 Governor Wright met with "several of the most sensible and dispassionate People from different Parts of the Province," including those of the "largest Property," and by his "arguments and reasoning with them, [they] seemed intirely convinced of their error, & the danger & folly of their late rebellious assembling." Although he

---

[41]Habersham to Whitefield, 27 January 1766; *Collections* 6:56.
[42]Wright to Conway, 31 January 1766, CRG, TS 37: 110-11.

thought that his diplomacy had generally succeeded, Wright recognized that "a knot of rebellious turbulent Spirits still remain here in Town, kept hot by their continual correspondence & intercourse with Charles Town." Even though he felt "that many of the better sort of People begin to see that my firmness . . . will redound to the interest and happiness of the Province & People in general," this "knot" remained even after Parliament repealed the Stamp Act, the news of which the colonists received on 16 June.[43] The crisis of confrontation had shaken the colony and then as quickly had passed; yet a fissure had developed with significant political and military implications for the future.

From a political standpoint, for the first time two factions, or parties, had emerged in political life in Georgia, although for awhile they no longer confronted each other face to face. The presence of this second party weakened the political power of Governor Wright and the Crown, for now their efforts could be countered at every turn by the Sons of Liberty. Second, Governor Wright realized that the confrontation had been a near thing; he wrote that "I must . . . declare that I have had the great mortification to see the Reins of Government nearly wrested out of my hands, His Majesties authority insulted, & the Civil Power obstructed."[44] Finally, the military and political imbroglios strained the prestige and personal influence that Governor Wright had so carefully cultivated.[45] In the eyes of many colonists he had chosen sides; he had placed the interests of the Crown before their own. The royal government would no longer operate without political dissent challenging each of the major steps taken by its leadership.

Parliament repealed the Stamp Act largely because of the combined reactions of the colonists of North America and the merchants of England. While setting a precedent for future resistance, the Sons of Liberty in Georgia, however, had not been able to overcome directly the firm stand made by Governor Wright against their efforts. Georgia was the only colony in which stamps had actually been distributed and used.[46] As one member lamented, "The number of the sons of liberty are too few here to make any head against the other party [including the merchants],

---

[43]Wright to Conway, 10 March 1766, ibid., 116-17; *CRG* 9:540.
[44]Wright to Conway, 31 January 1766, CRG, TS 37:103-104.
[45]Abbot, *Royal Governors*, 108, 123.
[46]Spindel, "Stamp Act Riots," 217-19; Alden, *History*, 69.

which is supported by the rangers of this province."[47] Of greater consequence than numbers, however, was the fact that the opposition had not been effectively organized. It had confronted the 100 men representing the authority of the king with a mob rather than an army. For the time being, the Sons of Liberty had failed to challenge the royal government decisively.

During the Stamp Act crisis, for the first time the royal governor of Georgia had used a military force, organized primarily for external defense, to intimidate and thus to quell an internal disorder, or civil disturbance. The governor did not use the Royal Americans; they were too few and were beyond his effective control. Although the governors of New Jersey, Massachusetts, and Maryland originally asked General Gage for regulars, only in New York City did the commander in chief assemble Redcoats as a show of force. Nor did Governor Wright call upon the militia, which in his eyes was truly a force of last resort in an internal confrontation.[48] Instead he relied upon the firm support of the rangers. Although members of provincial organizations, the rangers were volunteers, commanded by officers holding commissions from the governor and paid by the Crown. These soldiers were as much troops of the king as the regulars. Employed by the governor, they had a vested interest in following orders. The nature of the duties performed and the relative isolation of many of the garrisons they manned may have contributed to their loyalty by minimizing their contact with the general populace.

Furthermore, the rangers had been well led. The governor himself had provided personal leadership and acted "with unusual Firmness & Spirit."[49] He had appeared with them with his musket in hand and had personally patrolled the streets as well. Both troop leaders, John Milledge and James Edward Powell, who were also prominent political leaders, had warned Governor Wright of impending troubles, had responded immediately to his orders, and ultimately had remained loyal to the king. This dynamic leadership had obviously inspired and influenced the rangers to stand firm when faced with disadvantageous odds and to tip

---

[47]*Pennsylvania Gazette*, 13 February 1766, 2.

[48]Spindel, "Stamp Act Riots", 26; Alden, *History*, 72; Shy, *Toward Lexington*, 210-12.

[49]James Habersham to Revrd Mr. George Whitefield, 7 February 1766, *Collections* 6:57.

decisively the delicate balance in the first confrontation between the Sons of Liberty and the royal governor.

As the Stamp Act crisis passed into memory, the affairs of the colony, superficially, returned to normal. For a time the Royal Americans and the rangers went about their usual peacetime routines. Governor Wright, obviously mindful of the crisis that he had just faced, felt that there were never enough of these soldiers in the colony to satisfy him, and he made his needs known on several occasions. For example, in April 1767 he made an especially impassioned appeal to General Gage, commander in chief of British forces in North America. "For God sake Sir, is it possible to spare a few Troops from either of the Florida's, or from the Northward? an addition even of 100 Men would now in time of Peace sufficiently garrison Fort Augusta, & Fort George, leave 3 or 4 to take care that the Works at Frederica are not burn't &c & have enough here at Savanah [*sic*] to command some little respect."[50] These appeals went unanswered at the time they were offered, and with the passage of time, a mere 100 men would prove an insufficient force with which to counter a growing threat. As a consequence, Governor Wright found himself in the position of seeing already inadequate support eroding, even as he clamored for additional soldiers.

The rangers—the soldiers who had ably supported the governor and the king during the critical period from December 1765 to March 1766— were ironically the first to fall under the outside pressures of austerity. For a time, though, through 1766 and into the early months of 1767, they continued to perform their normal duties at a strength of 11 officers, 2 cadets, and 139 men. They experienced about the same turnover rate as earlier and even less turbulence after October 1767. As before, they, with the regulars, garrisoned the forts along the frontier. There were fifteen rangers at Fort Argyle, and twenty-five at Fort Barrington, although its enclosed caponier, was falling into such disrepair that Governor Wright was considering abandoning it. Augusta with thirty rangers (and regulars at Fort Augusta) and Fort George with nineteen were the remaining major links in the line of defense, backed by a reserve of sorts in Savannah.[51]

---

[50]Wright to Gage, 2 April 1767, CRG, TS 37:244; Wright to Board of Trade, 15 June 1767, ibid. 28, pt. 2B:496.

[51]"Georgia Pay Bill[s]," Gage MSS; "Answers" of Wright to Lords of Trade, 1766, CRG, TS 28, pt. 2A:431; Wright to Earl of Shelburne, 18 November 1766, ibid. 37:142;

Members of the latter garrison participated in the usual ceremonies marking the king's birthday in June 1766.[52] Above all else, the rangers were the force preferred by the governor to prevent "accidents. . . from Indians, or Negroes, or from the Insults of the People."[53]

Unbeknownst to Governor Wright, the distant British government, unmindful of his needs, was making moves to disband the rangers. At least as early as January 1766, General Gage, somewhat closer to the problem, had given thought to deactivating the rangers in Georgia and replacing them with regulars from West Florida.[54] Feeling that he lacked the authority to do this, Gage waited to act until February 1767, when he received the necessary orders from Secretary at War Lord Barrington. He then dispatched Captain Lewis Fuser, an officer of the Royal Americans, to Georgia with orders "for the dismission of those troops."[55] To Governor Wright, the orders, which he received on 26 March, were "a very sudden & great stroke to the [Province] & will be severely felt." In accordance with these orders, despite his own obvious misgivings, he discharged the rangers on 31 March.[56]

A definitive reason for abolishing the rangers did not appear at the time in any of the correspondence relating to them. Governor Wright, in writing to General Gage in April, said that "I own I apprehended it [the loss of the rangers], as the natural consequence of the Peoples strange conduct & behaviour."[57] Wright apparently felt that political dissent within the colony, the very thing the rangers had proven useful in quelling during the Stamp Act crisis, had influenced the decision to disband them.

Unfortunately, General Gage did not think highly of the rangers. He wrote in January 1766 that they were "an Expensive sort of Troops and some Companies of Foot might Answer the purpose full as well, if not better; Tho' it must be allowed that Cavalry may be of great use to the

Collections 3:169.

[52]*Gazette*, 15 June 1766, 3.

[53]Wright to Gage, 2 April 1767, CRG, TS 27:243.

[54]Gage to Lord Barrington, Secretary at War, 8 January 1766, Carter, *Correspondence* 2:324; Gage to Barrington, 7 May 1766; ibid., 352.

[55]Gage to Barrington, 22 February 1767, Carter, *Correspondence* 2:409.

[56]*Gazette*, 1 April 1767, 2.

[57]Wright to Gage, 2 April 1767, CRG, TS 37:243.

Southward in Time of Actual war with the Indians."[58] Regardless of the reason—austerity, retribution, or Gage's shortsighted, personal preference for infantry regulars—the rangers, as a component of the British establishment, disappeared from the seacoast and, for a time, from the frontier, and Governor Wright viewed his vulnerability with pessimism and dejection.

As a result of the passing of the rangers, James Wright felt that the colony had been stripped of its most important military resource and that he was now "destitute of all means of support."[59] First, a comparable number of regulars did not replace the rangers as Wright had believed would be the case and as Gage had intimated might happen in his letters to his superiors.[60] Second, only about twenty regulars remained in Georgia—an ensign and thirteen men at newly rebuilt Fort Augusta and six or seven men at Frederica.[61] For Governor Wright the paucity of full-time troops meant that "my situation my Lord is rather hard & difficult, not a soldier in the Province more than [the regulars] I have mentioned, either to protect it against Indians, or Negro Insurrections, or even to be the least check on the Licentiousness of the People, or command respect to His Majesties Authority."[62] The Stamp Act crisis and subsequent political clashes had apparently caused Governor Wright to view internal and external threats in much the same light; in fact, he now seemed to give increased priority to the former. Unfortunately, for him, as of mid-1767, he no longer had the solid, provincial troops upon whom he could rely, nor would he be able for much longer to call on the regulars, the only other royal force in the colony.

The Royal Americans in Georgia, a relatively inconsequential force aside from its symbolic value, fell victim to attrition and a change of colonial policy. From the peak of thirty men in 1764, their strength dropped to twenty-nine by January 1767 and to twenty-one by August.[63]

---

[58]Gage to Barrington, 8 January 1766, Carter, *Correspondence* 2:324.

[59]Wright to Gage, 2 April 1767, CRG, TS 37:243.

[60]Ibid.

[61]Ibid.

[62]Wright to Shelburne, 15 August 1767, ibid., 241.

[63]Captain-Lieutenant Ralph Phillips to Wright, 6 January 1767, *CRG* 14:413; Wright to Gage, 20 July and 6 August 1767, CRG, TS 37:247, 250; Wright to Shelburne, 15 August 1767, ibid., 241.

Governor Wright, bemoaning the loss of the rangers in April, felt very strongly that the regulars manning Fort Augusta and Fort Frederica were too far away and too few to take up the slack; more would be necessary to "prevent any attempt to insult His Majesties Authority, & the Officers of the Crown, & this my Lord may be the more necessary as the Rangers are disbanded."[64] As a result, he proposed to Captain Fuser, the local commander, that the small force should be redistributed so that twenty-one men would be stationed at Savannah and seven at Fort George. This would then ensure that "I may have Centinels at least in the day time."[65] Obviously, Governor Wright thought that the Royal Americans could be more useful to the Crown impressing tidewater Georgians rather than the Creeks or backcountrymen with the authority of the king.

Wright must have been shocked once again when he learned that the regulars, few though they were, would soon be leaving. On 17 August 1768 the *Georgia Gazette* reported that Captain Ralph Phillips and his Royal Americans had set out from Augusta for Charles Town, where they would embark for New York.[66] General Gage reported on 18 August to Secretary of State for the Colonies Lord Hillsborough that he had complied with his instructions and had ordered the three companies of the First Battalion "to join their Battalion in the Province of Quebec."[67] He reported on 9 September that part of this force had landed in New York and was already on its way to Quebec; the remainder were "daily expected."[68]

Lord Hillsborough and General Gage had compelling reasons for withdrawing the Royal Americans from Georgia. Of overriding importance, the removal of the detachment of the Sixtieth Regiment was only a part of a general relocation of troops from the interior to key garrisons along the eastern seaboard. This reflected the new colonial and territorial policies of the British cabinet in general and Hillsborough in particular.

---

[64]Gage to Shelburne, 3 April 1767, Carter, *Correspondence* 1:126; Wright to Hillsborough, 23 May 1768, CRG, TS 37:283; Wright to Shelburne, 6 April 1767, ibid., 216.

[65]Wright to Gage, 6 August 1767, CRG, TS 37:250.

[66]*Gazette*, 17 August 1768, 2.

[67]Gage to Hillsborough, 18 August 1768, Carter, *Correspondence* 1: 187.

[68]Gage to Barrington, 19 August 1768, ibid. 2:480; Gage to Hillsborough, 9 September 1768, ibid. 1:192.

The cabinet, in effect, revamped the Proclamation of 1763 and redrew the old Indian boundary line beyond the Appalachian Mountains, thereby allowing more westward settlement. In addition, the ministers now left the regulation of Indian traders and, for all practical purposes, settlers to the colonies. These measures saved money but, more important, allowed the removal of British troops from the frontiers. After all was said and done, these troops were now in a better position to respond to a revolt by the colonists, should one develop, or as the earl of Hillsborough wrote General Gage, "to serve effectually upon any emergency whatever."[69] This was equally evident to the Americans.

Aside from the perceived need for a redistribution of soldiers, the colonial response to the Mutiny, or Quartering, Act in general and Georgia's response in particular had had a bearing on the ministerial decision. In May 1765, on the heels of the Stamp Act, Parliament had passed the Quartering Act, which directly applied to the colonies the provisions of the English Mutiny Act relating to the regulars.[70] The new law, in addition to tightening military discipline, required the provincial assemblies to make arrangements to quarter British soldiers stationed there in barracks, inns, or other suitable, uninhabited buildings in the absence of the first two. Furthermore, they were to supply the troops with certain categories of rations and accessories. Led by New York, a number of colonies, including South Carolina and Georgia, interpreting this act to be a form of indirect taxation, refused to comply.[71] The controversy in Georgia, where troops were needed and repeatedly requested, surprisingly raged from 20 January until 29 October 1767, when the Commons finally agreed to provide £200 for items ranging from firewood to rum; these expenses were included in the tax act of 1 April 1768.[72] General Gage's insistence that he could not "send Troops into Forts where no provision is made to accommodate them with the Common necessaries of life" probably influenced the outcome.[73]

---

[69]Shy, *Toward Lexington*, 260-65; Alden, *History*, 92-94, quotation on 93; Jack M. Sosin, *The Revolutionary Frontier, 1763-1783* (New York: Holt, Rhinehart & Winston, 1967) 14-15.

[70]Greene, *Colonies*, 42-44.

[71]Ibid., 114-15; Alden, *History*, 86-87; Coleman, *Colonial Georgia*, 252-55.

[72]*CRG* 14:412-13, 476-80, 483-86; 19, pt. 1:44-45; *Gazette*, 4 November 1767, 3.

[73]Gage to Wright, 16 May 1767, CRG, TS 37:245; Shy, *Toward Lexington*, 272.

The change of heart by the Commons House of Assembly of Georgia came too late. General Gage could not justify supplying soldiers to a colony that would not support the few who were already there. Feeling as he did that "the Troops are not Stationed either in South Carolina or Georgia for the sake of Convenience, but for the Service of those Colonies only," General Gage apparently could not reconcile the reluctance by the Commons with their simultaneous request for additional troops.[74] Captain Fuser, the local commander, influenced Gage's thinking by complaining to him "that the soldiers at Fort Augusta lye upon the boards, & are continually seduced by the Country people to desert, for wch no satisfaction can be obtained."[75] Finally, the garrisons were simply too difficult to support, too small, and too dispersed to protect even themselves should the Indians have ever attacked in force.[76] So, ministerial policy and local irritants merged, and General Gage ordered the Royal Americans to Quebec. As far as Governor Wright was concerned, he no longer had "a single Soldier within this Province."[77] Although numerous pleas for such troops would be made in the future, the next regulars in the province would be Georgia Continentals, troops of the Continental Congress, in the midst of the American Revolution.

The demise of first the rangers and then the Royal Americans left both the frontier and the seacoast vulnerable, despite the continued presence of the militia. Of the two unprotected areas, Governor Wright and the members of the assembly appeared most alarmed initially by the loss of the ranger garrison at Fort George on Cockspur Island in the Savannah River. Consequently, the governor's first actions came while the regulars still protected the extremities of the frontier. On the very day that Captain Fuser arrived with the order to disband the rangers, Governor Wright explained to the council that he intended to petition General Gage for a number of regulars to garrison Fort George; in the

---

[74]Gage to Shelburne, 7 April 1767, Carter, *Correspondence* 1:134.

[75]Gage to Wright, 16 May 1767, CRG, TS 37:245; Wright to Gage, 6 August 1767, ibid., 250.

[76]Shy, *Toward Lexington*, 273.

[77]Wright to Lord Dartmouth, Secretary of State for the Colonies, 17 June 1773, CRG, TS 38, pt. 1:64.

meantime, he proposed that a force of one officer and ten men, supported by the province, be placed at this "key to our Port."[78]

Governor Wright had a number of reasons for rating Fort George as such a critical installation. He felt that the post, located as it was at the entrance to the Savannah River, commanded and enforced "a due Observation of Several of our Laws and which would otherwise be as mere dead Letters." In this regard, the garrison backed the customs officials as they attempted to limit smuggling and to "enforce due obedience to the Laws of Trade." Moreover, it provided a check against "Epedimecal, and Contagious diseases [which] might be brought into our Town, and possibly spread into the Country unknown to us, till it might be too late to prevent the fatal Consequences of them."[79] The garrison could basically enforce quarantines on ships with victims aboard who had apparently contagious diseases, such as smallpox; the infected were most often newly arrived slaves. The commanding officer at Fort George, the commander of the scout boat (the *Prince George* was still afloat), and the keeper of the lazaretto, the quarantine building on Tybee Island, would jointly share the responsibility for detaining ships at Tybee Creek or individuals at the lazaretto, apparently for up to forty days after the last person had recovered from the illness.[80]

Governor Wright and some of the "principal inhabitants of Savannah" who signed a petition in 1771 additionally recognized that a strong fort could "prevent Enemies Privateers from cuting [*sic*] out and carrying off our shipping or from coming up the River to plunder &c."[81] These justifications for a garrison of some type at Fort George highlighted the importance of the port of Savannah to the colony. As the Stamp Act crisis had demonstrated, the river and the harbor were the lifeline upon which the colonists depended. Convinced of its importance, Governor Wright set about to rectify the deficiency.

The governor wasted very little time in providing a garrison for Fort George after gaining the concurrence of the Council. While the regulars remained, he rejected the suggestion of the Commons that they be used.

---

[78]Wright to Shelburne, 6 April 1767, ibid. 37:188.

[79]These are summarized from Wright to Commons House of Assembly, 10 November 1769, *CRG* 15:41; *Collections* 3:168.

[80]*Gazette*, 27 July 1768, 3; 15 March 1769, 3.

[81]Memorial, 17 January 1771, *CRG* 16:268-69; *Collections* 3:168.

The Royal Americans were spread too thinly already, and if they were withdrawn from Fort Augusta, they would leave the inhabitants of that region to face both the Indians and the encroaching white "Crackers," who were, according to James Wright, "a set of Vagabonds often as bad or worse than the Indians themselves."[82]

Having no other immediate alternative, Governor Wright constituted a detachment—which by May numbered ten men—and placed Captain John Simpson in command; initially he paid their salaries out of his own pocket.[83] He viewed this, however, as only a temporary measure. With the support of the commons, he wrote General Gage and requested that additional regulars be sent to provide a garrison for Fort George and to bolster the contingent of Royal Americans at Fort Augusta and Frederica as well, little knowing at the time that even these would soon depart.[84] For the short term he expected the assembly to agree to support the men when it next met. If the members failed to help, he would "withdraw the Command, and the Province will be left intirely open."[85]

When the assembly met in late October, Governor Wright presented his plan and carefully explained that, if the legislative body refused to support the detachment, he would discontinue his own financial backing.[86] After considering this ultimatum, the Commons voted £210 on 30 October 1767 to fund an officer, now Captain James Edward Powell, formerly of the rangers, and five men for twelve months.[87] As the regulars departed and no replacements were forthcoming, the delegates continued to vote such appropriations through at least 1773.[88] By this time, although Fort George continued to be an issue of importance, it was "almost in ruins," and the one officer and three men still stationed there could do no more than just "make signals &c."[89] As highly as the

---

[82]*CRG* 14:474-75.

[83]Wright to Shelburne, 15 August 1767, CRG, TS 37:241; *Gazette*, 13 May 1767, 3; "Commissions," 153.

[84]Wright to Shelburne, 15 August 1767, CRG, TS 37:241; Gage to Shelburne, 27 May 1767, Carter, *Correspondence* 1:140; *CRG* 14:475.

[85]Wright to Shelburne, 15 August 1767, CRG, TS 37:241.

[86]*CRG* 14:481-82.

[87]Ibid.; *Gazette*, 19 August 1767, 2; "Commissions," 153.

[88]*CRG* 19, pt. 1:50, 128, 181, 492; the Commons finally reimbursed Wright in the amount of £184.8.4 for the period that he supported the garrison in December 1768 (ibid ., pt. 1:127).

[89]*Collections* 3:168.

colonists apparently rated the importance of Fort George, such a token force, even at its peak strength, was of no real consequence when balanced with the defensive needs of the entire colony. Nevertheless, in the absence of regulars and rangers, this provincial garrison, astride the lifeline of the colony, for a time served as the only paid, full-time force directly answerable to the governor.

The five years from 1763 to 1768 had been a time of considerable turmoil and change within the colony of Georgia and North America. Peace and prosperity had followed the Treaty of Paris. Despite this thriving situation, a number of Georgians, as well as other Americans, had begun to develop a new view of the relationship that existed between England and her colonies. All Americans had in some way been affected by the series of parliamentary and ministerial decisions designed to reassert British controls over an empire that for decades had effectively been adrift. The Stamp Act and then the Quartering crises placed the mother country and the colonies at odds. In both, Governor Wright proved that he and the Crown had the influence and, in the Stamp Act crisis, the force necessary to enforce the acts of Parliament. The victories would be relatively short-lived, as the crises were only the first of the clashes of American and English interests.

The three organizations within the military establishment of Georgia were involved in, and affected by, the political, social, and economic fallout from the changing pattern of colonial relations. The British regulars, first the Independents and then the Royal Americans, disappeared from the forts that they had garrisoned for most of the colonial era. The Crown disbanded the rangers at the peak of their power, although they had proven decisive in the first confrontation between the Sons of Liberty and the royal governor. By default, the militia remained the only force of any consequence within the colony to face the challenges of expansion, the Indians, and internal dissent during the years of changing peace.

Chapter 4

The Backcountry, the Creeks, and the Military

The period between the departure of the Royal Americans and the end of 1774, at first glance, did not appear to differ markedly in Georgia from the preceding years of peace. Despite the interruptions caused earlier by the disturbances of 1765 and 1766, the colony continued to grow and to prosper, thus fulfilling earlier expectations. Scattered among some 1,400 settlements, or "plantations," in twelve parishes, the population reached about 23,375 blacks and whites by 1770 and 33,000 by 1773.[1] With the signing of yet another treaty with the Indians in the latter year, an additional land cession of 2,116,298 acres expanded the northern frontier beyond the Broad River and raised the total holdings of the colony to an estimated 6,695,429 acres.[2] Exports of rice (20,192 barrels in 1774), indigo, deerskins, wood products, naval stores, and a host of other items reached a value of £68,688.10.2 by 1773, and the province, in James Habersham's words, "was making a rapid progress in her Commerce, Wealth and Population, and from the Situation I am now in, you must suppose, [as a merchant] I am loaded with Business."[3] In terms of overall expansion and commerce, the temporary breaches between the colonists and Great Britain caused by the Stamp and Quartering acts superficially seemed to have mended as quickly as they had appeared.

Although development continued, and no major internal upheavals or confrontations marred the relative calm of politics, a progression of seemingly minor political incidents, some of which could have gotten out of hand, occurred during these years. These minor events, in retrospect and taken as a whole, represented a significant pattern of growing dissent.

---

[1]Wright's estimate of settlements (*Collections* 3:160); see also *Historical Statistics*, 756; Greene, *Population*, 5-7, 182; there were 15,000 blacks in 1773.

[2]*Collections* 3:160.

[3]James Habersham to Henry Ellis, 27 January 1772, ibid. 6:162; 3:164-67; *Historical Statistics*, 767-68.

The colonial military establishment did not become directly involved in any of these political squabbles. As institutions of government, however, military units could not remain completely detached, and the pervading climate of political uneasiness affected each type of force in a different way.

The Stamp Act crisis, as the starting point, had raised issues, challenged fundamental beliefs, and altered existing relationships; these seeds of change, sown in crisis, matured with the passing of time. The political tensions of these years resulted from the friction between the two factions—the "friends of Government" and the Sons of Liberty. The former, led by Governor Wright, attempted to retain complete control, while the latter sought a greater share of political power. Available military forces would increasingly become a factor in the overall political equation.

The arena for the political struggle between the two competing factions was the assembly. Here in relative isolation, insofar as most issues were concerned, the members of the Commons, groping for a greater role in the political processes of the colony, challenged the royal prerogatives of the governor and the Upper House on several occasions between 1766 and 1774. These issues ranged from claims over responsibility for selecting the colonial agent to represent Georgia in London to contests over the right of free passage for postmen on the ferries.[4] Only one, the Quartering Act, directly impinged upon the military.

Debates over the authority of the governor to confirm the speaker of the assembly grew particularly heated, and support for nonimportation of certain English goods in protest against the duties of the Townshend Act of 1767 extended beyond the commons and threatened to boil over into a crisis of the magnitude encountered with the introduction of the Stamp Act. In the latter case, opposition began to coalesce in 1769 as the Amicable Society, a radical committee, engineered a mass meeting that adopted measures relating to nonimportation similar to those passed by South Carolina. The furor died as Parliament in 1770 repealed all of the irritating taxes, except the duty on tea.[5]

In each instance of opposition, the governor and the Upper House managed to head off the political challenge before serious inroads could

---

[4]Coleman, *Revolution*, 24-26.
[5]Ibid., 28-32, 34-37; Saye, *Constitutional History*, 80-81.

be made in the powers of the royal government.[6] Despite these temporary successes, due in large measure to the governor's personal loyalty and dedication as "a faithful servant" of the Crown, according to James Habersham, "the spirit of opposition never was more violent, than now."[7] The seeds of dissidence planted during the Stamp Act crisis were growing to maturity, and they forced Governor Wright to assess the strength of his government in a report to the ministry: "But my Lord things are not gone too far yet in this Province to be reduced to Proper order, & kept so, as I have not allowed them to make any innovation in my Power to prevent and if the Council are Supported every thing will, & must return & go in its proper Channel, but otherwise I think not."[8] On balance, Governor Wright concluded that he could maintain control if given proper support. Unfortunately, this support, which to Wright should have included a fairly large number of regulars, was not forthcoming. In fact, the governor had lost the military forces—the rangers and the Royal Americans—that he had felt were significant assets. Only the militia and the small garrison at Fort George remained.

With the disbanding of the rangers and the departure of the British regulars, the militia became, by default, the force upon which the colony and the governor, with obvious reluctance, would have to rely in any crisis. There was no other alternative in the colony at all between 1768 and 1773, and none readily at hand after that. For example, Governor Wright estimated that the British garrison at St. Augustine, East Florida, was "of no kind of use . . . their distance and Situation is Such."[9]

The militia only gradually assumed a more active role, however, since it had been eclipsed in importance by the rangers before and during the Stamp Act crisis. The reported militia strength had increased from 1,100 in 1765 to 1,800 by 1767; nevertheless, not a single new company had been added to the three regiments in the same period. The First

---

[6]Greene, *Quest*, 47.

[7]Wright to Earl of Shelburne, Secretary of State for the Southern Department, 18 November 1766, CRG, TS 37:143-44; Habersham to William Knox, 7 May 1768, *Collections* 6:64; for other self-evaluations and favorable assessments of Wright by Habersham, see Wright to Lord Hillsborough, Secretary of State for the Colonies, 6 August 1768, CRG, TS 37:354; Habersham to John Nutt, 28 November 1771, *Collections* 6:153; Habersham to Wright, 15 February 1772, ibid., 165.

[8]Wright to Shelburne, 6 April 1767, CRG, TS 37:187.

[9]Wright to Hillsborough, 13 December 1770, ibid., 501-502.

Regiment had held a general muster on 4 June 1766, but as previously noted, despite the opportunity for participation by the militia, the rangers had dominated the observance of the king's birthday.[10] Governor Wright's assessment of the militia had not changed and became more negative by 1770.

> What are a few Scattered Militia Suppose from 2500 to 3000. against an Invasion if any Such thing was to be Attempted. and of these Settlers Numbers would make off to the Neighboring Provinces on the first appearance of danger or Trouble. and Many others Would not Obey Orders, being neither in Pay, or Subject to discipline. and if under both, yet they Could not be drawn down to the Sea Coast from their Families, who Would Probably be Robbed and Murdered by the Indians during their absence, so that your Lordship Sees what a Situation we Shall be in if War happens. and I presume not one half of the above Number to be depended on in the whole for Every Place and Service.[11]

Despite Governor Wright's obvious misgivings, after 1768 the growth of the militia regiments and the activities in which the companies took part increased, if for no other reason than there was no longer another force upon which the governor could call. As a result, the vital signs of the militia became more vigorous, both in organizational expansion and in terms of increased participation in duties essential to the community as a whole.

The first sign was a faint stirring as the number of militia companies marginally increased. These changes were seemingly insignificant at first and reflected the relative peace of the times; there simply was no obvious impetus for immediate expansion. Governor Wright added a new company to the First Regiment in August 1767; it was distinctively named the Light Infantry Company and comprised volunteers, an innovative concept in Georgia without precedent in peacetime during the royal period. He commissioned Sir Patrick Houstoun, a prominent landholder (he owned 4,900 acres by 1774) and delegate to the assembly, as captain of this new company, for which he authorized fifty "Private Men" in addition to the necessary officers, four of whom the governor appointed at the same time. These volunteers were to come from the

---

[10]Greene, *Population*, 181; Wright to Shelburne, 18 November 1766 and 6 April 1767, CRG, TS 37:141-42, 180-81; "Commissions," 144-51; *Gazette*, 28 May 1766, 4.

[11]Wright to Hillsborough, 13 December 1770, CRG, TS 37:499-500.

three Savannah Town Companies of militia—the First, Fourth, and Eighth.[12]

A Grenadier Company of identical structure joined the First Regiment in June 1772; Captain Samuel Elbert, a merchant (of Rae, Elbert, Graham), landowner, and delegate to the assembly, was the commander.[13] Governor Wright gave no reason for the formation of either company, nor is there any way at present to determine the composition of the enlisted ranks. Nevertheless, he managed to create two distinctive volunteer units in Savannah and did so within the existing militia structure.

These two companies, raised five years apart, highlight a growth trend that continued and gradually increased over the next seven years. By December 1773 Governor Wright had added eight new companies to the three regiments, which brought the total number of companies to twenty-nine—all foot companies, as the Troop of Horse had disbanded, probably in 1771.[14] In addition, a separate organization, the Watch Company—perhaps not even technically a part of the militia, although it drew from the same manpower—formed in 1770. It had three officers, a drummer, and twenty-seven watchmen between the ages of eighteen and fifty-five to patrol the streets of Savannah. In all likelihood, the governor and the assembly patterned this company after a similar unit in Charles Town to maintain law and order, much like a police force, with the special responsibility of keeping slaves in line and thereby preventing insurrections. The strength of all of the militia companies by September was 2,828 officers and men.[15]

---

[12]A company of volunteers commanded by Captain William Moore was "raised for the Assistance of our Friends the Chikesaws against our Common Enemy the French" in May 1757, during wartime; the members may have been Indians ("Commissions," 61-63); for details on the Light Infantry Company, see ibid., 153-54. See also Lucas, *Index*, 305; Greene, *Quest*, 494.

[13]"Commissions," 187-88; Elbert had 1,445 acres of land by 1774; he would later become a general in the Georgia Continentals (Bryant and Hemperley, *English Crown Grants*; Lucas, *Index*, 185); see also Greene, *Quest*, 493.

[14]"Commissions," 174, 204, 205; the *Georgia Gazette* printed a reminder of the dissolution of the Troop of Horse "near" three years before (*Gazette*, 6 April 1774, 2).

[15]Wright to Dartmouth, 16 August 1773, CRG, TS 38; pt. 1:90-91; *CRG* 15:255; 19, pt.1:147, 488; "Commissions,"171-72; Peter H. Wood, *Black Majority: Negroes in Colonial South Carolina from 1670 through the Stono Rebellion* (New York: W. W. Norton, 1974) 273.

Fig. 12: James Habersham. Courtesy of the Hargrett Rare Book and Manuscript Library, University of Georgia.

The commissions given the officers of the militia were a further measure of growth and vitality. Governor Wright and, in his absence from 1771 to 1773, James Habersham seem to have been sensitive to vacancies created within the regiments and to have filled them with a fair degree of regularity. For example, President Habersham wrote in August 1772 to Colonel James Jackson of the Second Regiment in Augusta and discussed the problems of granting promotions. In part, he said, "When you was last here, I requested of you a Return of the Officers, and the Number of Companys in your Regiment, that any vacancies might be filled up, also to be informed, whether it was necessary to constitute any new Companys, and if so who would be proper to appoint Officers." He also made it clear that he, as acting governor, and, in all likelihood, Wright as well, relied a great deal upon the regimental commanders and captains of companies to supply them with names for vacancies and to help to determine when increases in population called for new units.[16]

Vacancies and changes in the ranks of the officers occurred frequently. For example, the Fourth Company, First Regiment, experienced officer turnovers in six out of the eight years between 1767 and 1775. In the same period, the colonelcy of the First Regiment changed three times.[17] These promotions resulted from officers' reaching the upper age limit for the active militia, from deaths, from transfers between units, and as a result of officers' moving out of the province altogether; Governor Wright removed an officer from command in only one documented case: he relieved Joseph Gibbons from the First Company, First Regiment.[18] In many instances, officers simply moved up the chain of command in their own companies.[19]

Regardless of these changes, the social composition of the officers' corps remained much the same as that of a decade before: 51 officers out of 102, exactly one-half, had more than 500 acres of land. The Third

---

[16]For Habersham's title, see *CRG* 15:316-19; Habersham to Colonel James Jackson, 8 August 1772, *Collections* 6:198.

[17]"Commissions," 139, 151-52, 163, 165, 178, 185-88, 206, 212, 217-18, 221.

[18]Ibid., 205.

[19]For example, in the Fourth Company, First Regiment, Samuel Elbert advanced from lieutenant to captain (ibid., 152, 165); in the Third Company, First Regiment, Richard Wylly moved from lieutenant to captain and Nicholas Horton from ensign to lieutenant to captain (ibid., 155, 175, 178, 187).

Regiment had fifteen landholders with more than 1,000 acres, as compared with eight for the First, three for the Second, and four for the Fourth. Six had served as delegates to the Commons House of Assembly, and a number of others had been justices of the peace, church vestrymen, and the like. The officers of the militia, as late as 1775, remained an influential and prominent body of social and political leaders.[20]

As organizational growth occurred, the colonial government, after a period of years, reaffirmed the militia law, which had theoretically disappeared in 1770 when the original law, reenacted since 1755, expired.[21] The political challenges of the period from 1768 to 1773 interfered with many of the routine affairs of the government, and the militia law had apparently been one of the victims.[22] For example, the assembly refused even to pass a tax bill during the 1770–1771 session because of a dispute over the nonrepresentation of the four new southern parishes.[23] Consequently, in 1770 a militia bill progressed through the entire legislative process beginning in November and then simply died when it was on the verge of becoming a law on 21 December.[24]

Some of the militia officers in 1772 felt that the elements of the militia system were no longer effective, since the law had expired; others were "afraid of ordering the usual Musters, for fear of being troubled with vexatious Suits in case of refusal or Contumacy of Persons not appearing." In spite of such objections, Acting Governor Habersham called a general muster for 4 June 1772.[25] As a result of such doubts, the legislature passed a new militia act in 1773 to which the governor assented on 29 September. The only obvious element changed was the title: "An Act for the better ordering the Militia." The life of the new statute—three years—would carry the law through the remainder of the colonial era.[26]

---

[20]Analysis based upon data in Lucas, *Index*; Bryant and Hemperley, *English Crown Grants*; and "Commissions." See also Greene, *Quest*, 493-95; *Collections* 3:171-74; *Gazette*, 19 April 1775, 2.

[21]"An Act for the better ordering the Militia of this Province," in *Acts*, 263, DeRenne MSS.

[22]Abbot, *Royal Governors*, 154-55.

[23]Coleman, *Colonial Georgia*, 258-59.

[24]*CRG* 15:224, 231-34, 246, 261.

[25]Habersham to Hillsborough, 30 April 1772, *Collections* 6:178.

[26]*CRG* 15:352; 19, pt. 1:291-332.

With the passage of time, as these positive organizational and legal changes took place, the companies of militia performed activities that had in the past fallen to the rangers. The first category of such duties was the maintenance of law and order: the militiamen aided the appointed justices of the peace in the respective parishes. For example, in June 1767 a guard of militiamen escorted five horse thieves (a sixth was killed resisting arrest) from Augusta to the jail in Savannah; it was quite possible that these same men captured the criminals in the first place.[27] In a similar affair, for which the assembly reimbursed the firm of James Jackson & Company in 1773, a party of militia pursued a band of horse rustlers.[28]

Aside from capturing and escorting criminals, the militiamen performed their legally required duty of patrolling for runaway slaves. Although it was quite possible that patrolling was performed routinely, the official attention paid to it apparently fluctuated. In 1769 Captain Lachlan McGillivray of the Troop of Horse presented a grievance to the grand jurors of the Court of General Sessions that cited the "great neglect of patrol duty in the parish of Christ Church" and singled out the Third Company, commanded by Captain James Cuthbert, as the derelict unit.[29] In December 1771 the Council ordered Colonel Philip Delegal of the First Regiment (Francis Harris had died in October) to ensure that his companies did patrol duty over the Christmas holidays.[30] The militiamen probably found patrolling to be a dull and usually uneventful routine, but they continued to do their legal duty as in the earlier years, at least when violations of the slave laws were numerous.

As the population of slaves in Georgia increased, the number of runaways multiplied accordingly. The governor and his council sent militiamen, as they had once sent rangers, after such escapees at least once a year from 1770 to 1773. For example, in December 1771 the Council alerted Captain Richard Wylly to have part of his Third Company, First Regiment, prepared to apprehend "a great number" of fugitive slaves who had committed robberies between Ebenezer and Savannah. Similar transgressions and responses occurred the next year,

---

[27]*Gazette*, 3 June 1767, 2.
[28]*CRG* 19, pt. 1:500.
[29]*Gazette*, 10 January 1770, 2.
[30]*CRG* 12:147; CRG, TS 37:567.

when slaves burned a house on Black Creek, killing a child, and then on the Savannah River stopped and robbed a boat, owned by Captain John Stirk of the Fourth Company, First Regiment. In this case, even the *Prince George* joined in the search.[31] The white members of southern society viewed fugitive slaves as financial losses and as security threats; as a result, the militia, by rounding them up, carried out the will of the community of which it was a significant part.

In contrast to their previously conspicuous absence from mention in accounts of important events, the militia began to appear and to play a primary part in ceremonies. This occurred gradually, for the *Gazette* mentioned no military units in the ceremony marking the king's birthday in 1767, some two months after the rangers disbanded, although militia officers accompanied the governor on his walk from the council house to Fort Halifax and attended the "entertainment" at the courthouse.[32] By comparison, at similar events in both 1768 and 1769, Governor Wright reviewed several companies of militia drawn up "on the Bay" alongside the river.[33] President James Habersham reported to the absent Wright that, in the course of a similar ceremony on 6 June 1772, he was "surprised to see so respectable an Appearance" as the militia made.[34] Finally, in February 1773, when Sir James Wright, now a baronet, stepped ashore from the scout boat after his stay in England, Sir Patrick Houstoun's company of light infantry, Captain Samuel Elbert's grenadiers, and "the other companies of militia" most likely of the First Regiment were drawn up to receive him.[35]

The training and appearance of the different companies of militia varied, despite the militia law and the fact that ceremonies and musters were held fairly often.[36] The inhabitants of the tidewater and the back

---

[31]*CRG* 19, pt. 1:185, 501-502; 12:146, 325.

[32]*Gazette*, 10 June 1767, 2.

[33]Ibid., 8 June 1768, 2; 7 June 1769, 2.

[34]Habersham to Wright, 6 June 1772, *Collections* 6:183-84.

[35]*South Carolina Gazette*, 1 March 1773, 2; some of the cracks in the power of Wright appear here. Before his return, the Commons voted not to make repairs to his house; with some difficulty it passed a motion to have a committee greet the governor upon his return (*CRG* 15:381, 384-85).

[36]Company musters were not well documented; the scattered evidence seems to indicate that this may have been because they were held rather routinely; see *Collections* 3:167; *Gazette*, 11 May 1768, 3; 9 August 1768, 2; Lilla Mills Hawes, ed., *The Journal*

country obviously had different priorities and cultures that were reflected in the militia. A journal entry and an excerpt from a letter permit a side-by-side appraisal of two militia companies, the First Company of the Second Regiment, from Augusta, and the Light Infantry Company of the First Regiment, in Savannah, at similar ceremonies held the same day in different parts of the province.

In the first, David Taitt, an Indian commissioner, recorded a most revealing passage in his journal in June 1772 after having observed the militia participants in the annual ritual in Augusta. "This being His Majestys Birth Day, I went to see the Malitia of this place Reviewed by their Officers. The men made a very Sorry Appearance, some having old rusty firelocks, others Riffles, and some being well Clothed and Others with Osnaburgh Shirts and Trousers; they fired platoons as ununiformly as their Acuttrements and dress."[37]

By the military standards of the British regulars with whom Taitt was apparently comparing them, these frontier militiamen, or "Banditto" as he referred to them, obviously did not impress him as soldiers. Perhaps his views were colored by the stereotype that inhabitants of the coastal areas had of the settlers of the backcountry. James Habersham, for example, referred to some of the men of the region north of Augusta as "Crackers": "Persons, who have no setled Habitations, and live by hunting and plundering the industrious Setlers."[38] Governor Wright also wrote to Lord Hillsborough that many of the people in the "Back Settlements" were of the "same stamp" as the Regulators, who had

---

of the Reverend John Joachim Zubly A.M., D.D., March 5, 1770 through June 22, 1781 (Savannah: Georgia Historical Society, 1989) 9; Thomas Lee, the gunner for Savannah and a lieutenant in the Eighth Company, First Regiment, apparently taught "Military Discipline" and related drill (see *Gazette*, 24 February 1768, 1).

[37]Newton D. Mereness, ed., "Journal of David Taitt's Travels from Pensacola, West Florida, to and through the Country of the Upper and the Lower Creeks, 1772," in *Travels in the American Colonies* (New York: Macmillan, 1916) 563.

[38]Habersham to Wright, 20 August 1772, *Collections* 6:204; Habersham to Hillsborough, 12 August 1772, ibid., 201-202; Edward J. Cashin, " 'But Brothers, It is our Land We are Talking About': Winners and Losers in the Georgia Backcountry," in *An Uncivil War: The Southern Backcountry during the American Revolution*, ed. Ronald Hoffman, Thad W. Tate, and Peter J. Albert (Charlottesville: University Press of Virginia, 1985) 244.

fought against officials—and the militia—of the colonial government of North Carolina.[39]

Although some backcountrymen deserved the pejorative labels, most were subsistence farmers, trappers, traders, and woodsmen who had been hardened by exposure to the harsh realities of the frontier and lived in almost daily fear of Indian raids. Reflecting the types of men in their units and the different pursuits of the frontier, the officers included fewer large landowners (only three had more than 1,000 acres in 1775) than were present in the other three regiments.[40] Captain Fuser of the Royal Americans in 1767 felt that the backcountrymen around Augusta were capable of defending themselves reasonably well; they were, according to him, "used to arms, & may call themselves good Rangers and where some of the Gen'n have Forts, & better housed than the Kings."[41] Obviously not as polished at drill as the militiamen of the tidewater, these backcountrymen had a higher stake in the militia system than the companies farther from the Indian threat: their stake was survival.

After watching the First Regiment in Savannah, James Habersham provided quite a different impression than had Taitt. "The light Infantry made a good Appearance as usual, and went through their Exercise to the Satisfaction of myself and many present—Coll. Delegall [the commander] said, they performed as well as the Regulars."[42] Like their southern brethren from Virginia, the planters, the merchants, and other residents of the coastal towns and surrounding areas were removed from the day-to-day fears of the frontier. This relative freedom from major defensive concerns allowed some of the militia companies of towns along the coastal belt to evolve into social as well as military organizations. This was particularly true of the Grenadier Company, the sister unit of the Light Infantry

---

[39]Habersham, for instance, noted that many of these people were "great Villians [sic], Horse Stealers . . . and were amongst the North Carolina Regulators" (Habersham to Hillsborough, 12 August 1772, CRG, TS 38, pt. 1:6). See also Wright to Hillsborough, 13 December 1770, ibid. 37:501-502; Davis, *Fledgling Province*, 42-43, 85-86. Many of these settlers were poor, religious, and political dissenters or descendants of dissenters of one type or another, seeking to make a new life for themselves beyond the centralized control of the British government.

[40]See analysis based on data in Lucas, *Index*; Bryant and Hemperley, *English Crown Grants*; and "Commissions" above and n. 20.

[41]Wright to Gage, 6 August 1767, CRG, TS 37:250.

[42]Habersham to Wright, 6 June 1772, *Collections* 6:183.

Company. The members of this company, apparently well-to-do citizens of Savannah, petitioned the royal council in 1773 to allow them to become "incorporated" and to be "exempted from serving the office of the Constable." They explained that they were extremely proficient at drill and had "sent to England at a very great expence for Necessary Cloaths and Accoutrements, which they daily expect."[43] Some years later a gentleman reported that "he dined with the Grenadiers."[44] Because of the obvious social nature of this volunteer unit and others like it, such as the Light Infantry Company, their appearance and proficiency with drill did not constitute prima facie evidence that they would excel in combat.

The striking differences between the scruffy, ill-disciplined militiamen of the frontier and the apparently immaculate, well-drilled volunteers of Savannah, who had "at much trouble acquired a proper exercise," resulted in large measure from their social composition, distance from the Indian boundary line, and the demands placed upon them.[45] The comparison may have been equally misleading in terms of military proficiency. Precision on the peacetime parade ground would not necessarily guarantee victory for the militia—or regulars—on the field of battle. The British and the Continental armies would have to grapple with this dilemma throughout the American Revolution. The company from the backcountry was at least as likely to be proficient, given a proper test, in fighting against the Indians as the company from the town would be if it campaigned alongside a British unit, after which it was obviously modeled. Had either been faced with the opposite conditions, the results might have been equally disastrous.

Appearances aside, the ultimate test of either type of company could, however, be made only under the stress of combat or of an internal disorder. Both tests would come for militiamen throughout the colonies.[46] Interestingly enough, William DeBrahm, surveyor general of the Southern Department, praised the Georgia militia in 1772, noting that its three

---

[43]*CRG* 15:374; Millett and Maslowski, *For the Common Defense*, 4; Aldridge, "Colonial Virginia," 236-37.

[44]Deposition of Thomas Gunnersall, 7 June 1775, in Wright to Dartmouth, 9 June 1775, CRG, TS 38, pt. 1:454.

[45]*CRG* 15:374.

[46]Leach, *Arms for Empire*, 38.

regiments were "all better trained than formerly a Militia in Europe."[47] Two factors, the Indians and slaves, continued to provide the motivation for training and preparedness prior to the American Revolution.

A final duty of the militia companies—frontier patrols—resulted from the fears of the Indians and tested the military capabilities of the militiamen. These patrols called as much for constraint as for proficiency in combat. The governor and his council knew that a minor incident with the Creeks might possibly spark a frontier war that could have a devastating effect on the colony as a whole. The chances of this happening had lessened somewhat, as the Creeks had had their attention diverted from the colonials since 1765 by a war against the Choctaws. The royal government nevertheless had to protect the settlers as they occupied newly acquired lands.[48]

On one occasion in 1767, as a result of a quarrel between a settler (Mills) and an Indian (Saucy Jack), two men from East Florida had been killed and another had been wounded. These casualties had prompted the settlers near the Satilla River to flee their homes, and a group of forty or fifty Creeks had scavenged the abandoned farms. In response, the Council directed Captain George McIntosh to take a detachment of fifty or sixty men from the Southern, or Third, Regiment to the Satilla River and to induce the Indians there to return property that they had stolen from the settlers' houses. The instructions to Captain McIntosh cautioned him, "by no Means to use force." The warning proved unnecessary, as the militiamen did not see "more than one Indian" during their entire patrol.[49]

At about the same time, Creeks threatened a colonist (Charles Watson) in the same general area, who, they claimed, had settled on tribal lands. The Council directed Mr. Moses Nunes Rivers, formerly an officer in the rangers and now the Creek interpreter, to take an officer and ten men from the Ebenezer companies of militia (probably the Fifth

---

[47]Louis DeVorsey, Jr., *DeBrahm's Report of the General Survey in the Southern District of North America* (Columbia: University of South Carolina Press, 1971) 162.

[48]Alden, *John Stuart*, 224; David Taitt to John Stuart, 3 January 1774, Great Britain, PRO, Colonial Office, America and West Indies, Military Correspondence, December 1773–April 1776, CO 5/91, 92, 93 (1), 249, on microfilm, William R. Perkins Library, Duke University, hereinafter cited as "Military Correspondence"; Taitt to Stuart, 17 January 1774, ibid., 270.

[49]*CRG* 10:332; 19, pt. 1:48, 51, 501; Wright to Shelburne, 24 October 1767, CRG, TS 37:258.

and Ninth companies of the First Regiment) and to advise the Indians that the line agreed upon in 1763 would be surveyed in a short while to clear up confusion. The Council alerted a detachment of twenty-five or thirty men from the same companies to be prepared to provide assistance to the inhabitants, should the Indians carry out their threat. Again the officer in charge received the warning to be cautious and to prevent a "rupture" with the Indians.[50]

Nothing of note occurred on these occasions, but the militia did not always show such restraint. In August 1770 a party sent by Governor Wright to investigate the slayings of two settlers—Thomas Jackson and George Buck—burned a Creek village on the Oconee River in retaliation, despite the attempts of its officers to restrain them.[51] Although these were minor incidents in their own right, each potentially represented the single spark necessary to light the fuse to an uprising of the Creeks. Should such a crisis occur, the untried militia and a newly formed troop of rangers would be all that stood between survival and disaster.

Despite the minor clashes along the Indian boundary line, a delicate state of equilibrium and of uneasy peace had characterized Creek colonial relations since the Congress of Augusta in 1763. Nevertheless, Governor Wright personally remained pessimistic about the possibility of maintaining lasting peace with them. After 1770 he became increasingly concerned as the Creeks and the Choctaws, after years of war, appeared to be reconciling their differences. Such a reconciliation, he thought, would leave the Indians with "nothing to amuse themselves, . . . and as they are a People who cannot rest long without having their hands imbrued in blood, its [sic] highly probable that they will pick a quarrel with us."[52]

Although intertribal warfare continued, Governor Wright still believed that the Creeks were to be feared, as he reported in 1773:

---

[50]*CRG* 10;333-34; a similar event took place in April–May 1768; see ibid., 491.

[51]Wright to Hillsborough, 22 August 1770, CRG, TS 37:474; 8 October 1770, ibid., 484; John Stuart to Hillsborough 2 December 1770, K. G. Davies, ed., *Documents of the American Revolution, 1770–1783*, 21 vols. (Shannon, Ireland: Irish University Press, 1972–1981) 2:280-83; Alden, *John Stuart*, 297.

[52]Alden, *John Stuart*, 224; Wright to Hillsborough, 20 July 1770, CRG, TS 37:464.

The Creeks say they might easily break up and ruin this Province and even distress the Province of South Carolina. But in the end, it would turn to their ruin likewise. Considerations of this sort weigh with some of the most sensible and prudent. But I am well satisfied at the same time that there are a great many amongst them, probably the greatest part of them who would, and are disposed to promote a War at all Hazards and Events, and they certainly are a most base treacherous people and in whom you can have no confidence or dependence.[53]

He also included an estimate of the strengths of each of the Indian tribes on the periphery of the colony. He placed the Creek population as 12,000 people, among whom 4,000 were estimated to be warriors. He reckoned the total population of Georgia, by way of comparison, to be 18,000 whites and 15,000 blacks.[54]

Several months later the governor made a prediction of the outcome, should a war with the Indians break out.

Your Lordship will be pleased to consider the Situation we shall be in if there should be an Indian war. A Province without Men or Money for what is 2000 or suppose it was 2500 militia, scattered over a large Extent of Country, who have their Children and Property to take of. And if not, are undisciplined and not one in five or ten that would face an Enemy. . . . [O]n the other [side] 4000 savages. . . . [W]e had not a single Soldier in the Province and that if a Rupture should happen with the Indians the Province must be over-run and destroyed.[55]

Governor Wright's concern about the Indians and the frontier in general had intensified after 1770 as the areas along the Indian boundary line assumed an increasing significance.

New settlers continued to drift to Georgia's backcountry in search of unsettled land. By 1770 two new settlements in particular—Wrightsborough, near the Little River, about thirty miles from Augusta, and Queensborough, off the Ogeechee River on Lambert Creek, some fifty miles to the southeast of Augusta—had begun to fill with settlers, Quakers in the former and Scotch-Irish in the latter.[56] As a result of this

---

[53]Wright to Dartmouth, 17 June 1773, CRG, TS 38, pt. 1:63-64; David Taitt to John Stuart, 3 January 1774, "Military Correspondence," 249; *Collections* 3:170.

[54]*Collections* 3:167, 169.

[55]Wright to Dartmouth, 31 January 1774, CRG, TS 38, pt. 1:170-71.

[56]For a general discussion of the settlements, see Coleman, *Colonial Georgia*, 226-28, 235; also see Davis, *Fledgling Province*, 23-26; E. R. R. Green, "Queensborough

growth and the threats from the Creeks, Governor Wright raised a "Scout," a body of troops comprising a captain, a lieutenant, and ten mounted men, to protect these settlers on the fringes of the province from the "insults of Straggling Indians." The Commons supported this small force with an appropriation, not to exceed £100.[57] The ground work had now been laid for the revival of the rangers.

A second major development occurred in June 1773, when Governor Wright skillfully acquired 2,116,298 acres of land from the Creeks and Cherokees in exchange for relief from their debts with the Indian traders.[58] Between June and September 1773 he organized a troop of rangers, to be supported from land sales from the cession, ostensibly to protect the settlers and the land venture itself from "Straggling Indians." He commissioned Captain Edward Barnard, a former second lieutenant in the rangers and the lieutenant colonel of the Second Regiment of Foot Militia, as commander and authorized a strength of three lieutenants, a quartermaster, a surgeon, three sergeants, a drummer, and sixty-five privates.[59]

The instructions for Captain Barnard and the commissions of the other officers clearly spelled out, in great detail, their responsibilities and duties and the nature of the troop. Of primary importance, they were "to keep good order amongst, and for the protection of the Inhabitants of the new ceded Lands above Little River," which began twenty-two miles north of Augusta. The governor appointed the officers to the positions of

---

Township: Scotch-Irish Emigration and the Expansion of Georgia, 1763–1776," *William and Mary Quarterly* 17 (April 1960): 185; *CRG* 11:85-86; DeVorsey, *Boundary*, 159; by 1773 Wrightsborough had twenty houses; the Indian trade and agriculture were sources of commerce and subsistence; see WilliarmBartram's account in Francis Harper, ed., "Travels in Georgia and Florida, 1773–1774: A Report of Dr. John Fothergill," *Transactions of the American Philosophical Society* 33, pt. 2 (November 1943): 139; Sosin, *Revolutionary Frontier*, 65; Mark Van Doren, ed., *The Travels of William Bartram* (New York: Facsimile Library, 1940) 55.

[57]"Commissions," 172-74; *CRG* 19, pt. 1:183.

[58]David H. Corkran, *The Creek Frontier, 1540–1783* (Norman: University of Oklahoma Press, 1967) 281. Wright received approval from the king to acquire this land from the Indians while he was in London (Davis, *Fledgling Province*, 29; *Collections* 3:160). By February 1774 the sale of land had brought enough settlers to add about 700 men to the militia (Wright to Dartmouth, 24 February 1774, CRG, TS 38, pt. 1:160).

[59]"Commissions," 208; Wright to Hillsborough, 1771, CRG, TS 28, pt. 2B:777, 780; Wright to Dartmouth, 17 June 1773, ibid. 38, pt. 1:61; *Collections* 3:171-74.

Fig. 13: A Map of the Lands Ceded to His Majesty. Philip Yonge. 1773. MPG 2 (extracted from CO 5/662 f. 132), Public Record Office. Crown copyright material published by permission of the Contoller of Her Majesty's Stationary Office.

justices of the peace to give them additional civil authority.[60] Enlisted in the manner of a British regular, each private, from his monthly pay of two pounds, was expected "to victual" and to provide himself a uniform consisting, by specification, of a blue coat, "faced with Red," a red jacket, blue or buckskin "Breeches," cloth boots, and other accessories. Each mounted ranger also was to have a rifle, two dragoon pistols, a hanger (sword), a powder horn, a shot pouch, and a tomahawk.[61]

The rangers of the Ceded Lands seemed to have been of the same breed of men who had enlisted in the earlier troops of rangers. These men, as had their predecessors, led a relatively isolated existence on the fringes of civilization, an existence filled with both the possibility of danger and the reality of monotony. A few owned and worked small farms, averaging 250 acres, most within the Ceded Lands and fairly close to Fort James, their home base; some apparently had families. Several were settlers from North Carolina, South Carolina, New Jersey, and Pennsylvania, seeking a place to live; others may very well have been so-called Crackers looking for jobs.[62] The officers, with one exception, Second Lieutenant Edward Keating, were large landowners. Captain Edward Barnard and (after Barnard's death on 6 June 1775) his successor, Councillor James Edward Powell, both former officers in the rangers, owned 5,610 and 5,665 acres respectively. First Lieutenant Thomas Waters claimed 3,950 acres of land near the Broad and Savannah rivers, with a two-story dwelling house. Even Lieutenant Keating owned 450 acres and had some twenty-four slaves.[63]

---

[60]*Gazette*, 16 June 1773, 1; "Instructions to Edward Barnard," in claim of Thomas Waters, PRO, Audit Office, Georgia Loyalist Claims, AO 13/37, on microfilm at Georgia Department of Archives and History, Atlanta, hereinafter cited as "Instructions to Edward Barnard"; *CRG* 12:390-91.

[61]"Instructions to Edward Barnard"; Van Doren, *Travels*, 264-65.

[62]"Georgia. Pay Bill of His Majestys Troop of Rangers," in the claim of Thomas Waters, PRO, Audit Office, Georgia Loyalist Claims, AO 13/38, on microfilm at Georgia Department of Archives and History, for the period 6 September 1773 to 6 March 1776, hereinafter cited as "Pay Bill," Waters's Claim; Lucas, *Index*; Caroline Price Wilson, comp., *Annals of Georgia: Important Early Records of the State*, 2 vols. (Savannah: Braid & Hutton, 1933); affidavit, Ceded Lands, 22 July 1776, Cuyler MSS.

[63]Information compiled from Lucas, *Index*; Wilson, *Annals of Georgia*; Bryant and Hemperley, *English Crown Grants*; "Schedule to which the Annexed Memorial refers," 3 June 1783, in "Pay Bill," Waters's Claim. Also see "Commissions," 223.

Fig. 14: A Ranger in the Ceded Lands.
Drawing by Jean Schucker.

Considering the duties of the rangers, the troop, after an initial period of instability, experienced surprisingly little turnover. After September 1774 the greatest number of enlisted men mustering out or dying in a pay period was four, with one man enlisting; there was only one deserter. In the year from 6 March 1775 to 6 March 1776, of those who had served at least one year, only three men—one of whom died—left the unit. A total of ninety-seven privates served at one time or another during the lifetime of the unit, two and one-half years; of these, sixty-two men served for the entire period. The officers experienced only two changes: James Edward Powell replaced Edward Barnard after his death, and Timothy Barnard resigned after serving only six months.[64] The Troop of Rangers, insofar as its personnel were concerned, seemed capable, over time, of doing the tasks that Governor Wright had in mind.

The rangers garrisoned Fort James, which they had built at the fork of the Broad and the Savannah rivers near Dartmouth. This fort, covering about an acre of ground and complete with buildings for the officers and barracks for the troops, was "a four square stockade, with salient bastions at each angle, mounted with a block-house, where are some swivel guns, one story higher than the curtains, which are pierced with loop-holes, breast high, and defended by small-arms."[65] Operating from this base, the troop, consisting usually of five officers, a cadet, three sergeants, a drummer, and some sixty-two to seventy-one privates, had three divisions, with at least an officer, a sergeant, and one-third of the men in each. One of these divisions was always to be on duty and was to "Range or Patrole about the Country to prevent any Quarrels or Squabbles between the White People and any scattering or straggling parties of Indians who might come into the said Lands."[66] Prevention of

---

[64]Based on an analysis of "Pay Bill," Waters's Claim, 6 September 1773 to 6 March 1776. From 5 March 1774 to 5 June 1774, the troop lost fifteen men while enlisting the same number. In the next pay period, thirteen men left, and twelve men enlisted. Although a shorter total period of time was involved, the turnover on the average was less than that experienced in the two troops of rangers earlier; see above, chap. 3.

[65]The planned specifications for the fort were given in the sales instructions to the commissioners, quoted in Alex M. Hitz, "The Earliest Settlements in Wilkes County," *Georgia Historical Quarterly* 40 (September 1956): 270; the fort itself was described by William Bartram in 1775 (see Van Doren, *Travels*, 264-65). For the maps showing the travels, see Cappon, *Atlas*, 33.

[66]"Instructions to Edward Barnard"; "Pay Bill," Waters's Claim.

squatting by settlers on Indian lands and preservation of order among the whites also had a priority, as the instructions specified that the rangers were "to see what people are settled on any part of the said lands, without proper Authority for so doing, and to compel them to Remove off, by enforcing the Vagrant Law to the Utmost of its Extent against them."[67] In December 1773 Governor Wright personally toured the Ceded Lands, most certainly accompanied by the rangers, and may have visited Fort James. During the course of the trip he doubtless felt, as he had predicted in a letter on 10 August to Lord Dartmouth, the secretary of state, that, with the rangers in the Ceded Lands, he would no longer need to "fear reducing these Villains [Crackers—not to mention the Creeks] and keeping them in good order."[68]

As for the colony as a whole, the presence of a troop of rangers at this time was less significant than the presence of the two troops six years before. The Troop of Rangers in the Ceded Lands was a smaller force by one-half. With their responsibilities limited to the outermost extent of the colony, they were beyond the effective call and control of Governor Wright. Since they had been raised specifically for duty in the Ceded Lands and were paid from the proceeds of land sales by the provincial government rather than as members of the British military establishment, there was no assurance that these rangers would prove as loyal to the governor as their predecessors had been. Thus, it seemed the rangers were unlikely to play a decisive role in any internal disorder centered in Savannah. Together with the militia, however, they might have to fight Indians, should a war such as Governor Wright feared break out.

As Governor Wright had predicted, in late December 1773 the first of a series of swift and brutally destructive attacks by Creeks shattered, for a time at least, the grudging accord between the whites and the Indians. On Christmas Day a party of about seven Creeks murdered William White and his family of five at their homestead on the North Branch of the Ogeechee River.[69] This single incident was not so unusual

---

[67]"Instructions to Edward Barnard."

[68]Wright was noting the murder of two Cherokees by a white man (Wright to Dartmouth, 10 August 1773, CRG, TS 38, pt. 1:82); see also Wright to Dartmouth, 27 December 1773, ibid., 158; William Bartram noted the presence of a "Retinue" with the governor when he passed him on 8 or 9 May 1773 (Harper, "Travels," 137).

[69]Wright to Dartmouth, 31 January 1774, CRG, TS 38, pt. 1: 163-65; Taitt to Stuart,

by itself, as Indians had occasionally killed settlers throughout the history of the colony. However, on 14 January 1774 some seventeen Creeks attacked the "plantation" of the William Sherrill family, located four miles from the Whites'. The family included five white men, three black men, and twelve women and children of both "colours"; the attack occurred while the men were erecting a stockade.[70] "By the encouragement and good example of a Negroe fellow, who shot one of the Head Indians through the eye," the surviving settlers skirmished the Indians for six hours. The attackers, while losing at least two of their number, killed seven people, including Sherrill, and wounded five more. These two incidents, in apparent retaliation for the death of an Indian in a dispute over stolen horses, seemed at the time to signify that a war might be in the offing.[71]

The militia and the rangers in the area of the incidents responded almost immediately to counter the encroachment of the Indians. Captain Barnard with 40 men, probably including some rangers, investigated the Sherrill massacre, and Lieutenant Colonel James Grierson of the Second Regiment assembled a force of 101 militiamen and some 25 rangers and marched them to William's Creek, where they camped for several days. On 23 January he dispatched a mounted scouting party of about thirty-five men, comprising some twenty-five militiamen and ten or eleven rangers, under the command of Second Lieutenant Keating, to escort several survivors back to the Sherrill homesite to remove some personal effects. On the twenty-fourth this group was

> riding briskly, and rather unguardedly, as apprehending no enemy near, they discovered two Indians at a small creek before them, who upon seeing our men, threw off their blankets, and ran up the hill, seeming frightened, upon which the foremost of our people pushed after them as fast as they could, but were stopt on a sudden by the appearance of a large body of Indians who had kept themselves concealed near the top of the hill behind long grass, and now appeared in two ranks firing upon our people.[72]

27 January 1774, "Military Correspondence," 269; for a general account, see Sosin, *Revolutionary Frontier*, 84.

[70]The size of the party was found in Alden, *John Stuart*, 306.

[71]*Gazette*, 2 February 1774, 2; CRG, TS 38, pt. 1:190-91; see John Stuart to Dartmouth, 13 February 1774, Davies, *Documents* 8:48-49.

[72]Wright to Dartmouth, 31 January 1774, CRG, TS 38, pt. 1:163-65; John Stuart to

Surprised by Big Elk and his band of from seventeen to sixty Indians, the militia and rangers, after firing a few shots, "rode off full speed to the camp." Lieutenant Daniel Grant and two other men—Weatherford and Hammond—were killed, and their bodies abandoned; another died the next day at Wrightsborough. When this part returned to the camp with the story of the reversal, all but thirteen or fourteen men in Captain William Goodgion's First Company and five or six others—perhaps rangers— deserted their officers and fled. Lieutenant Colonel Grierson and this small party prudently followed the next day.[73]

These encounters, marked by brutality, underscored the intensity of the cultural conflict between the whites and the Indians and the plight of those in the backcountry as compared to the situation enjoyed by the dwellers along the coast. It was possible that Lieutenant Grant, and perhaps the other two casualties left behind as well, were only wounded initially and that the Creeks killed them later. Two reports, perhaps exaggerated, published in the *South Carolina Gazette* after Lieutenant Grant's body was recovered, indicated that this was the case. The first said that Grant was only stunned when the ambush was initiated. The Indians then "returned, seized and bound him to a Tree, then retired to some Distance, and shot 30 arrows into his Body; after which they cut off his Genitals, struck a Tomahawk into his Head, another into his Fundament; and burnt the Body." The second stated that "his Body was found tied to a Tree, a Gun Barrel, supposed to have been red hot, was thrust into, and left sticking in, his Body; his Scalp and Ears taken off, a painted Hatchet left sticking in his Scull, twelve Arrows in his Breast, and a painted War-Club left upon his Body."[74] Such accounts help to explain the intensity of the reaction to the Indian encroachments that started with the retreat of the militiamen.

Major General Frederick Haldimand, 3 February 1774, "Military Correspondence," 117-18; *Gazette*, 9 March 1774, 2; 16 February 1774, 2.

[73]The reported number of Indians in the ambush varies from account to account. There were probably as many as sixty men, women, and children altogether; see Stuart to Dartmouth, 13 February 1774, Davies, *Documents* 8:48-49; *Gazette*, 16 February 1774, 2; 16 March 1774, 2.

[74]*South Carolina Gazette*, 14 February 1774; generally verified in Stuart to Dartmouth, 13 February 1774, Davies, *Documents* 8:48-49.

Fear and panic spread throughout the province and even into South Carolina and Virginia. The *South-Carolina Gazette* reported that "the whole Western Frontier of Georgia has been thrown into the utmost Consternation, and is abandoning fast; and that the Inhabitants of our own Back Settlements are not a little alarmed."[75] Rumors added to this sense of panic. For instance, the *Georgia Gazette* on 9 February reported another skirmish between militia and Indians that was discounted as false in the edition of the next week. The *Gazette* also reported that a letter from Augusta, dated 9 March, announced that Big Elk had been killed and scalped on his way back to one of the Cherokee towns; allegedly, he had Lieutenant Grant's scalp.[76]

The colonial government in Savannah reacted, or overreacted, as quickly as the distances from the incidents allowed. Governor Wright, in an address to the Commons House of Assembly on 28 January, explained that he had drafted one-third of the militia for the protection and the safety of the inhabitants of the province and directed that the settlers build stockade forts where necessary. The commons agreed to provide support for the militia on "actual Service" and petitioned the king and General Frederick Haldimand, acting commander in chief of British forces in North America at the time, to send immediate assistance, soldiers, "to strike a terror into the minds of the Indians." The Upper House added, in a similar address, that at least 1,000 men would be necessary in the event of war to protect them against a tribe of Indians "so powerful" as the Creeks.[77]

In a related political move, a committee of the Commons proposed on 10 March that three companies of rangers with seventy-five men in each be raised and stationed on the frontier to quiet the apprehensions of the settlers of the backcountry.[78] There is no evidence that this action was completed. As time passed and no other incidents occurred, the governor,

---

[75]*South Carolina Gazette*, 31 January 1774, 3; Panic in Georgia was reflected in Habersham to Mrs. Mary Bagwith, 3 February 1774, *Collections* 6:234.

[76]*Gazette*, 9 February 1774, 3; 16 February 1774, 3; 23 March 1774, 2.

[77]*CRG* 15:538-40. A fort was actually built at Wrightsborough (*The Proceedings and Minutes of the Governor and Council of Georgia, October 4, 1774, through November 7, 1775, and September 6, 1779, through September 20, 1780*, ed. Lilla Mills Hawes, vol. 10 of *Collections* [Savannah: Georgia Historical Society, 1952] 5); see also *CRG* 15:544-45: 17:771-72.

[78]*CRG* 15:545-46; CRG, TS 38, pt. 1:237.

accepting these infractions at face value—as isolated attacks and not as
a part of an overall war effort—concluded that peace could be salvaged.
He met with several Creek headmen in Savannah in April and demanded
satisfaction in kind for the murders of fifteen whites and two blacks.
Furthermore, the Creeks were to return all blacks and all horses taken
from settlers since the incidents started; until such time as the demands
were met, Governor Wright suspended trade with the Creek nation as of
22 April.[79] With negotiations under way and although General Haldimand
had turned down the request for regular forces, the colony gradually
began to return to normal insofar as the Indians were concerned.[80]

The disastrous events on the frontier receded in importance as the
likelihood of war diminished, and the inhabitants of Georgia celebrated
the king's birthday as usual. The governor reviewed the militia, as had
become the custom, and the account of the occasion in the *Gazette* noted
that Captain Samuel Elbert's Grenadier Company and Captain Thomas
Netherclift's Light Infantry Company "made a fine appearance, and went
through their exercise with great dexterity and exactness."[81] This public
display, as much as anything, symbolized the colony's ultimate commit-
ment to and dependence on the militia; at the same time it indicated the
social status of the volunteer militia companies. Indeed, during this
period, the fear of the Creeks had motivated the governor to pay more
attention to the militia even while he asked for regulars.[82] James
Habersham in 1772 had summed up the rationale behind the practical
adjustment to reality, when he had explained to Colonel Jackson of the
Second Regiment that his companies must "be ready to appear without
Confusion, and we not know, how soon they may be wanted—I do not
mention this from any present apprehension of our Peace being disturbed,
but as alarming Events sometimes suddenly and unexpectedly happen, we
ought to be prepared."[83] Not surprisingly then, to be better prepared and
to keep up with growth, on 18 February 1774 the governor had added

---

[79]*Gazette*, 20 April 1774, 2; 27 April 1774, 1.
[80]Haldimand to Dartmouth, 6 April 1774, "Military Correspondence," 273-74.
[81]*Gazette* 8 June 1774, 3.
[82]Gage to Dartmouth, 29 August 1774, Carter, *Correspondence* 1:368-69.
[83]Habersham to Jackson, 8 August 1772, *Collections* 6:198.

from St. George Parish the Fourth Regiment of Foot, with eight companies. Four more companies joined the Third Regiment in March.[84]

When the Indian congress was held in October at Savannah to settle the differences from earlier in the year, light infantrymen and grenadiers provided the escorts for some of the Indians during their journeys through the settlements.[85] A detachment of Captain Bernard's rangers escorted another small group from Augusta.[86] With this last act, the immediate crisis with the Creeks ran its course, but the fundamental issues of Indian-white conflict were only set aside until the American Revolution presented an opportunity for them to erupt once again.

The last years of the uneasy 1760s and the first years of the turbulent 1770s had reflected the dynamics of colonial expansion in Georgia and the shifting relationships between the colonies and Great Britain. Growth toward the frontiers and prosperity had been balanced by political tension and Indian scares. In this period, despite the presence after 1773 of the small and geographically isolated Troop of Rangers, the militia had gradually assumed a greater military role in the community. Organizational expansion continued, despite Governor Wright's obvious disdain for the militiamen as soldiers. The militia necessarily assumed an increasing number of responsibilities and apparently never failed to answer when called upon by the governor to act.

Unfortunately the actions of the militia under fire (and those of the rangers, for that matter) had confirmed Governor Wright's expectations; while the ambush of the small force in January 1774 under disadvantageous conditions may have been an unfair test of the ultimate usefulness of the militia as a military force, it nonetheless called into question its combat effectiveness. (Even Braddock's Redcoats had been unable to respond effectively to a French and Indian ambush in 1755.) Militiamen during the American Revolution would fight best from behind defensive works and when supported by Continentals. Of greatest importance, the

---

[84] "Commissions," 211-14.

[85] *Gazette*, 20 April 1774, 2; 5 October 1774, 2; *Collections* 10:1; Alden, *John Stuart*, 311; Corkran, *Creek Frontier*, 206.

[86] *Gazette*, 12 October 1774. 2.

Creek crisis of 1774 pointed out the obvious: in the absence of British regulars, the militia, alive and well, as yet constituted the only military force of any consequence *in the colony*. A true test of its military and political worth was just around the corner as the colonies and the mother country drifted further apart.

Chapter 5

The Militia: An Instrument of Power, 1774–1776

The progression in Georgia from colonial subordination to Great Britain in 1773 to the brink of armed rebellion against her late in 1775 was neither an unbroken continuity nor, at any stage along the way, a foregone conclusion. Yet in the youngest and least-developed colony (discounting the loyal and dependent Floridas), as in the other twelve, forces were clearly at work transforming old relationships and perceptions.[1] Both the militia as an institution and the individual militiamen of whom it was composed reacted to, and took part in, the transformation from colony to state.

The Stamp Act crisis of 1765 and 1766 had delineated a recognizable beginning to opposition against the royal government headed by Sir James Wright. The Sons of Liberty, members of an informal opposition party, from this time until the summer of 1774 attempted to redefine the existing division of power between the royal governor and the Commons House of Assembly. By 1773 the power struggle had reached an equilibrium of sorts, which had been reinforced in early 1774 by the Creek crisis, a symbolic reminder of Georgia's dependence upon the military, diplomatic, and economic resources of Great Britain.[2] Although deeply divided, reluctant to act decisively out of perceived self-interest, and thus out of cadence with the more vocal inhabitants of other colonies such as Massachusetts and South Carolina, Georgians by mid-1774 were

---

[1]East and West Florida had been English colonies since 1763 (Wright, *Florida*, 17-19); this discussion applies only to the original thirteen colonies that rebelled against the Crown. The best source for tracing this development in the colonies is Pauline Maier, *From Resistance to Revolution: Colonial Radicals and the Development of American Opposition to Britain, 1765–1776* (New York: Vintage Books, 1972).

[2]Abbot, *Royal Governors*, 159.

becoming increasingly sensitive to the metamorphosis taking place in the old familial ties between the mother country and her American colonies.[3] From this point on, the political equilibrium began to disintegrate as Georgians, almost 33,000 in number, both as citizens and as militiamen, found themselves embroiled in controversy and then conflict.[4]

By the summer of 1774 both the scares posed by the Creeks and the political isolation in relation to the other colonies fostered by such concerns began to dissipate, and Georgians became more and more tied to events outside the colony. When Parliament moved in the spring of 1774 to blockade the port of Boston in retaliation for the Boston Tea Party in December 1773, the inhabitants of Georgia felt the reverberations. Although opponents of the resultant Coercive, or Intolerable, acts met in Savannah and Midway on 27 July, 10 August, and 30 August, they failed to gain sufficient support in the divided colony to act decisively, and the delegate, Dr. Lyman Hall, who was elected to the First Continental Congress, to be held in September, declined to attend for this reason. The Indian problems were too fresh in the minds of the people of the backcountry.[5]

James Wright, who possessed substantially more power than most of his fellow governors, from this point on began to sense that his position, initially weakened in the Stamp Act crisis and challenged on numerous occasions during the previous decade, was beginning to erode. He wrote in August 1774,

---

[3]Edwin C. Bridges, "The Handbill of July 14, 1774, and the Beginning of the American Revolution in Georgia," Atlanta, 1975, 3-5.

[4]Stella H. Sutherland, *Population Distribution in Colonial America* (New York: Columbia University Press, 1936) 259; some 15,000 of these 33,000 people were blacks.

[5]Coleman, *Revolution*, 43-44; Lawrence Henry Gipson, *The Triumphant Empire: Britain Sails into the Storm, 1770–1776*, vol. 12 of *The British Empire before the American Revolution* (New York: Alfred A. Knopf, 1965) 229-38; petitions protesting these meetings and stressing military dependence upon England appeared during this period; see *Gazette*, 12 October 1774, 1; Bridges, "Handbill," 8; John W. Blassingame, "American Nationalism and Other Loyalties in the Southern Colonies, 1763–1775," *Journal of Southern History* 34 (February 1968): 73; Carol R. Cunningham, "The Southern Royal Governors and the Coming of the American Revolution, 1763–1776" (Ph.D. diss., State University of New York at Buffalo, 1984) 235-41.

If these Calls & meetings are considered as *illegal & improper* it will require the interposition of *higher authority* to remedy the Evil, for the executive Powers of Government in the Colonies are too Weak to rectify such abuses, and Prosecutions would only be Laughed at and no Grand Jury wou'd fine [*sic*] a Bill of Indictment and the Persons ordering & carrying them on Probably [would be] insulted and abused.

In December 1774 he lamented that "our Liberty Folks are really very active in Fomenting a Flame throughout the Province," but with "but 200 Soldiers & a Sloop of War I think that I should be able to keep every thing quiet & orderly." He realized, however, that he had at present "not the least support . . . beyond the Kings officers & a great Number of Gentlemen."[6] By late 1774 Governor Wright accurately perceived that, without assistance, his position would finally become untenable.

Since the Stamp Act crisis, Governor Wright had faced political opposition from the Sons of Liberty, or Whigs, but in January 1775 the Whigs tried new tactics and began to infiltrate or bypass existing institutions. They first undermined the colonial legislative bodies. One day after the royal assembly met, on 18 January 1775, an extralegal provincial congress met in Savannah with delegates from five parishes in attendance. Following the lead of the Continental Congress, these men agreed to a diluted "non-importation, non-consumption, and non-exportation" association and elected three members—Noble Wimberly Jones, formerly of the rangers, Archibald Bulloch, and John Houstoun— to attend the next meeting of the Continental Congress on 10 May 1775. Of the forty-five signers of the association, sixteen were active officers in the militia; eight were field-grade officers or captains, including Colonel James Deveaux and Major Philip Box of the First Regiment.[7] This congress adjourned on 25 January, and Governor Wright prorogued the Commons on 10 February rather than take the risk that it might support

---

[6]Wright to Dartmouth, 24 August 1774, *Collections* 3:181; Wright to Dartmouth, 20 December 1774, CRG, TS 38, pt. 1:367-68.

[7]Coleman, *Revolution*, 46-49; White, *Historical Collections*, 58-61; Allen D. Candler, ed., *The Revolutionary Records of the State of Georgia*, 3 vols. (Atlanta: Franklin-Turner, 1908) 1:65-66, hereinafter cited as *RRG*; Bridges, "Handbill," 6; *Virginia Gazette*, Williamsburg, 19 January 1776, 3; "Commissions"; five of these same officers had signed an "Oath of Allegiance and supremacy to the King," on 4 June 1774 (*Early History of Georgia Documents* [n.p., n.d.] 41).

the actions of the congress. As it turned out, the royal assembly would not meet again until considerably later in the Revolution. With the assembling on 4 July 1775 of the members of the second provincial congress, including eighteen militia officers with the regimental commanders of the First and Third Regiments, the Whigs controlled the only legislative body in the colony.[8] They had effectively bypassed the legislative powers of Governor Wright, and this was only the first step.

The Whigs next countered the executive powers of the governor in June by creating a council of their own—the Council of Safety. The so-called Associators in South Carolina did likewise. Acting as a guiding body when the provincial congress was not in session, the Council of Safety, counting among its members four officers of the militia, aided by parochial committees "of the Lowest People," acted with the authority formerly possessed by Wright and his council.[9] Without troops, Governor Wright, as early as February before the Council met, wrote that his executive powers were so weak that, even "where it is Wished to Support Governmt and keep things in Due Order, there is not the Means of doing it." By September he reported that "Government [was] totally Annihilated, and Assumed by Congresses, Councils, and Committees."[10] The governor and his council continued to perform some of the normal routines of government, including granting appointments and commissions, through January 1776. By September at the latest, they fully realized, however, that they did so at the pleasure of the Whigs, who now virtually possessed the executive power. The judiciary was gradually

---

[8]Coleman, *Revolution*, 56-57; Bridges, "Handbill," 7; "Proceedings of the First Provincial Congress of Georgia, 1775," vol. 5, pt. 1 of *Collections* (Savannah: Georgia Historical Society, 1901) 1-2; Wright to Dartmouth, 17 June 1775, *Collections* 3:186; "Commissions"; Colonel Philip Delegal, formerly the commander of the First Regiment, was also a delegate.

[9]"Proceedings of the Georgia Council of Safety, 1775 to 1777," *Collections* 5, pt. 1:18; Wright to Dartmouth, 19 December 1775, ibid. 3:228; *RRG* 1:63; Harrold, "Colonial Siblings," 740-43.

[10]Wright to Dartmouth, 24 February 1775, CRG, TS 38, pt. 1:395-96; Wright to Dartmouth, 23 September 1775, *Collections* 3:212-13; Cunningham, "Southern Royal Governors," 265, 274-84.

isolated so that the legal practices would be preserved. Court orders were ignored; juries failed to meet; and assistant justices failed to sit.[11]

As the Whigs overtly gained control of the institutions of government in Georgia, they also moved surreptitiously to undermine the will and the resources of the royal leadership and its Loyalist supporters. With each challenge Governor Wright was confronted with growing Whig strength and confidence as his own and that of his government conversely diminished. The first of these actions took place on 15 February 1775 and was remotely similar to the Boston Tea Party, which had unfolded several months earlier. Disguised as sailors, a group of townspeople from Savannah, with blackened faces on that February night reclaimed sugar and molasses seized earlier in the day by the customs collector. The mob threw into the water two sailors from His Majesty's Schooner *St. John* (eight guns), sent by the captain, Lieutenant William Grant, to guard the goods; one of these men drowned.[12]

The tempo picked up after the news of Lexington and Concord reached Georgia, and on the night of 11 May, certain individuals broke into the king's powder magazine in Savannah and removed 600 pounds of powder.[13] Henry Laurens, a prominent South Carolinian merchant and Whig, wrote that this act, which took place "under the Nose of the Governor," was symptomatic of the "commotion" in the province and indicated that "a large majority of the Inhabitants [of Savannah are] ready to participate in the measures of their American Brethern."[14] Doctor Noble Wimberly Jones, a leading Whig in Georgia, supported this analysis in a letter to Benjamin Franklin by estimating that this majority was actually "perhaps 9 out of ten or more"; however, Sir James Wright felt

---

[11]Appointments are reflected in "Commissions" through 17 January 1776, 220-23; *Collections* 10:47-48; Coleman, *Revolution*, 63-64; Wright to Dartmouth, 14 October 1775, *Collections* 3:217; 14 October 1775 and 11 December 1775, ibid., 215, 227; for outside views, see Governor Patrick Tonyn [East Florida] to Gage, 14 September 1775, William Bell Clark and William James Morgan, eds., *Naval Documents of the American Revolution*, 9 vols. to date (Washington: U.S. Government Printing Office, 1964) 2:104, hereinafter cited as *Naval Documents; Gentleman's Magazine*, October 1775, 495.

[12]Log of H. M. Schooner *St. John*, 15 February 1775, *Naval Documents* 1:91; 2:742; Coleman, *Revolution*, 50.

[13]Wright to Dartmouth, 12 May 1775, CRG, TS 38, pt. 1:429; *Collections* 10:22; Bridges, "Handbill," 7.

[14]Henry Laurens to William Manning, 22 May 1775, *Naval Documents* 1:509.

in early June that there were "still many Friends of Government here, but they begin to think they are left to Fall a sacrifice to the Resentment of the People, for want of proper support & Protection And for their own Safety & other Prudential Reasons, are falling off & lessening every day."[15] Wright's assessment about Loyalist sentiment was reinforced by a Whig, Peter Taarling, who hoped, as late as October, that "a few months more, may arouse us."[16] Subsequent events served to raise the hopes of the Whigs and to dampen further the spirits of the "Friends of Government."

The king's birthday once again, as it had in past years, served as an early indicator of the temper of the times. On 2 June an unknown group of men spiked twenty-one guns, probably located in a battery at or near the remains of Fort Halifax. These guns, normally used to fire salutes, were rolled down the bluff overlooking the Savannah River. Some of the guns were drilled out again, mounted, and fired on Sunday. Although the governor's customary entertainment followed, the next day another affair of a different sort mocked it as a number of men erected a Liberty Pole and spent the evening at Tondee's Tavern "in utmost harmony" drinking toasts to the discharge of a cannon of their own.[17] On the thirteenth, a crowd of about 300 people paraded through the town and "put up a Liberty Tree & a Flagg." On 17 June, when the governor wrote the letter to Lord Dartmouth complaining of this event, both the flag and the Liberty Pole were still up "in Contempt & Defiance of the Court, & of all Law & Government & which here, as well as elsewhere Seems now nearly at an End."[18] Lieutenant William Grant of the *St. John*, which continued to remain on station near Tybee, agreed "that Anarchy and a total subversion of Government has taken place in Georgia as well as, in the other provinces."[19]

---

[15]Jones to Benjamin Franklin, 16 May 1775, N.W. Jones MSS; Wright to Dartmouth, 9 June 1775, CRG, TS 38, pt. 1:446-47.

[16]Peter Taarling to John Houstoun, 24 October 1775, John Houstoun Papers, Georgia Historical Society, Savannah GA.

[17]*Gazette*, 7 June 1775, 3; Lieutenant William Grant to Vice Admiral Grave, 18 June 1775, *Naval Documents* 1:716; the commissary officer was to have removed the guns from Fort Halifax in 1773 (*CRG* 19, pt. 1:489); also see Wright to Dartmouth, 17 June 1775, *Collections* 3:187.

[18]Wright to Dartmouth, 17 June 1775, CRG, TS 38, pt. 1:466; *Collections* 3:183.

[19]Grant to Graves, 18 June 1775, *Naval Documents* 1:716-17.

Other blows, which even more clearly showed the hopelessness of the royal situation, followed in quick succession. On 17 June, as fervor ran high in Savannah, Whigs from both Georgia and South Carolina forced John Stuart, the British superintendent of Indian affairs, to flee first Charles Town and then Savannah. Despite his denials, they claimed that he had attempted to stir up the Cherokees. He sought and gained refuge aboard the *St. John*.[20] To facilitate blocking the Savannah River, armed parties of perhaps fifty to eighty men from both provinces took control of Tybee Island and the lighthouse, over which a liberty flag flew; they even fired on the British schooner before it sailed for St. Augustine.[21] Lieutenant Grant continued to observe boats passing from South Carolina to Tybee and men on the island after he returned later in the month.[22] When he sailed for the Bahamas on 9 July, he had aboard "Some Gentlemen and their Servants" who had escaped "the Violence of the Mob" in Savannah. For instance, a mob of Liberty Boys, including several gentlemen and prominent merchants who were also militia officers, tarred and feathered John Hopkins, a Savannah mariner. With the departure of the *St. John*, Governor Wright and supporters of the Crown were entirely on their own to face increased antigovernment activities.[23]

In Savannah, meanwhile, the Whigs continued to defy openly the remaining authority of the Crown. On 4 July George Baillie, the commissary general, reported to the Council that the cannon and stores of the town were being removed from storage. The governor directed Mr. Baillie to have them returned and to forbid the men involved from continuing this activity "at their Peril." They continued in spite of the warning and, as an indication of their growing confidence, told the com-

---

[20]Wright to Dartmouth, 20 June 1775, *Collections* 3:189; journal of *St. John*, 17 June 1775, *Naval Documents* 1:712. Stuart probably was innocent of the charges against him; see Alden, *John Stuart*, 170; Corkran, *Creek Frontier*, 289; Philip M. Hamer, "John Stuart's Indian Policy during the Early Months of the American Revolution," *Mississippi Valley Historical Review* 17 (June 1930–March 1931): 360; John Stuart to the Committee of Intelligence of South Carolina, 18 July 1775, in Peter Force, comp., *American Archives*, 4th ser., 6 vols. (Washington: M. St. Clair and Peter Force, 1837–1846) 2:1681.

[21]Journal of *St. John*, 18 June 1775, *Naval Documents* 1:715; Wright to Dartmouth, 20 June 1775, *Collections* 3:189.

[22]Journal of *St. John*, 29 June and 3 July 1775, *Naval Documents* 1:783,812.

[23]Ibid, 5 July 1775, 1:824, 848, 924; "Deposition," 25 July 1775, in Wright to Dartmouth, 29 July 1775, *Collections* 3:202.

missary general that they would leave a list of their names and the stores that were being taken after they had finished. In exasperation the governor asked the Council "what could be done to put a stop to such Lawless Proceedings?" The Council responded that, "as his Excellency has no Force at all to prevent such daring and Unlawfull Proceedings nothing more can be done at present but to take Affidavits of the Matters." By October the Council of Safety had essentially closed the port, causing the residents of Savannah "to feel the ill Effects . . . Bread being excessive scarce; & Flour in Town nearly consumed, Rum & Sugar very scarce and dear." This power extended to the regulation of the slave trade and to the emasculation of the Customs Service. The Council of Safety was obviously operating from a position of growing strength.[24]

The gunpowder issue became even more critical later as the Whigs outfitted their own vessels, including at least one schooner, the *Liberty*, with eight to ten cannons. Operating from Tybee Island, these ships began to capture gunpowder, much of which was intended for the Indian trade, before it reached the government and merchants in Georgia.[25] For example, on 8 July the *Liberty* and boatloads of armed men from Georgia and South Carolina took six and one-half tons of powder from the merchant ship *Philippa*. The Parochial Committee offloaded the remaining musketballs, firearms, and lead on 12 July and stored them in Savannah's powderhouse. South Carolina received 5,512 pounds of powder, six kegs of lead, and some firearms. The Whigs also shipped two and one-half

---

[24]At one point in September Governor Wright allegedly fled to a sloop of war (M. Smith to the Rev. M. Smith, 25 September 1775, CO 5/134, GA, MSS, UGA); see also *Collections* 10:28-29; the Whigs finally seized the magazine in early August (Wright to Dartmouth, 7 August 1775, ibid. 3:205). In Sunbury, "armed men" seized a confiscated sloop with over 100 cases of gin and "conducted the Vessell to Sea" (ibid. 10:28); the Parochial Committee tied up a cargo of slaves (Wright to Dartmouth, 14 October 1775, ibid. 3:215); see also Thomas Skinner to James Hare, 18 September 1775, CO 5/134, GA, MSS, UGA; William Brown to Board of Customs at Boston, 23 March 1776, T 1/520, ibid.

[25]*Collections* 10:24, 46-47; the Indian situation was a ticklish matter for both sides; see Wright to Dartmouth, 8, 10, 18 July, 23 September, and 1 November 1775, ibid. 3:191, 194, 198-99, 212, 218-19; Governor Patrick Tonyn of East Florida to Dartmouth, 21 July 1775, *Naval Documents* 1:949; Wright to Dartmouth, 23 September 1775, ibid. 2:191-92; voucher, 4 July 1775, Edwin Parsons Collection, Georgia Historical Society, Savannah GA, hereinafter cited as Parsons MSS.

tons of gunpowder to George Washington's Continental Army in Boston. On 17 September the Whigs seized from the *Polly* 250 barrels of powder intended for the Indians and fifty muskets intended for the Light Infantry Company.[26]

While the seizures of powder and arms bolstered the resources of the Whigs, they also increased the likelihood of war with the Indians. On top of everything else, Whig recruiters for "one of the Regiments now raising in South Carolina" freely traversed the province. When Chief Justice Anthony Stokes sentenced one of them—Ebenezer McCarty—to the jail, he was soon chagrined to find that the Whigs had released him. The governor summed up his feelings of impotence in a letter to Lord Dartmouth on 8 July: "Powers of Government are wrested from my Hands, that Law & Government are nearly if not quite annihilated & a mere Nominal Governor can be of little use & to me a most disagreeable Situation & its [*sic*] not in my Power to support either any longer."[27] As each day passed and brought greater disillusionment, Governor Wright and his council stood helplessly by, apparently convinced that the resources were not available with which to contest the growing power of the Whigs.

Throughout the early months of 1775 Governor Wright recognized that without soldiers to enforce the royal prerogatives, he would be unable to stem the tide of protest that was gradually engulfing him and the royal government. Although the rangers and the militia were near at hand and at least potentially available, he clung to two alternatives, both beyond his personal control, for possible military support during the year—British regulars and a sloop of war. His wish for the former was apparently fulfilled when he received a letter from General Gage written during April in which the general explained that the king had directed Gage to send 100 regulars from St. Augustine to Georgia.[28]

---

[26]Wright to Dartmouth, 23 September 1775, *Collections* 3:212; Thomas Skinner to Mr. James Hare, 18 September 1775, CO 5/134, GA, MSS, UGA. Sheldon S. Cohen, "The *Philippa* Affair," *Georgia Historical Quarterly* 69 (Fall 1985) 345-52.

[27]Wright to Dartmouth, 8 July 1775, *Collections* 3:192; 10:29; Wright to Dartmouth, 7 August 1775, ibid. 3:204-205.

[28]Dartmouth to Gage, 28 January 1775, Carter, *Correspondence* 2:183; Gage to Dartmouth, 19 April 1775, ibid. 1:395; Gage to Wright, 16 April 1775, *Collections* 3:188.

By this time, however, the governor viewed an inadequate force as being worse than no troops at all. In July, he and the Council decided that so few regulars would probably only "Inflame the People, and that they would only be Subject and Exposed to Insult and Danger" themselves.[29] In a letter written earlier to Lord Dartmouth, he had explained his position.

> What might have been easily done with 100 men 5 or 6 Months ago, I fear Could not now, with less than 4 or 5 Times that Number, and I Apprehend a few Coming here may only help exasperate the People, And to be Plain my Lord I see Nothing but a Prospect of a General Rebellion throughout America.[30]

General Gage and the king had made their offer based on limited resources and higher priorities to the north in Massachusetts. To Governor Wright and the Council these priorities must have seemed misplaced; at any rate, they refused the offer because it was too little and too late. The regulars were now beyond reach, for a time, and the Royal Navy held out the only other outside hope.

Governor Wright had good reason to believe that some type of naval support would be forthcoming. The earl of Dartmouth had written to Wright on 1 February 1775, informing him that the king had directed Admiral Graves "to station one of his small Cruisers in the River Savannah."[31] The governor obviously felt that a small warship might be able to back his position as decisively as the *Speedwell* had done in the Stamp Act crisis. Although operationally ineffective against the Whigs, the *St. John* for a short time fulfilled a morale-boosting role, but only unofficially, as its assigned station was the Caribbean; it would be almost a year before the promised naval support finally arrived. In no fewer than ten letters between June and December 1775, Governor Wright repeatedly

---

[29]Wright to Dartmouth, 1 February 1775, CRG, TS 38, pt. 1:373; Wright to Dartmouth, 17 June 1775, *Collections* 3:187; *CRG* 12:420.

[30]Wright to Dartmouth, 25 May 1775, *CRG*, TS 38, pt. 1:445.

[31]Wright had asked for such a ship as early as 1770; see Wright to Hillsborough, 13 December 1770, ibid. 37:503; Dartmouth to Wright, 1 February 1775, ibid. 38, pt. 1:363-64; *Naval Documents* 1:387.

reminded Lord Dartmouth in one way or another that "no Sloop of War or Cruizer is come yet."[32]

Admiral Graves, in spite of his orders, felt that Georgia had no urgent need for such a vessel. He based his estimate upon information from someone he felt to be a reliable source: Governor Wright himself, or so he thought. Wright had, in fact, written the admiral in June explaining the needs of Georgia in great detail; however, the letter never reached him.[33] In its place, Whigs of the Secret Committee in Charles Town had substituted a forged letter that said in part, "It gives me [Governor Wright] the highest pleasure to acquaint you, that I now have not any occasion for any vessel of War, and I am clearly of opinion that his Majesty's service will be better promoted by the absence than the presence of vessels of war in this port."[34]

The Whigs' subterfuge worked with surprising success. In a letter written in reply in August, Graves expressed relief over the improved state of affairs in Georgia and the fact that his inability to supply a ship had not "been detrimental to the Kings Interest within your Government"; he promised to send "a Sloop whenever it is in my Power."[35] Wright continued to hope, but as time passed, he must have recognized that external help of sufficient strength was not going to materialize. Massachusetts was the focal point of British official attention; resources were just too few to support every colonial government. As the Whigs closed his political options one by one and his superiors failed to provide adequate military support, Governor Wright nonetheless was left with two potential assets, the rangers and the militia, with which he might uphold royal authority.

The rangers constituted, as they had since their reestablishment in 1773, only a very tenuous military alternative in the heightening political storm. Governor Wright never mentioned in correspondence these mounted soldiers on the far frontier of the newly acquired Ceded Lands

---

[32]Wright to Dartmouth, 29 July 1775, *Collections* 3:201; other letters can be found in ibid., 187, 190, 208, 211-12, 216, 224, 226, 229.

[33]Wright to Graves, 27 June 1775, *Naval Documents* 1:764-65.

[34]Substitute letter, ibid., 765.

[35]Graves to Wright, 22 August 1775, ibid., 1204; Graves to Philip Stephens, Secretary of the British Admiralty, 29 July 1775, ibid., 1002.

and so may have felt them too far beyond reach to consider seriously. He may have even doubted their loyalty.

Fort James was indeed isolated in relation to Savannah, and the seventy-two rangers stationed there to protect the settlers from Indians were a very small force with which to intervene in a situation much different from, and against an opposition much stronger than, that contained by their predecessors during the Stamp Act crisis.[36] As Governor Wright continued to feel that the Creeks were "Strange Treacherous Faithless Wretches," he may have decided that the rangers were more useful on the frontier as a buffer against the Indians.[37]

Although the rangers remained in service in the Ceded Lands until 6 March 1776, they were no longer a factor in the political crisis after October 1775, if indeed they ever had been.[38] In a letter written to Lord Dartmouth on 14 October 1775, Sir James reported that a "Party of the Back Country People" had compelled the rangers to surrender "a small Stockade Fort," probably Fort James, and then returned it to their control upon the receipt of orders from the Council of Safety.[39] The Council perhaps recognized the political impotence of the rangers and the potential danger presented by the Creeks if these frontier soldiers were to be withdrawn before they could be replaced by Whig units. The rangers were then almost a neutral force, directed at a common problem—the Creeks; during the critical months of 1775 Governor Wright, for all practical purposes, was left, as he had been for long periods before, with only one military alternative: the militia.

Throughout the history of Georgia the militia had always formed the backbone of the local defensive forces upon which the survival of the colony might depend. Although the presence of full-time soldiers had often overshadowed the continuing role of the militiamen, the absence of these professionals thrust the citizen-soldiers into prominence, as not only

---

[36]"Pay Bill," Waters's Claim, March 1775–March 1776.

[37]No evidence apparently exists to provide concrete reasons; see Wright to Dartmouth, 24 April 1775, CRG, TS 38, pt. 1:424.

[38]Pay vouchers reflect service; see "Pay Bill," Waters's claim; *Collections* 10:16; Harper, "Travels," 192.

[39]Wright to Dartmouth, 14 October 1775, *Collections* 3:215; verified by Colonel W. Thomson to the South Carolina Council of Safety, 29 September 1775, "Papers of the First Council of Safety," *South Carolina Historical and Genealogical Magazine* 2 (1901): 171; Coleman, *Revolution*, 63.

the last, but the only resort. Recognizing the importance of military resources, Governor Wright, while at least tacitly supporting the growth of the institution, had never seemed to consider the militia seriously as a military force upon which he could call with confidence, particularly in an internal struggle. To him, *soldiers* and *militiamen* were not synonymous terms, as indicated by his remark to Lord Dartmouth on 1 February 1775: "We have not a Single Soldier, or so much as a Sloop of War or Armed Schooner here."[40] His disdain for the militiamen had been evident in his correspondence as early as his first evaluation in December 1760.

Apparently the governor's attitude toward these part-time soldiers never completely changed, as the Stamp Act crisis convinced him of their unreliability and the performance of members of the Second Regiment in the Creek crisis in 1774 demonstrated their weakness in combat. At the same time, he could not neglect the militia for several reasons: the Indians still remained a threat; no regulars were available; commissions in the militia were important patronage; and these companies represented to the settlers themselves local forces of some magnitude and thus importance. The events that occurred during the early months of 1775 partially opened Wright's eyes to the worth of the militia, but unfortunately for him and his government, his education came too late.

As the political assaults of the Whigs gained momentum in the spring of 1775 and as Governor Wright's pleas for adequate military and naval support went unanswered, the local militia companies constituted an as yet untapped resource with which the Loyalists might check the rapidly deteriorating political situation. Sir James and the royal council took a tentative step in this direction on 11 May in response to the theft of powder from the local magazine. In their session the following day they ordered a patrol formed for "this Time of publick disputes" to prevent "Violent and unwarrantable behaviour of Riotous and disaffected Persons to Government."[41]

Significantly, at this point the governor, despite his own reservations, still felt that he exercised control over the militia under his nominal command. He could issue orders and was reasonably certain, he thought, that some militiamen would still respond. A patrol notice for the First Company of the First Regiment supported this notion, since it appeared

---

[40]Wright to Dartmouth, 1 February 1775, CRG, TS 38, pt. 1:374.
[41]*Collections* 10:23.

in the *Gazette* in June, apparently in response to the governor's directive.[42]

The royal leadership never followed up its first feeble efforts to assert its legal authority over the militia. During the public demonstrations of June and July, Governor Wright failed to call out the militia companies to act against the "Rebels." Furthermore, probably guided by the same rationale he had used in the Stamp Act crisis, he chose not to avail himself of the opportunity to muster them in a show of force on the king's birthday; however, he did invite a number of officers to his "genteel entertainment" at the courthouse on 5 June.

The public confidence in the governor shown by a group of militia officers should have signaled to him the possibility of additional support from some number of militiamen at a time when events, which called for desperate measures, were obviously getting out of hand. The thought obviously occurred to him, since, after learning several days later that some South Carolinians were planning to come to Georgia to capture him, he called several officers together and asked them if they would stand by him. The officers "in & near Town" said that he could depend on them but "that they Cannot answer for their Men, who they Apprehend will be much divided." They proposed that a Highland Company be formed to act as Wright's "life guards."[43]

The Savannahans' show of support balanced the earlier refusal of the officers of the Grenadier Company, all three of whom were members of the Council of Safety, to obey the governor's orders. To symbolize their defiance, these grenadiers, according to a letter in the *Virginia Gazette*, "threw down their commissions, and declared they would fight in defence of their liberties." Perhaps stung by this public disloyalty and obviously forgetting his own precedent of aggressive leadership when he had used a small band of rangers during the Stamp Act crisis against a much larger force, Wright chose not to take advantage of the support of the loyal officers and failed to make a bid to win the militiamen over whom they had influence. Instead he fearfully asked, "But what can the Officers or

---

[42]*Gazette*, 28 June 1775, 2.

[43]Wright to Dartmouth, 9 June 1775, CRG, TS 38, pt. 1:447-48; Grant to Graves, 18 June 1775, *Naval Documents* 1:716; John Houstoun to George McIntosh, Joseph V. Bevan Collection, 1733–1825, Force Transcripts, Library of Congress, Washington, DC, hereinafter cited as Bevan MSS.

a few People do?"[44] At that point he tacitly relinquished control of the militia as an instrument of Crown authority to the Whigs, who were actively moving to exploit that very force.

Not sharing Governor Wright's reservations and perhaps remembering the hard lessons of the Stamp Act crisis, the Whig leaders initiated a series of actions in July to gain control of the militia companies. On 15 July the members of the provincial congress appointed a committee of four men "to report their opinion with respect to the better governing the Militia of this Province." This was obviously a step toward drafting a new militia law or set of regulations, although none was immediately forthcoming.[45]

The Council of Safety next began to subvert the governor's power to commission militia officers. Choosing a different approach from that of the officers of the grenadiers, Captain John Stirk of the Fourth Company, First Regiment, made the first attempt within the existing legal system. He forwarded a letter of resignation to the governor that the Council addressed in its session on 1 August.[46] In the letter Captain Stirk claimed that he had been asked by the men of the Fifth Company to assume command of their unit because "their present Capt. [Jacob Meyer] neither knows or ever Attempts to Train them in the Militia Art." These men, he said, had understood that the provincial congress had recommended that each company should elect its own officers, "if those Already appointed should be thought Incapable or unfit"; they had subsequently elected him captain and directed him to apply to the governor for commissions for himself and his subordinate officers.[47]

The Council dismissed this petition on two grounds. The members found that it was "Irregular and Improper" because it seemed to be based on a resolution of the provincial congress, and even if it were "regular and Proper," no other complaint about their military fitness had been made against the present officers.[48] The findings of the royal council had

---

[44]*Collections* 5, pt. 1:18; letter, dated 10 June 1775, *Virginia Gazette*, 15 July 1775, 2; Wright to Dartmouth, 9 June 1775, CRG, TS 38, pt. 1:447-48.

[45]White, *Historical Collections*, 79; Wright to Dartmouth, 11 December 1775, *Collections* 3:226.

[46]*Collections* 10:36; Coleman, *Revolution*, 63.

[47]John Stirk to Wright, 29 July 1775, *Collections* 10:36.

[48]Ibid., 36-37.

not the least significance insofar as Captain Stirk or the Council of Safety was concerned. The royal councillors soon found out the actions of the Whigs had rendered their own moot. In another letter Lieutenant William Stephens and Ensign William Johnston, formerly Stirk's subordinates, complained that, when they had not signed the association, or petition, "to abide by the orders and direction of the Continental and Provincial Congress" at a muster on 28 July, their company had proceeded "to the choice of other officers in their stead." The militiamen elected John Martin as captain, William Moore as first lieutenant, and William Evans as second lieutenant.[49]

The Council of Safety followed Stirk's lead and presented an application for the recommissioning of officers that was considered as the others had been, only two weeks later. The signatories, three of whom held royal militia commissions, stated in their letter that they had been informed that many of the officers presently commissioned in the militia were "disagreeable to the People over whom they Command." Such officers should, therefore, be removed because of the "danger of the times . . . as no set of Men could be Expected to fit under Banners, for which they had no good Opinion or respect."[50]

As reported in the minutes of the Council, the governor opined that this "Application appears to him to be of a very extraordinary Nature and to have a dangerous Tendency . . . That it seems Calculated, to wrest the Power and Command of the Militia from the Crown, and out of his hands and to Vest it in the Congress and Committees." Moreover, the present officers, according to the Council, were "at least equally well Qualified to serve their Country as Officers of Militia as those said to be chosen by the People."[51] The Council, therefore, agreed that there was no need for reform of the militia and that the officers chosen by the members of the companies would not be granted royal commissions. The Council sent a letter to that effect to the petitioners.[52]

This legalistic charade did not deter the efforts of the Council of Safety; it now simply ignored the existing system. Accordingly, this

---

[49]Ibid., 37, 43-44; for the text of the "Association," see Wright to Dartmouth, 17 June 1775, *Collections* 3:185-86.

[50]Council of Safety to Wright, 8 August 1775, ibid. 10:37-38.

[51]Ibid., 39, 40-42.

[52]Wright to William Ewen and other Gentlemen, 17 August 1775, ibid., 43.

Council quickly gained control over other companies, for the royal councillors considered letters from officers who had been displaced in the First, Eighth, and Light Infantry Companies of the First Regiment.[53] The governor could now do no more than lament the loss of the force to which he had been generally indifferent. In a report to Lord Dartmouth on 17 August, he enclosed the minutes from the sessions of the Council and noted that they showed "the Scheme and Attempt to Wrest the Command of the Militia out of my Hands and it is said the Committee of Safety are to Give Commissions to the People who are to Chose [*sic*] Officers in the Room of those who refuse to Sign the Association." He added in an update on 16 September that every company of militia in the province had chosen officers and that "the Whole Executive Power is Assumed by them, and the King's Governor remains little else than Nominally so."[54]

Even at this late stage, Governor Wright may have been short-sighted. There were indications that not all of the members of these companies signed the association, as there are occasional references to "parts" of these units performing activities. Additionally, Captain Thomas Netherclift, formerly of the Light Infantry Company, pledged to the governor that he was recruiting a new company, "in which I have made considerable progress."[55] The fact that the officers and the men of the militia companies were divided in loyalty suggests that Governor Wright might have had some chance of success if he had chosen to exploit the militia himself. Since he did not, by September the Council of Safety had gained de facto control of the commissioning process. It formally granted sixteen commissions on 11 December.[56] While apparently retaining the existing regimental structure, the Council also extended this authority, as the governor had traditionally done, and created new units by authorizing

---

[53]Lieutenant John Charles Lucena and Ensign John B. Randall to Wright, 3 August 1775; Thomas Netherclift to Wright, 10 August 1775; James Robertson to Wright, 14 August 1775, ibid. 10:43–45.

[54]Wright to Dartmouth, 17 August 1775, 16 September 1775, *Collections* 3:207, 209.

[55]Netherclift to Wright, 10 August 1775, ibid. 10:44.

[56]Ibid. 5, pt. 1:17; many of the officers had been chosen long before; for example, see above and Evan Haines, Pension Haines, Pension Claim #W8897, Military Service Records, National Archives, Washington DC.

positions for officers in areas throughout the province. The officers elected for these vacancies were then certified by the Council.[57]

Having gained the semblance of legal authority, the Whig leaders began to use the militia, now about 1,000 strong, to solidify their political power operationally.[58]The earliest recorded use of a reconstituted force of militia occurred during the height of the commissioning controversy. In early August a party of Whigs tarred and feathered Thomas Brown, who later was an infamous Tory leader. The Whigs charged him and Colonel Thomas Fletchall, a loyalist and commander of a regiment of militia in South Carolina, with attempting "to Spirit up the back In habitants in favor of Government." Brown, upon being set free the next morning, allegedly sought the assistance of his supposed collaborator and asked him to use his command of 700 or more men "to make reprisals" against the responsible culprits.[59]

The Whig Parochial Committee of Augusta applied to the Loyalist Lieutenant Colonel James Grierson to call out his Second Regiment of militia to protect the inhabitants against this expected retaliation. Grierson, faced with this very peculiar situation, refused to comply without the approval of the royal governor; Wright, with the assent of the Council, supported his decision and directed the regimental commander not "to order out the Militia on any such occasion as mentioned, without his Express direction."[60] The Council of Safety, obviously without the approval of the governor, exercised its newly acquired power and, beginning in early August, dispatched militia units to back up the local committee.[61]Portions of Captain John Stirk's Fifth Company of Ebenezer and Captain Thomas Chisolm's Tenth Company from the Ogeechee River area of St. Matthew's Parish joined members of the Grenadier Company,

---

[57]Receipt, 6 February 1776 to William Farrell, Cuyler MSS; *Collections* 5, pt. 1:31, 33-34, 36, 37.

[58]George White, *Statistics of the State of Georgia* (Savannah: W. Thorne Williams, 1849) 64.

[59]All of the correspondence incorrectly mentioned Fletcher instead of Fletchall (*CRG* 12:434-35); see Edward J. Cashin, *The King's Ranger: Thomas Brown and the American Revolution on the Southern Frontier* (Athens: University of Georgia Press, 1989) 27-29.

[60]*Collections* 10:46; Coleman, *Revolution*, 66.

[61]Letter, Committee of Augusta, 20 October 1775, Cuyler MSS; receipt for fifty pounds of "bar lead," Committee of Augusta to Barnard Hunt & Goodgion, 5 September 1775, ibid.

commanded by Captain Samuel Elbert, and the Light Infantry Company, now commanded by Captain William Candler, as these representatives of the First Regiment marched to Augusta.[62]

The total force may have numbered as many as 138 men, including Captain John Conyers with 25 men, probably from the First Company of the Fourth Regiment from St. George's Parish, and militiamen of the Second Regiment from Captain Thomas Pace's Tenth from Wrightsborough and Captain John Lamar's First from north of Augusta.[63]No confrontation apparently took place once these forces arrived in Augusta.

The Council of Safety exercised its power beyond the boundaries of Georgia on at least two occasions as militiamen assisted fellow Whigs in South Carolina. In July 1775 Major James Mayson, acting under orders from the Council of Safety of South Carolina, with at least two companies of South Carolinian rangers, had captured Fort Charlotte, across the Savannah River from Augusta. He had also taken possession of some artillery pieces, ammunition, and powder stored there. This had touched off a response from some 200 Loyalists commanded by Major Joseph Robinson and Captains Robert and Patrick Cunningham, who recaptured some of the supplies that Mayson had taken to Ninety-Six Court House, South Carolina. After confining Mayson for a time to the jail, they released him on bail. Rumors later circulated that some of these forces, under either Colonel Fletchall or former Captain of the Carolina Rangers, Moses Kirkland, intended to capture Augusta, perhaps to avenge the punishment that Thomas Brown had received there.

The South Carolina Council of Safety dispatched Commissioner William Henry Drayton to command the militia units opposing Colonel Fletchall's forces. In September Georgians, numbering some 84 to 200 men and including the company of Captain Richard Austin from the

---

[62]Based on an analysis of expense vouchers and commissions to make matchups in some cases between royal and Whig units. For this period, at least, it seems that company designations remained the same and that former royal officers, now Whigs, continued to serve in them after elections; see accounts, Committee of Augusta, 5 August 1775, Cuyler MSS; claim of John Chapman, ibid.; voucher of Thomas Chisholm, C. C. Jones MSS; Wright to Dartmouth, 17 August 1775, *Collections* 3:208; "Commissions," 204.

[63]*Collections* 5, pt. 1:18; roster of Thomas Pace's Company, 30 August–19 September 1775, voucher to LeRoy Hammond, 4-8 September 1775; voucher of John Lamar, 1775; accounts of Humphrey Wells, 15 August 1775; receipt of James Murphy, 1 September 1775, Cuyler MSS; "Commissions," 204, 219.

Fig. 15: A Map of South Carolina and a Part of Georgia. John Stuart. 1870. Courtesy of the Hargrett Rare Book and Manuscript Library, University of Georgia.

Ceded Lands near Fishing Creek, crossed the Savannah River to Captain Hammond's farm, Snow Hill. These Whig units, which would finally comprise some 1,200 militiamen and rangers, forced Colonel Fletchall to sign a truce at Ninety-Six on 16 September and dispersed a party of men under Kirkland, who subsequently fled to Charles Town and sanctuary aboard the sloop of war *Tamar*. He joined Governor William Campbell, who, on 15 September, had found Whig pressure to be too great to remain in town. Governor Josiah Martin of North Carolina had made a similar assessment in July after the Committee of Safety called out the militia, ostensibly to protect the colony against a slave uprising. He fled to HMS *Cruzier*.[64] This pattern would be repeated later in Georgia.

Several other companies of Georgians, including eighteen volunteers from Captain Jacob Colson's company and possibly the company of Captain Leonard Marbury, may have assisted the South Carolinians again when Patrick Cunningham and a party of Loyalists broke the truce forty-eight days later by seizing near Ninety-Six 1,000 pounds of powder and 1,000 pounds of lead destined for the Cherokees. The Whigs, numbering some 4,000 men, of whom about 900 were from North Carolina,

---

[64]For the background of the incidents, see Martha C.S. Cohn, "Thomas Browne: Loyalist" (Master's thesis, Louisiana State University, 1972) chap. 2; Sosin, *Revolutionary Frontier*, 99-100; James Mayson to Lieutenant Colonel Thomson, 18 July 1775, "Papers of the First Council of Safety," *South Carolina Historical and Genealogical Magazine* 1 (1900): 44-47; Henry Laurens to William Henry Drayton, 5 September 1775, ibid., 197-98; Laurens to South Carolina Delegates to Congress, 18 September 1775, ibid., 285-87; William Henry Drayton to South Carolina Council of Safety, 21 August 1775, R. W. Gibbes, ed., *Documentary History of the American Revolution*, 2 vols. (New York: D. Appleton, 1855) 1:149; A. Williamson to Captain John Caldwell, 21 August 1775, ibid., 154; Drayton and William Tennent to South Carolina Council of Safety, 7 August 1775, ibid., 132-33; Tennent to South Carolina Council of Safety, 10 September 1775, ibid., 169; Drayton to Council, 11 September 1775, ibid., 173-74, 184-86; Drayton to South Carolina Council of Safety, 30 August 1775, ibid., 162-63; diary of Rev. William Tennent, 4 September 1775, ibid., 235; Drayton to South Carolina Council of Safety, 11 September 1775, 17 September 1775, ibid., 173, 187-90. Adam transported at least 253 men between 1 August and 20 September (voucher of John Adam, ferryman, 1 August–20 September 1775, Cuyler MSS); see also roster of Captain Richard Austin's Company, 11 November 1775, ibid.; voucher of LeRoy Hammond, 8-10 September 1775, ibid.; for details, see Loulie Latimer Owens, "A Nail in Time," *Sandlapper* 9 (January 1976): 16-22. Also see Jerome A. Greene, *Historic Resource Study and Historic Structure Report. Ninety-Six: A Historical Narrative* (Denver: National Park Service, 1979) 66-73; Cunningham, "Southern Royal Governors," 261-62, 308.

recovered the powder and captured most of the leaders of the Loyalists; Cunningham escaped. These actions effectively ended organized Loyalist activity in South Carolina for several years. Governor Campbell left the colony for Savannah on 6 January 1776.[65]

Meanwhile in Savannah, the Whig militia, under the orders of the Council of Safety, without interference assumed tasks that had formerly been performed by the royal militia under the orders of the royal governor. In early August Whigs took possession of the public powder magazine; a captain with twenty men guarded it around the clock.[66] The Council of Safety in December directed the officers of the First Regiment to ensure that patrol duty was performed during the Christmas holidays.[67] Additionally, on 2 January 1776 Lieutenant Seth John Cuthbert, Eighth Company, First Regiment, and William Moore, Fourth Company, First Regiment, received orders to "arm and array" sufficient men of their companies to recover from a Mr. John Spencer four indentured servants who had been improperly enlisted by him and to return them to Captain William Manson.[68] Although these were tasks of a somewhat routine nature, each indicated the degree of control that the Council of Safety exercised over the militia, which had formerly responded to the commands of the royal governor. Such control would soon prove necessary, as a crisis was brewing that would test the solidarity of the Whig cause in general and the militia in particular.

---

[65]Drayton to South Carolina Council of Safety, 9 November 1775, William Edwin Hemphill and Wylma Anne Wates, eds., *Extracts from the Journals of the Provincial Congresses of South Carolina, 1775–1776* (Columbia: South Carolina Archives Department, 1960) 103-104, 110; *South-Carolina and American General Gazette.* 24 November–8 December 1775, 2; George Thrasker, Pension Claim #W2373, Military Service Records, Record Group 15, National Archives, Washington DC, 330; Walter Clark, ed., *The State Records of North Carolina*, 25 vols. (Winston: M. I. & J. C. Stewart, 1886–1907) 11:264-65. Also see Greene, *Historic Resource Study*, 73-75, 203; Cunningham, "Southern Royal Governors," 312; for more details, see Cashin, *The King's Ranger*, 35-36.

[66]Wright to Dartmouth, 7 August 1775, *Collections* 3:205.

[67]Ibid. 5 pt. 1:23.

[68]Ibid., 26; these servants had apparently enlisted in one of the companies of volunteers.

In December 1775 the people of Georgia teetered on the edge of momentous change. Ambivalence had characterized the social and political life of the colony since the Stamp Act crisis. Two competing groups—the Liberty Boys and the "Friends of Government"—had existed side by side since this confrontation had irrevocably altered the old order. The subsequent decade of relative peace had been gradually disrupted after the effect of the Coercive Acts, following the Boston Tea Party, had been felt on even the distant southern frontier. In a matter of eighteen months effective power passed from the royal government to the Whig Council of Safety.

The militia companies, largely purged of Loyalist officers by September 1775, had been the ultimate guarantor for the Whigs in this political shift of power. Governor Wright had failed to assert his authority over this force, the last possible means on hand for enforcing the royal prerogatives. The Whig leaders, perhaps remembering the Stamp Act crisis, seized control of the militia companies and actively used them to solidify their political position, to eliminate dissent, and to enforce their policies. The militia, in short, had emerged for the Whigs as a decisive instrument of political power. As the two governments (if James Wright's regime was yet worthy of the title) coexisted in the waning days of 1775, the fates of both seemed to hang in the balance as a British naval force sailed toward Tybee Island.

Chapter 6

Confrontation in Savannah

As the new year of 1776 dawned, the citizens in the divided colony of Georgia found that they once again faced a military crisis, not unlike others in the past. For Governor Wright and the Loyalists, the anticipated arrival of British men-of-war must have seemed the answer to their numerous, passionate pleas for support. To the Whigs, led by the Council of Safety, the British expedition could only be viewed as a threat to the cause of liberty, which they had worked so hard to advance over the past decade. After these years of dissension, it now seemed that, at least in Georgia, military force would finally decide the issue of Crown or Whig rule as it had in Massachusetts some nine months before. The militia companies, always a major component of the military establishment of Georgia, would come face to face with British regulars after whom they had been patterned.

On 7 January 1776 President George Walton, since March 1775 the captain of the Eighth Company, First Regiment (a town company), called the Council of Safety together for a special meeting to discuss the grave warning received from the Whig committee in South Carolina. This report explained that two British ships of war—the sloop *Tamar* (sixteen guns) and the armed vessel *Cherokee* (six guns and eight swivels) and a transport had sailed from Rebellion Road in Charles Town and were believed to be destined for Georgia to secure livestock or to support the exportation of local produce contrary to "Continental restraints."[1] The Council responded immediately to the threat and appointed Samuel Elbert, formerly the commander of the grenadiers, as colonel and "Chief in Command," Stephen Drayton, as lieutenant colonel, and Joseph Habersham, also a grenadier, as major. These men were to assume command of the militiamen being ordered to duty in Savannah. The Council of

---

[1]*Collections* 5, pt. 1:27-28; journal of H. M. Sloop *Tamar*, Naval Documents 3:666; Master's log of H. M. Armed Vessel *Cherokee*, ibid., 67.

Safety also ordered Josiah Barrington, James Read, and a party of five men (in all likelihood, militiamen) to seize Captain Osborn's sloop, which was attempting to sail from St. Simons Island with a load of lumber, contrary to the nonexportation agreement.[2]

These measures and others taken by the executive arm of the provincial congress to bolster the overall defensive posture of Savannah and the province proved timely, as the intelligence from South Carolina was, in fact, quite accurate (only two small ships short) in its assessment of the composition of the vanguard of the British expedition. Unfortunately for the Whigs, other ships were also en route to the colony.

In mid-December 1775 Major General Sir William Howe, the commander in chief of British forces, had ordered an expedition formed to sail to Georgia to purchase rice and "other Articles of Provision" for the garrison in Boston. As a consequence, Vice Admiral Samuel Graves had constituted a naval force under the command of Captain Andrew Barkley of the post ship Scarborough (twenty guns). In addition to this ship, Barkley initially controlled the armed schooner *Hinchinbrook* (six guns), the armed transport *Symmetry*, and the transport *Whitby*. On board were some 175 to 200 marines and light infantrymen commanded by Major James Grant of the Fortieth Regiment of Foot. Additionally, there were 160 seamen manning the two warships. At noon on 5 January 1776, these ships had weighed anchor in Boston harbor and made sail for Georgia.[3]

As Captain Barkley's ships were departing Boston, other British vessels were preparing to sail from South Carolina to the neighboring province. By 18 January the ship *Syren* (twenty-eight guns), the sloops *Raven* (fourteen guns) and *Tamar*, and the armed vessel *Cherokee*, with several tenders and captured prizes, had departed Charles Town and now rode at anchor off Tybee Island. With the arrival of the fleet from Boston

---

[2]*Collections* 5, pt. 1:28; *RRG* 1:102; receipts of Josiah Barrington, 6 January 1776, and James Read, 7 January 1776, Cuyler MSS.

[3]"List of His Majesty's Ships & Vessels . . . 17 Augt. 1775," *Naval Documents* 2:742-43; Major General William Howe to Lord Dartmouth, 19 December 1775, ibid. 3:166; Vice Admiral Samuel Graves to Captain Barkley, 26 December 1775, ibid., 254-56; journal of H. M. S. *Scarborough*, 26 December 1775, ibid., 319; Wright to Dartmouth, 10 March 1776, *Collections*, 3:233-34; narrative of Vice Admiral Graves, 3 January 1776, *Naval Documents* 3:584; journal of *Scarborough*, 5 January 1776, ibid., 633.

in early February, a formidable naval force, comprising five men-of-war and other support ships with more than 390 seamen and some 200 soldiers aboard the two transports, would be assembling in the Savannah River.[4] Since the mission of these vessels was as yet unknown to the Whigs, for the first time since the Stamp Act crisis it appeared that the British government was confronting open rebellion in Georgia with naked force.

To James Wright, the purpose of the British fleet certainly seemed obvious: it had come to punish the rebels, just as the Whigs suspected. And so he told Doctor Noble Wimberly Jones and Joseph Clay on 18 January that

> he was very Certain their [the ships'] orders were to treat any of the Colonies who were in Arms, had raised Fortifications, Seized any of the Crown Officers, or Kings Stores, as in a State of Rebellion, and woud, if in their power destroy their Towns and Property wherever they woud come at them and that he apprehended they would look on us as in that State and as Far as in their power, treat us Accordingly.[5]

This assessment was understandable, as the governor had been requesting a naval presence in the colony since the early 1770s. Unfortunately, Wright's uninformed threat to use force could prove counterproductive to the success of Captain Barkley's actual mission. While Barkley apparently had enough firepower and soldiers on hand to seize the needed rice, he would prefer, and was prepared, to purchase the commodity, if such

---

[4]Journal of H. M. S. *Syren*, 12-19 January 1776, *Naval Documents* 3:777, 867; journal of *Tamar*, 12-28 January 1776, ibid., 829-30, 898, 1027; journal of H. M. Sloop *Raven*, 15-16 January 1776, ibid.; 840; journal of *Syren*, 19 January 1776, ibid., 867. The *Tamar* needed provisions and repairs, and the *Raven*'s crew was unhealthy after the voyage from England to Charles Town to Savannah (Captain Tobias Furneaux to Philip Stephens, 22 January 1776, ibid., 932). The *Syren* sailed from the Savannah River on 26 January (journals of *Raven* and *Tamar*, 22 and 26 January 1776, ibid., 932, 1027; "Disposition of the Fleet. . . ," 27 January 1776, ibid., 1008). By 9 February 1776 all of the ships had arrived in the Savannah River from Boston (ibid., 1142, 1155, 1165; *RRG* 1:98; Captain Thomas Sherman to Mr. Drayton, 7 January 1776, Gibbes, *Documentary History* 1:253).

[5]"Information to the Town of Savannah from Govr. Wright by Doctr. Jones & Jos. Clay," 18 January 1776, *Naval Documents* 3:852, and Bevan MSS; summary of conversation, 22 January 1776, ibid.

a peaceful transaction was possible. Governor Wright's interpretation had simply muddied the waters.

Confused as to the British intentions and confronted by what could only be construed as a hostile force anchored one-half mile from Cockspur Island, the Whig leaders stepped up their activities to prepare Savannah for a British attack, should one develop. The first order of business was to secure sufficient weapons, powder, and ammunition with which to oppose British advances. Steps had already been taken before the Georgians had even received notification that a direct attack was materializing. On 2 January the Council of Safety had appointed a three-man committee to procure 400 muskets and bayonets, 20,000 pounds of gunpowder, 60,000 pounds of ball, and bullets, bar lead, grape, swan and goose supplies. These were housed at Fort Fredericka on St. Simons Island.[6]

With the approach of hostile ships, the need for ordnance of various types became even more urgent. The Council ordered the removal of the cannons from Fort George on Cockspur Island so as to prevent them from falling into British hands and subsequently to make them available for use in the defenses to be constructed around Savannah.[7] Furthermore, the executive committee directed militiamen to confiscate muskets and ammunition from the houses of both overseers and slaves in Georgia and along the eastern bank of the Savannah River in South Carolina. Overseers could keep only one musket and thirteen cartridges. This served the twofold purpose of gathering additional small arms, while, at the same time, depriving slaves of weapons should the British attempt to incite them to rebel against their masters as Lord Dunmore had done in Virginia in April 1775. (He had raised some 200 to 300 "Loyal Ethiopians" by promising freedom in exchange for their service to the Crown.)[8] Finally, to prevent the needless wastage of powder and musket balls and to guard against false alarms, Colonel Elbert received the authority to detain any individual who "idly" fired his weapon "in the Town or Common of Savannah."[9]

---

[6]*Collections* 3:26-27
[7]*RRG* 1:94.
[8]Ibid., 92; Alden, *History*, 190; Cunningham, "Southern Royal Governors," 295.
[9]*RRG* 1:99.

With efforts now underway to procure and regulate weapons, the Council of Safety turned its attention to the development of the defenses of Savannah. The Whigs sank a ship in a narrow part of the Savannah River about two or two and one-half miles below the town, probably near Fig Island. They hoped that this obstacle would block the channel in such a way as "to prevent any Ship of Force getting up" the river. A guard force stationed at the nearby Brewton plantation watched over the sunken hulk, adding to its defensive value. In the event the British found a way to bypass this hazard, the Georgians erected two batteries of cannons to cover the main channel. The primary battery on the "Savannah Bluff," containing some eight to ten pieces, several of which were eighteen-pounders, was located outside of town on a hill some forty feet high, quite possibly in the old Trustees' Garden near the former site of Fort Halifax. Gun crews also manned a two-gun battery on one of the wharves at the foot of Savannah's sandy bluff to repel a direct attack against the town itself.[10] Additionally, the council ordered Colonel Elbert to place a lookout at Causton's Bluff, overlooking Augustine Creek, to send a warning "of any boats which may be sent from the men of war."[11] These measures provided a basis for future action to bolster the defenses, should time and manpower permit.

Realizing that the defense of Savannah and Georgia depended on the number of troops available to man the fortifications, the Council of Safety, as early as the end of December, had begun to order militia companies to march to the capital. The three town companies of the First Regiment—the First, the Fourth, and the Eighth, in all likelihood—

---

[10]Captain Andrew Barkley to Major General Henry Clinton, 23 February 1776, *Naval Documents* 4:59-60; the locations of the batteries were deduced by comparing their descriptions with the bearings to them taken by the watches aboard the ships in Barkley's expedition; because of the topography, later generations of forts (e.g., Fort Wayne) were built at about the same location as the large battery, based largely upon the topography (letter, 24 March 1776, in the *Morning Chronicle and London Advertiser*, 14 May 1776, ibid., 493-94); see also Barkley to Vice Admiral Clark Gayton, 21 March 1776, ibid., 443-44; receipt, the Commissioners of the Battery to Samuel Killpatrick, 31 January 1776, Cuyler MSS; chart of the Savannah River, John McKinnon, 1825, photostat in Georgia Surveyor General Department.

[11]*Collections* 5, pt. 1:38.

received the initial call to arms.[12] As the threat of British intervention surfaced on 7 January, notification went out to the St. John's Riflemen and to Captain John Stirk of Ebenezer, who was ordered to have one-third of his Fifth Company, First Regiment, in Savannah by noon of the next day.[13]

From this time on, drafts and volunteers from militia companies from as far away as the parish of St. George, drawing a shilling and six pence per diem, rotated to Savannah. For example, during the period from 9 to 31 January, Captain John Adam Treutlen divided his company of thirty-eight men from Ebenezer into three divisions of fourteen, twelve, and twelve men, each of which rode to Savannah and then returned home after nine days of travel and duty.[14] This pattern would be repeated by at least nine other companies from the western parishes alone over the course of the next several months. For instance, Captain John Conyers and fifteen men of his First Company, Fourth Regiment, marched five days to Savannah from the parish of St. George, spent nine days in town, and returned home in four days.[15] As a result of this orderly system, by

---

[12]Memorial of Mordecai Sheftall, 12 February 1796, Mordecai Sheftall Papers, 1780–1796, Georgia Historical Society, Savannah GA; receipt, Adam F. Brisbane, 2 January 1776, Read MSS. The organization of the militia was in a state of flux; it seemed to rely to some extent on the old regimental system; companies bore the names of their captains or had a title (receipt, Wm. Farrell, 6 February 1776, Cuyler MSS).

[13]*Collections* 5, pt. 1:27-28, 32, 37.

[14]Receipt, John Adam Treutlen, 9-24 January 1776, Cuyler MSS; certificate, John Adam Treutlen, February [?] 1776, Read MSS; pay order for John Adam Treutlen, 17 February 1776, Felix Hargrett Collection, Special Collections, University of Georgia Libraries.

[15]The Council of Safety issued the order for the mobilization of one-third of the militia companies of the western parishes on 18 January 1776 (*RRG* 1:102; "Acct. of Money. . . ," 17 February 1776, GA Misc. MSS); many of these companies were from the old Fourth Regiment from the parish of St. George (see Cuyler MSS for the following items: account, Levi Sheftall, n.d.; receipt for nine men for six days, Matthew Lyle, January 1776; receipt for thirty-two men over the period 25 January to 3 February 1776, Captain Luke Mann's Company, 28 January 1776; receipt for twenty-seven men for eleven days, Captain James Lambert's Company, n.d.; receipt for eleven men for twelve days, Captain John Duhart and Company, 3 February 1776; receipt for thirteen meals [men?] for five days, Captain Francis Stringer's Company, 3 February 1776; receipt for twelve men for dinner on 30 January 1776, John Ryal; receipt for twelve men for seventeen days, Captain Joseph Atkinson's Company, 8 February 1776; receipt for twelve men for eleven days, Joseph Atkinson and Company; receipt for twenty-one men for

early March some 300 to 400 militiamen (Governor Wright estimated 800) from throughout the province were in Savannah.[16]

Not every company, of course, responded with such dedication to the Whig cause. Since the political loyalties of Georgians were divided, some companies, even after the purge, maintained their avowed allegiance to the king. Captain James Goldwire, who commanded a company in St. Matthew's Parish, had received an order similar to that given to Captain Stirk. He consequently assembled the requisite one-third of his company and ordered them to march to Savannah. The men of the contingent did not move; moreover, every man in the company, with one exception, refused to obey. Captain Goldwire claimed that two men—James Pace, a tavern keeper, and John Hall, a planter—were avowed king's men and had "excited" the men to disobey.[17]

In response, the Council of Safety ordered Colonel Stephen Drayton on 12 January to assume command of all of the militia units in the parishes of St. Matthew, St. George, and St. Paul and to assemble a force to arrest the two Loyalists, Pace and Hall; of particular importance, he was to suppress any other opposition—a function that the American militia was to perform very well over the course of the war.[18] This expedition, comprising detachments of at least two companies—Captain Thomas Chisholm's and Captain Philip Howell's—was then marching

---

eleven days, John Gasper Grenier and Company, 3 February 1776; receipt for adjutant of militia of the parish of St. George, n.d.; receipt for twenty men for six days, David Russall; receipt, John Conyers and Company, 3 February 1776; certificate, John Conyers, 14 February 1776; see also receipt, John Conyer's Company, 7 February 1776, Georgia, Executive Department, Incoming Correspondence [File II, Names], 1754–1800, Georgia Department of Archives and History; receipt for twenty-four horses for eleven days, Israel Bird, 4 February 1776, Read MSS).

[16]Lachlan McIntosh to George Washington, 8 March 1776, *The Papers of Lachlan McIntosh, 1774–1779*, ed. Lilla Mills Hayes, vol. 12 of *Collections* (Savannah: Georgia Historical Society, 1957) 1; Governor Wright estimated that the officers of the Continental Battalion had recruited almost 200 men (Wright to Dartmouth, 10 March 1776, ibid., 3:234). The concentration of the different militia companies in Savannah obviously caused some problems because the Council of Safety appointed a committee "to enquire into the cause of the discontent" among them (ibid. 5, pt. I :41).

[17]*Collections* 5, pt. 1 :34.

[18]Ibid., 35; Barnett, *Britain and Her Army*, 217.

into the interior of the parish of St. Matthew, seeking out Tories, while compatriots were augmenting the defensive strength of Savannah.[19]

Even as the members of the Council of Safety were calling out the companies of citizen-soldiers for part-time duty to defend the province and to root out political dissent, the provincial congress, meeting on 20 January, was taking tentative steps toward the development of a force of Continentals, or regulars, to add a degree of permanence to the military establishment and to take at least some of the burden of defense from the militia. The Continental Congress on 4 November 1775 had authorized a Continental battalion of eight companies made up of a total of 728 officers and men for the defense of Georgia; this battalion was to be similar to a battalion to be raised in South Carolina.[20] Notification of this authority reached Georgia by mid-December, and the Council of Safety discussed the organization in a session on the nineteenth of the month.[21] Despite the urgency apparent in the other military matters, the provincial congress did not officially choose the officers for the battalion until 29 and 30 January 1776.[22]

The nominating process for the Continental officers was complicated by the presence of political factions within the Whig movement. Button Gwinnett, a prominent planter and radical from St. John's Parish, initially appointed as the commander, refused to accept the bid, preferring instead to serve as a delegate to the Continental Congress. As a result, the more conservative Lachlan McIntosh, a prominent landholder from St.

---

[19]*Collections* 5, pt. 1:37; Cuyler MSS inlude the following: receipt for three men for five days, Lieutenant Daniel Bonnel of Captain Thomas Chisolm's Company, 1 February 1776; account for two detachments of militia from the District of Great Ogeechee in the parish of St. Matthew, 20-28 January 1776; receipt for eight men for nineteen days and twelve men for fourteen days, Captain Chisolm's Company, n.d. (despite the lack of a date, these detachments were probably a part of the expedition, based upon internal evidence, such as the per diem rate).

[20]Journal of the Continental Congress, 4 November 1775, *Naval Documents* 2: 884; Collections 5, pt. 1:21-22.

[21]*Collections* 5, pt. 1:21-22.; Wright to Dartmouth, 19 December 1775, ibid. 3:227-28.

[22]McIntosh to Washington, 16 February 1776, White, *Historical Collections* 93; a "Return of the Officers chosen for the Battalion . . ." is in ibid., 94; the Continentals are discussed in detail in Gordon B. Smith, "The Georgia Continentals," Savannah, 1976, chap. 2, p. 1. A copy of Second Lieutenant John Berrien's commission, 30 January 1776, may be found in the Berrien-Burroughs Papers, 1761-1823, Georgia Historical Society.

Sketch by H.B. Hall, from a Drawing in Collection of Dr. J.A. Emmet 1871.

Button Gwinnett

Fig. 16: Button Gwinnett. Courtesy of the Hargrett
Rare Book and Manuscript Library, University of Georgia.

Engraved by Hoppner Meyer from a Painting by J.B. Longacre after an original Portrait.

GENERAL LACHLAN McINTOSH.

Lach. McIntosh

Fig. 17: General Lachlan McIntosh. Courtesy of the Hargrett
Rare Book and Manuscript Library, University of Georgia.

Andrew's Parish with little military experience, received the colonelcy; Samuel Elbert became the lieutenant colonel, and Joseph Habersham, the major. The subordinate officers obviously reflected a compromise between the two extremes. This split within the ranks of the Whigs led to a duel between Gwinnett and McIntosh in May 1777, and Gwinnett died of his wounds from the affair. The fissure was thus serious and would plague the war effort for the remainder of the Revolution.[23]

The selection of officers for the Continental Battalion, of course, represented no more than the first step toward the creation of a force of regulars. These men now had to recruit troops to fill the ranks of the companies. Because of Georgia's limited population (Colonel McIntosh estimated that there were only 3,000 white men available for service in the province), not to mention the unattractiveness of service in the Continentals as opposed to the militia, and because of the higher incentives offered by South Carolina, filling the ranks proved to be a difficult and time-consuming task.[24] As a result, by early March, Colonel McIntosh effectively commanded in Savannah only twenty to thirty green Continentals.[25] With his own fighting force in an embryonic state, he, by virtue of his position as de facto commander in chief, would have to depend upon the local militia companies and whatever assistance arrived from outside the province to handle the immediate crisis.[26]

As the preparations for the defense of Savannah proceeded, there was as yet one unfinished piece of political business: the governor and his council, all influential men, remained at large, conducting their affairs as usual. A British government, however impotent, thus continued to exist

---

[23]Joseph Habersham to William H. Drayton, February 1776, Gibbes, *Documentary History* 1:259; also see Smith, "Continentals"; Harvey H. Jackson III, "General Lachlan McIntosh, 1727–1806: A Biography" (Ph.D. diss., University of Georgia, 1973) 232-33, and his book *Lachlan McInrosh and the Politics of Revolutionary Georgia* (Athens: University of Georgia Press, 1979) 64-65; George R. Lamplugh, "Politics on Periphery: Factions and Parties in Georgia, 1776–1806" (Ph.D diss., Emory University, 1973) 6, 10-11.

[24]McIntosh to Washington, 16 February 1776, White, *Historical Collections,* 93; for an insight into recruiting, see Arthur Carney to Colonel McIntosh, 24 March 1776, Parsons MSS; also see Colonel Stephen Bull to Mr. Henry Laurens, 14 March 1776, Gibbes, *Documentary History* 1:268.

[25]McIntosh to Washington, 8 March 1776, *Collections* 12: 1.

[26]Ibid., 1-4.

as a rallying point for internal resistance against the Whig regime. As late as 3 January 1776, this body of Crown officials seemed totally without power, as Governor Wright lamented that he had

> no Troops, no Money, no Orders, or Instructions and a Wild Multitude gathering fast, what can any man do in such a Situation? no Arms, no Ammunition, not so much as a ship of war of any kind, and the Neighboring Province at the same time threatening [*sic*] Vengeance against the Friends of Government and to send 1000 Men to Assist the Liberty People if they want assistance, all these things My Lord are really too much.[27]

And then, some two weeks later, British men-of-war encouragingly rode at anchor at the mouth of the Savannah River. The implications were not lost upon the Loyalists or the Council of Safety.

On 18 January, after the British warships had worked their ways to new anchorages off Cockspur Island, the Council of Safety, reacting to the perceived danger from these nearby forces, met in special session that night and drafted an order to Lieutenant Colonel Elbert of the militia (and Continentals); he was, it said, to "secure" Governor Wright and Councillors John Mullryne, Joseph Tattnall, and Anthony Stokes, until he received further orders.[28] Accordingly, Major Joseph Habersham, that very night, followed shortly thereafter by "two companies of riflemen" who later served as guards, arrested Governor Wright at the Government House, his home, where he was meeting with the members of his council. Other Whig officers secured several of the council members who either were not present at the late-night meeting or who had fled.[29] With most of the former royal officials now paroled to their own homes, the transfer of power begun almost a year before and a reality as early as the end of the summer of 1775 was now officially completed.

---

[27] Wright to Dartmouth, 3 January 1776, *Collections* 3:229-30.

[28] *RRG* 1:101

[29] "Reminiscences of Dr. William Read, Arranged from his Notes and Papers," Gibbes, *Documentary History* 2:251; White, Historical Collections, 195; *RRG* 1:102-105, 269; Coleman, *Revolution*, 68; a guard was maintained in Savannah both at Governor Wright's house and, since 6 January, at the courthouse, (Anthony Stokes to Lords Commissioners of Treasury, 5 January 1778, CRG, TS 39:39-40; Henry Preston Paper, 23 January 1776, Georgia Historical Society, Savannah GA); twenty to twenty-five rations were drawn each day by a guard force, which may have been stationed in Savannah (accounts, Captain James Pearse, 2-22 January [1776?], Cuyler MSS).

While the capture of the royal governor by the Whig militiamen represented a decisive break with the political system and traditions of the past, this act in no way was a clear indicator that the colony—which was now, for all practical purposes, independent—would enjoy unanimity in its political future. Although the Whigs, themselves divided, were presently controlling local affairs and many of the supporters of the king were, for good reasons, attempting to remain inconspicuous, even at this late date a significant number of Georgians were as yet unwilling to renounce their loyalties to the Crown. In fact, James Wright, while under arrest himself, wrote Lord Dartmouth on 3 January 1776 that "if we had Proper Support and Assistance, I think Numbers would Join the King's Standard."[30]

Major Joseph Habersham and Colonel Stephen Bull of South Carolina, each examining the state of affairs in Georgia from different perspectives, arrived at the same conclusion reached by Governor Wright and feared the consequences.[31] The presence of the British fleet obviously heightened their concern. No less a Whig political leader than the president of the provincial congress, Archibald Bulloch, however, realized and eloquently stated the very painful choices now being confronted by Georgians throughout the province. After reading a letter from Wright, he wrote to the former members of the governor's council that

> we feel a most inexpressible Reluctance & pain at being obliged to consider those as Enemies, whom we but lately loved as Friends, and Fellow Citizens; And on the other, we find ourselves necessitated by the Laws of self-Preservation & Defence in some measure to regulate our Conduct by the Idea.

He added that he found the "necessity of setting up a Distinction between Englishmen & Americans" even more disturbing since all desired "nothing but the rights of Englishmen."[32] Rife with political factions and

---

[30]Wright to Dartmouth, 3 February 1776, *Collections* 3:229-30.

[31]Joseph Habersham to William Henry Drayton, February 1776 [?], Gibbes, *Documentary History* 1:259; Colonel Stephen Bull to Mr. Henry Laurens, 12 March 1776, ibid., 266.

[32]Archibald Bulloch to the Honorable Members of his Majesty's Council, 16 February 1776, Henry Laurens Collection, South Caroliniana Library, University of South Carolina, Columbia, hereinafter cited as Laurens MSS.

many uncommitted citizens, the colony was far from "unified and harmonious," facts that concerned more than Georgians alone.[33]

The Council of Safety of South Carolina viewed with alarm the presence of both a relatively large number of Tories, or at the least uncommitted Georgians, and a threatening British fleet in the Savannah River. Because of their physical proximity, the destinies of both South Carolina and Georgia had been intertwined throughout their early histories. Insofar as Georgia was concerned, the leadership of South Carolina had two fundamental concerns: that its neighbor remain friendly and that the merchants of Savannah, primarily, not violate the provisions of the Continental association relating to the nonexportation of produce to Great Britain approved by the First Continental Congress in September 1774 and amended in November 1775 to include rice.[34]

Prodded by the report of "great opposition" in Savannah to the nonexportation resolution from a committee recently returned from Georgia and perhaps even by the memory of the assistance given by militiamen from Georgia in 1775, on 29 January 1776 the South Carolina Council of Safety ordered Colonel Stephen Bull to march with 200 "good men" to Savannah.[35] Although the majority of these militiamen did not reach Georgia until 11 March, 113 men were present for duty in Savannah, under Major John Bourguin, and 40 were in Ebenezer by the be ginning of the month of March.[36] Some 442 men from Charles Town companies and the Granville County Regiment subsequently served in the province until their departure on 26 March.[37] By the first of March, the militiamen of Georgia, bolstered by a handful of Continentals and the

---

[33]Bridges, "Handbill," 8.

[34]Worthington Chauncey Ford, ed., *Journals of the Continental Congress, 1774–1789*, 34 vols. (Washington: U.S. Government Printing Office, 1904–1937) 3:314.

[35]Hemphill and Wates, *Extracts*, 217-18; Henry Laurens to Provincial Congress at Savannah, 24 January 1776, *Naval Documents* 3:986.

[36]Hemphill and Wates, *Extracts*, 218; *South-Carolina and American General Gazette*, Friday, 23 February, to Friday, 8 March, 3; *Naval Documents* 4:246; "General Return of the Different Detachments at Purrysburg, March 10, 1776," Gibbes, *Documentary History* 1:261-62; Colonel Stephen Bull to Henry Laurens, 12 March 1776, ibid., 264-65; "A General Return of the Different Detachments on Duty at Savannah in Georgia, under the Command of Colonel Stephen Bull," 15 March 1776, ibid., 272.

[37]Stephen Bull to Henry Laurens, 26 March 1776, *Documentary History* 1:273; accounts, Levi Sheftall, March–May 1776, Cuyler MSS.

vanguard of the expedition from South Carolina, waited for the opening British move.

As January slipped into February and the days of February moved inexorably toward March, a state of equilibrium, of sorts, existed in Georgia as both sides played their hands cautiously; events were nevertheless drawing to a climax. James Wright was the first to up the ante on 12 February, when he broke his parole and fled with his son and two daughters downriver to the refuge of the *Scarborough*[38] This precipitous exit from the colony may have been prompted by his concern for his own safety and that of his family; he wrote his former council members, however, that he had felt it urgent to "have an interview" with the British officers conducting the operation to Georgia.[39] With this act, James Wright, temporarily at least, removed himself from the affairs of the colony with which he had been faithfully and fully involved for almost sixteen years. Crown policy was for the time being almost completely in the hands of the British military.

Despite the best efforts of James Wright, now merely a mediator, Captain Barkley, and Major Grant to convince the Whigs that the expedition "wanted but a friendly intercourse and a supply of fresh provisions," the British leaders soon decided that, at the minimum, a show of force would be necessary to gain the needed supplies. Fortunately for the commodore, a fleet of about twenty-six merchantmen, many of which were laden with rice, lay at anchor opposite the wharves of Savannah, unable to sail because of the nonexportation provisions of the Continental association.[40] If a feasible plan could be devised, the rice was there for the taking, loaded and ready to transport.

By mid-February, Captain Barkley had in hand all of the military assets that he could reasonably expect. In addition to his own ship, the *Scarborough*, he now commanded the sloops *Tamar* and *Raven*, the

---

[38]Journal of *Scarborough*, 12 February 1776, *Naval Documents* 3:1239; Henry Laurens to John Laurens, 28 February 1776, ibid. 4:115.

[39]"Reminiscences of Dr William Read," Gibbes, *Documentary History* 2:252; *RRG* 1 :269-70.

[40]*RRG* 1:270; Captain Andrew Barkley to Wright, 19 February 1776, *Naval Documents* 4:16; Barkley to Wright, 19 February 1776, *Collections* 5, pt. 1:42; Archibald Bulloch to the Members of His Majesty's Council, 16 February 1776, Laurens MSS; William Brown to Board of Customs, 23 March 1776, GA, MSS, UGA.

armed schooner *Hinchinbrook*, the armed vessel *Cherokee*, the two transports *Symmetry* and *Whitby*, and a number of smaller vessels.[41] The weight of naval guns and the 500 to 600 sailors, soldiers, and marines on board the ships represented considerable combat power relative to that of the Georgians, but it would be difficult to bring most of it to bear against the "rebels" entrenched some ten to twelve miles up the partially obstructed Savannah River. Most of this became obvious to the captain after he made a reconnaissance upriver on 19 February.[42]

Although Captain Barkley, after he had personally surveyed the Whig fortifications and the difficulties of the river itself, would have preferred to have a greater number of soldiers, he was determined to take possession of the 3,000 or so casks of rice, "if it is found practicable."[43] He consequently set in motion a plan to seize the ships upon which this needed commodity was loaded. In a nutshell, he decided to use the smaller vessels in his flotilla to sail behind Hutchinson Island, "up the back river, a river not at all suspected by the inhabitants."[44] He would then put the troops ashore and march them across the island to capture the merchant ships tied up to the wharves on its south side. These ships would subsequently be maneuvered upriver, around behind the island, and finally downstream to Tybee. On 23 February the designated ships—the *Cherokee*, the *Hinchinbrook*, the armed sloops *St. John* and *East Florida*, three schooners, and the transports *Symmetry* and *Whitby*—made ready to begin the time-consuming task of "working up the River."[45]

As the British vessels slowly made their way up the Savannah, Colonel Lachlan McIntosh and the Council of Safety feverishly prepared for their arrival. The actions of the, Council were given further impetus by the imminent expiration on 1 March of the Continental association.

---

[41]Journal of *Scarborough*, 3-5 February 1776, *Naval Documents* 3:1142; journal of *Raven*, 4-12 February 1776, ibid., 1142, 1239; Master's log of *Cherokee*, 4-6 February 1776, ibid., 1155; journal of *Tamar*, 4-7 February 1776, ibid., 1165; Henry Laurens to Joseph Brown, 16 February 1776, ibid., 1326; journal of *Tamar*, 19 February 1776, *Naval Documents* 4:16.

[42]Journal of *Scarborough*, 19 February 1776, *Naval Documents* 4:24; Barkley to Major General Henry Clinton, 23 February 1776, ibid., 59-60.

[43]*Naval Documents* 4:59-60

[44]Letter, 24 Match 1776, in *Morning Chronicle*, 14 May 1776, ibid. 94.

[45]Journal of *Scarborough*, 25-26 February 1776, ibid.; journal of *Tamar*, 25-26 February 1776, ibid.; Master's log of *Cherokee*, 22-27 February 1776, ibid 4:106-107.

Unless the Council acted quickly, the merchantmen would be able to sail legally. Unwittingly, this would, of course, make the task of the British simple indeed. So, at the eleventh hour, the Council considered and passed a resolution forbidding any ship loaded "with rice, or any other article of produce," from leaving the harbor. To ensure that the merchant captains obeyed this legal sanction, President William Ewen instructed Colonel McIntosh to use the militiamen at his disposal to unship the rudders and to remove the rigging and the sails from the designated ships.[46] These actions would compel Captain Barkley to play out his hand.

While the merchantmen, with their cargoes of rice, were obviously of great importance to the British, Colonel McIntosh was equally concerned for the safety of the town and inhabitants of Savannah as well. As a matter of fact, he was convinced that the British "meant to land at or near the town, destroy it, and carry off" the ships anchored in the river. In other words, McIntosh, influenced perhaps by James Wright's earlier assessment that the British soldiers were in Georgia to crush a rebellion, thought that Savannah was the primary objective of the British. Once the militia had been driven from the town, he thought that the British could then appropriate the rice in their own good time. This evaluation of the importance of Savannah guided Colonel McIntosh's defensive plans and the actions taken by him to counter Barkley's moves. It even prompted the Council of Safety to make plans to burn the town should defensive measures fail "so that the minions of the King would find themselves in possession, not of a town, but a heap of smoldering ruins."[47] The fact that the Council even considered such extreme measures was an indicator of the degree to which positions were beginning to harden.

Since Colonel McIntosh obviously could not divine Captain Barkley's exact plan, he had to distribute his small force and build fortifications in such a way as to cover a number of possible landing

---

[46]White, *Historical Collections,* 90; Provincial Congress of South Carolina to Stephen Bull, 2 March 1776, *Naval Documents* 4:145.

[47]McIntosh to Washington, 8 March 1776, *Collections* 12:1; Journal of the Provincial Congress, *RRG* 1:272-73; the Council of Safety accordingly ordered an appraisal of all of the houses of Whigs, widows, and orphans in case such drastic measures became necessary (ibid., 110-11, 113; *Naval Documents* 4:146-47)

sites. By defending Savannah, he would be providing some protection as well for the merchant ships, particularly since they were to be rendered incapable of moving from their moorings. He had at his disposal some 300 to 400 militiamen from the province, 100 to 150 militiamen from South Carolina, and 25 to 30 Continentals. The crisis affected the attendance at church meetings; the minutes of the Midway Congregational Church reported that on Wednesday, 6 March, "few met, this Province being in a State of Alarm, and the major part of the men of this District being at Savannah."[48] So as to learn of British intentions as early as possible, he "placed guards everywhere the enemy could land, and ambushes in the different roads leading to it. "

Colonel McIntosh chose to concentrate 150 men under Colonel Archibald Bulloch at Brewton's plantation, since this seemed a logical landing site for troops attempting to take Savannah from the direction of Tybee that would at the same time minimize the exposure of the British ships to artillery fire. In addition, he had smaller detachments manning outposts along Augustine Creek to the south of Causton's Bluff: an officer and ten men at Half Moon Bluff and an officer and twelve men at Thunderbolt Bluff, all guarding roads leading to the west toward Savannah.[49] Although this line of outposts was necessary to prevent the British from making an undetected approach, it reduced the size of the reserve force left in town with which Colonel McIntosh could react once the British main attack became obvious.

As the first of March came and then passed and the merchant ships remained at Savannah, Captain Barkley realized that he would have to implement his plan for taking them. Anticipating this, Barkley had ordered the redistribution of marines, seamen, and cannons so as to

---

[48]McIntosh to Washington, 8 March 1776, *Collections* 12:1; an assessment of the militia as being "thoroughly organized and drilled" was given in the Journal of Provincial Congress (*RRG* 1:273); see also James Stacy, *History of the Midway Congregational Church, Liberty County, Georgia* (Newnan GA: S. W. Murray, 1899, 1903; reprint, 1951) 30.

[49]A great deal of information about the Whig defenses is contained in "The Publick of Georgia to Levi Sheftall for Contingent Expences," 1-31 March 1776, Cuvler MSS; for example, on 4 March Captain John Martin led a patrol at night along the Ogeechee Road for which he drew a ration of rum (McIntosh to Washington, 8 March 1776, *Collections* 12:1; letter, 24 March 1776, in *Morning Chronicle*, 14 May 1776, *Naval Documents* 4:493-94).

augment the firepower and the strength of those ships making the actual attack. As a consequence, on 26 and 27 February two lieutenants, twenty-three seamen, and eighteen marines from the *Scarborough* and a lieutenant, a petty officer, twenty-six seamen, and thirteen marines from the *Tamar* had boarded the sloops, schooners, and other vessels sailing up the back river. The sloop *St. John* had even received four of the *Cherokee*'s three-pounders.[50] With all in apparent readiness, at 2:00 P.M. on Saturday, 2 March, Captain Barkley, accompanied by a party of marines from the *Cherokee* and five seamen from the *Scarborough*, stepped aboard the *Hinchinbrook*, his flagship for the operation, and ordered Lieutenant Ellis to begin the run up the river.[51]

Captain Barkley's first task was to gain possession of the ships loaded with rice. As an initial step, so as to provide naval gunfire to support the landings of the soldiers and marines, he planned to sail with the *Hinchinbrook* and the *St. John* around the rear of Hutchinson Island and to descend the main channel of the river. He would then place his

---

[50]Journal of *Scarborough*, 26 February 1776, *Naval Documents* 4:94; journal of *Tamar*, 26 February 1776, ibid.; Master's log of *Cherokee*, 26-27 February 1776, ibid. 107.

[51]This account of the subsequent actions was synthesized from the following sources: Master's log of *Cherokee*, 1-4 March 1776, *Naval Documents* 4: 166-67; William Ewen to the South Carolina Council of Safety, 4 March 1776, ibid., 169-71, and in White, *Historical Collection*, 88-89; journal of *Hinchinbrook*, 1-9 March 1776, *Naval Documents* 277-78, Master's log of *Cherokee*, 8-9 March 1776, ibid., 279, letter, 24 March 1776, in *Morning Chronicle*, 14 May 1776, ibid., 493-94; enclosure to Edward Stanley to William Knox, 9 May 1776, ibid., 1112-14; *Public Advertiser*, 9 May 1776, ibid., 1114-15; Major General William Howe to Lord George Germain, 7 May 1776, ibid., 1437-38; Wright to Major General Henry Clinton, 10 March 1776, ibid., 293-94; Henry Laurens to William Manning, 16 March 1776, ibid., 370; John Conyers, Pension Claim #S31617, Military Service Records, National Archives, Washington DC; Wright to Dartmouth, 10 March 1776, *Collections* 3:234; McIntosh to Washington, 8 March 1776, ibid. 12:1-4; William Brown to Board of Customs, 23 March 1776, T 1/520 GA, MSS, UGA; Captain Hugh McCall, *The History of Georgia* (Savannah GA, 1816; reprint, Atlanta: A. B. Caldwell, 1909) 2:66-67; Jones, *History*, 226-27; Journal of the Provincial Congress, *RRG* 1:272. The best secondary sources are Harvey H. Jackson, "The Battle of the Riceboats: Georgia Joins the Revolution," *Georgia Historical Quarterly* 58 (Summer 1974): 229-43, and idem, McIntosh, 35-39. Also see Robert S. Davis, Jr., "The Battle of the Riceboats: British Views of Georgia's First Battle of the American Revolution," in *Proceedings and Papers of the Georgia Association of Historians* (Marietta GA: Georgia Association of Historians, 1983).

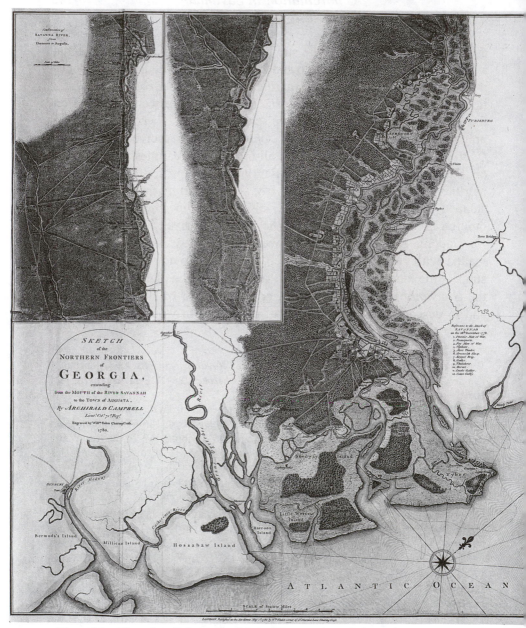

Fig. 18: Sketch of the Northern Frontiers of Georgia. Archibald Campbell. 1780. Courtesy of the Hargrett Rare Book and Manuscript Library, University of Georgia.

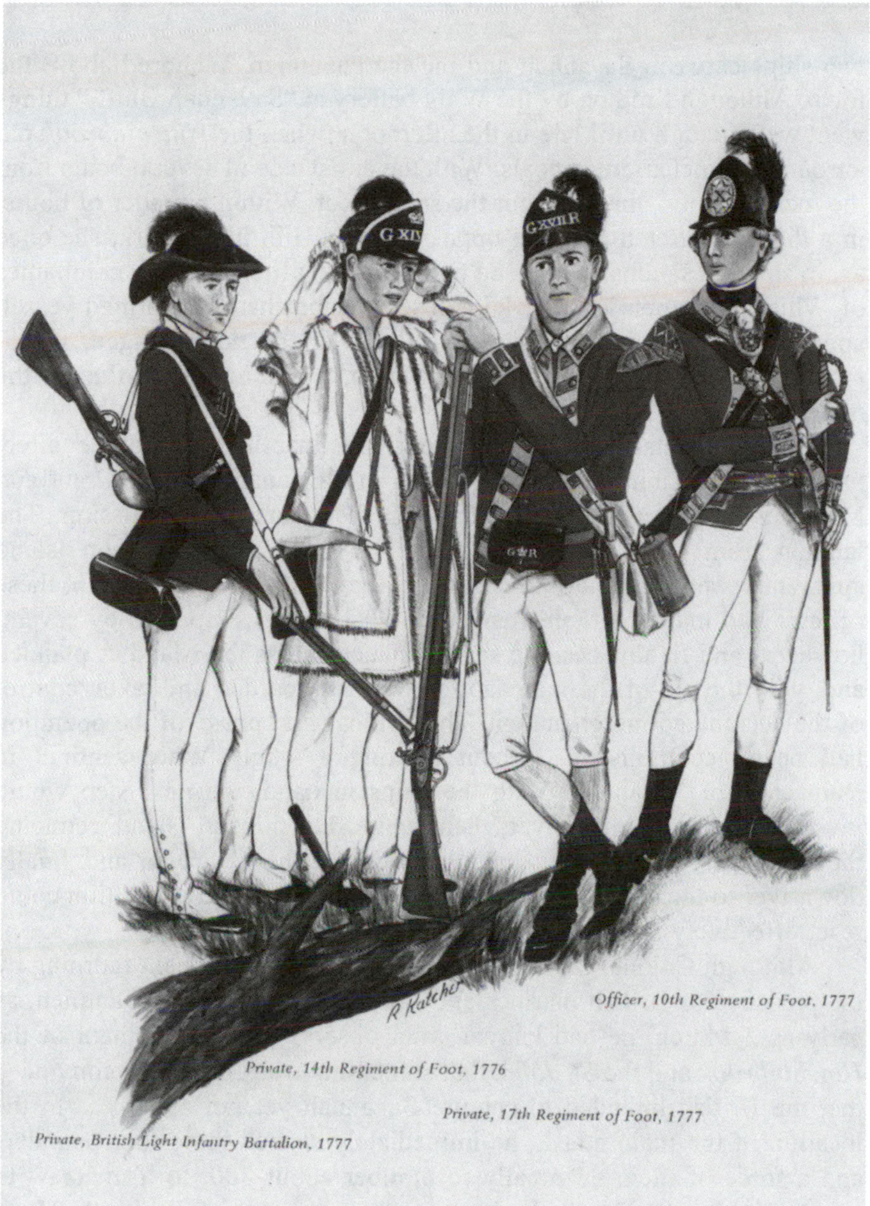

R Katcher
Officer, 10th Regiment of Foot, 1777
Private, 14th Regiment of Foot, 1776
Private, 17th Regiment of Foot, 1777
Private, British Light Infantry Battalion, 1777
British Light Infantry, 1776–1777
Plate No. 453

Fig. 19: British Light Infantry.
Courtesy of the Company of Military Historians.

two ships between Savannah and the merchantmen, anchored above the town. Although fired on by the Whig battery at "Savannah Bluff," things went well enough until late in the afternoon, when the *Hinchinbrook* ran aground on unchartered shoals. With the assistance of several boats from the merchantmen, the crew got the ship afloat. Within a matter of hours, in a different stretch of water opposite Rae's Hill, in the dark, she once again struck a sandbar. Harassed by small-arms fire from two companies of Whig militiamen led by Major Joseph Habersham, the armed vessel, apparently soon joined by the *St. John* after the tide changed, would remain aground until 4:00 P.M. on 3 March, too far away to influence the main action.[52]

Despite Captain Barkley's unfortunate inability to provide direct naval support against the Whig forces in Savannah, Majors Grant and Maitland had no major problems with their part of the mission. The landing from the transports on the north bank of Hutchinson Island apparently went without a hitch. By 3:00 or 4:00 A.M. on 3 March, these officers had marched their men, some 200 strong, supported by several howitzers and fieldpieces. the short distance across the island as planned and, with the aid of the merchant crews, had boarded and taken control of the designated merchantmen. This critical first phase of the operation had been accomplished without alerting a single Whig sentinel in Yamacraw or Savannah. With the ships in hand, the next step would involve moving them upriver, then behind Hutchinson Island, retracing the previous route of the *Hinchinbrook* and the *St. John*, and finally downriver to the anchorage off Tybee Island, before the opposition could react effectively.

Although Colonel McIntosh would be surprised the next morning by the presence of British marines and sailors aboard the merchantmen, as early as 2 March, he had known, after observing the movement of the *Hinchinbrook* and the *St. John*, that something was afoot. Still convinced that the British intended to capture Savannah yet not certain as to the location of the main attack, he immediately shifted three four-pounders and a force of men, eventually to number about 300, to Yamacraw to counter any landing by the Redcoats to the northwest of Savannah. These

---

[52]Journal of *Hinchinbrook*, 3 March 1776, *Naval Documents* 4:277-78; Whig riflemen wounded five seamen who were displacing the kedge anchor. Barkley later rejoined the landing forces (McIntosh to Washington, 8 March 1776, *Collections* 12:2).

soldiers hastily erected entrenchments and breastworks and concentrated the cannons into a single battery. Still in the dark as to the British intentions, Colonel McIntosh and his men awaited the next British move, little suspecting that it was already underway.

Captain Joseph Rice, who commanded "a Boat of Observation," was the first, to his detriment, to learn that British troops had captured the ships containing the rice. About 9:00 A.M. on Sunday, 4 March, following the orders of the Council of Safety, he had moved upriver to the anchored merchantmen to direct and to oversee the removal of the rigging by the respective crews. As his boat came alongside the *Charming Nancy*, he found to his consternation that he and his crew were staring into a number of upraised British muskets. Hustled aboard ship, Rice and his men would be spectators to a rapidly unfolding drama.

The "kidnapping" of Captain Rice and his men had somehow gone unnoticed across the river, but the Americans soon received their first clue that something was amiss. At about 9:30 A.M., two sailors came ashore ostensibly to get their clothes, and "gave Information [to Colonel McIntosh] of the Troops being on board the Shipping and of Rice's being taken." McIntosh then sent First Lieutenant Daniel Roberts of the St. John's Rangers and Captain Raymond Demeré of St. Andrew's Parish to confirm this report and to demand the release of the prisoners. A black rowed these two unarmed emissaries out to the *Charming Nancy,* where, "contrary to all the Principles which cement Society, and govern Mankind," the British detained them as well.[53]

After half an hour had elapsed with no word from Roberts and Demeré, the Americans, realizing these men too were now captives, began to take forceful action to secure their release. After trying to negotiate through a speaking trumpet and hearing only "insulting Answers" in return, they fired several rounds from the battery of four-pounders at the ships directly opposite. This elicited a written invitation, signed by Roberts and Demeré to treat with two suitable Whig representatives.[54]

---

[53]McIntosh to Washington, 8 March 1776, *Collections* 12:1-4; Major General William Howe to Lord George Germain, 7 May 1776, *Naval Documents* 4:1437-38; Ewen to South Carolina Council of Safety, 4 March 1776, ibid., 169-70.

[54]Ewen to South Carolina Council of Safety, 4 March 1776, *Naval Documents* 4:169-70; letter from Raymond Demeré and Daniel Roberts, 3 March 1776, Force, *American Archives* 5:600.

Captain James Screven of the St. John's Rangers and Captain John Baker of the parish's Riflemen responded, in a sense, to this offer and took matters into their own hands. "Chagrined no doubt, the former particularly, on Account of his Lieutenant, by the detention of our Deputies," these officers with a dozen riflemen rowed out to the *Georgia Planter* and peremptorily demanded the return of the detained Whigs.

Frustrated by the lack of a satisfactory response, Captain Baker fired on the British aboard Captain Inglis's ship and, as an answer, received a "Discharge, down directly upon them, of near two hundred Shot, both from swivels and small Arms." The riflemen returned the fire as the boat withdrew—many of them allegedly fired three times—and miraculously escaped with only one man wounded.[55] This fire fight triggered a general exchange of "ball, langrage, and small-arms" between the shore battery and the swivels aboard one of the merchantmen and be tween the entrenched militiamen and the marines and light infantry men aboard the ships that lasted from about noon until 4:00 P.M.[56] Throughout this skirmish, not a single American was killed or wounded, although the British apparently suffered a few casualties.

By 4:00 P.M. the battle between the British and the Americans was reaching a climax. With the tide now providing the opportunity for the merchantmen to sail upriver, the Americans had to make a desperate bid of some type to prevent the escape of the rice-laden vessels. An attempt to recapture them was out of the question, as the Georgians had "neither boats, Sailors, or arms Proper for the attempt, and the oars of the few Boats we had were previously stole away."[57] The Council of Safety, in a hastily convened meeting, decided that, rather than allow the British to use the rice, they would destroy both the merchantmen and their much-needed cargoes. The Council accordingly issued orders to Colonel McIntosh to burn the ships.

The Whig militiamen, led by Captain (later Commodore) Oliver Bowen, selected the *Inverness*, loaded with both rice and deerskins, to be the fireship, since it lay below the other merchant ships and could drift with the tide into the others. The men accordingly set the ship afire and cut it loose. Unfortunately, because it was fully loaded and thus had too

---

[55]Ewen to South Carolina Council of Safety, 4 March 1776, *Naval Documents* 4:170.
[56]McIntosh to Washington, 8 March 1776, *Collections* 12:3.
[57]Ibid.

great a draft, the *Inverness* ran aground. The Whigs quickly chose a nearby schooner and rigged its sails. They then fired it and sent it among the exposed shipping. It collided with the *Nelly*, which, with the *Polly* and two other schooners, was soon aflame. These ships, reduced to burning hulks, would pass back and forth during the night with the changes of the tide. They were for the Whigs "a subject only of Gratulation and Applause."[58]

The approaching fireships had panicked the British soldiers and sailors. Many of the troops scrambled overboard in confusion onto Hutchinson Island. Their plight was worsened by the marshy conditions of the shore and the "galling" musketry and grapeshot of the Whig militiamen. Crews frantically cut loose the ships that could be moved, while individual seamen desperately towed the burning ships toward the shore. As a result, some thirteen ships with over 1,500 barrels of rice successfully escaped out of the range of the Whig guns and to the protection of the *Hinchinbrook* and the *St. John*. In the meantime, the British soldiers who had jumped ashore made their way "in a laughable manner." according to Lachlan McIntosh, to the transports and other ships at the upper end of the island. So disoriented were they that they left behind two field guns.[59]

Although the so-called Battle of the Riceboats, for all practical purposes, had come to an end, both the British and the Georgians had challenges still to face.[60] While Commodore Barkley now possessed, at the cost of only four to six men wounded, the rice for which he had ventured to Georgia, he still had to get the ships back to Tybee without having them run aground or stopped by the Americans. He did everything that he could about the first danger by having the crews throw overboard part of the cargoes—including rice—to lighten the ships to the point that they drew only nine feet of water. Despite the commodore's precautions,

[58]Ibid.; McCall, *History* 2:67; RRG 1:272; Jones, *History*, 1:227; Ewen to South Carolina Council of Safety, 4 March 1776, *Naval Documents* 4:171; *Public Advertiser*, 9 May 1776, ibid., 1114-15; letter, 24 March 1776, in *Morning Chronicle*, 14 May 1776, ibid., 494.

[59]McIntosh to Washington, 8 March 1776, *Collections* 12:3; Howe to Germain, 7 May 1776, *Naval Documents* 4:1438; enclosure to Stanley to Knox, 9 May 1776, ibid., 1113-14; "A List of the Ships and Vessels Liberated from the Rebels. . . ," ibid., 172.

[60]The name of the battle was apparently coined by Jackson, "Battle," 229.

the larger ships experienced difficulties throughout their passage of the back channel.[61]

Preceded by the *Cherokee*, the transports, the *Hinchinbrook*, and the other support vessels spent the next five days laboriously maneuvering down the river, at various times towing stranded merchantmen from the hidden sandbars. The *Cherokee* and the *Whitby* fired broad sides at the Whig force at Brewton's plantation for an hour as they proceeded down the river. By 7:00 P.M. on 9 March the expedition, now swelled by "Thirteen sail" of merchant ships laden with rice, anchored alongside the *Tamar* and *Scarborough* between Tybee and Cockspur Islands. Following the orders of Captain Barkley, the British sailors transferred the valuable rice from the merchant ships to the two naval transports and prize ship *Rittenhouse*. With this process completed, the masters of the various ships awaited their sailing orders.[62]

Navigation had proven to be the major task confronting Captain Barkley's seamen because the Whigs, for all practical purposes, had not tried to stop the withdrawing British ships. They really did not have a great deal of choice in the matter, since, aside from the few remaining merchantmen and the scout boat *Prince George* (in Whig hands since January), they possessed no vessels of any consequence with which to challenge the British men-of-war.[63] The only alternative was to bombard the vessels from the shore batteries or to harass them with the available small arms. They closed out this option by granting the British a

---

[61]For the assessments of casualties, see journal of *Tamar*, 8 March 1776, *Naval Documents* 4:249; Henry Laurens to John Laurens, 14 March 1776, ibid., 343; Wright to Dartmouth, 10 March 1776, *Collections* 3:233-34; William Brown to Board of Customs, 23 March 1776, T 1/520, GA, MSS, UGA; enclosure, Stanley to Knox, 9 May 1776, *Naval Documents* 4: 1113.

[62]Master's log of *Cherokee*, 4 Match 1776, *Naval Documents* 4: 166-67, 279, 329, "A List of the Ships and Vessels Liberated from the Rebels. . . ,' ibid., 172; journal of *Scarborough*, 8-12 March 1776, ibid., 327-28; journal of *Raven*, 12-13 March 1776, ibid., 327; journal of *Hinchinbrook*, ibid., 277-78; enclosure to Stanley to Knox, 9 May 1776, ibid., 1113; deposition of Thomas Tallemach and James Jones, 1 May 1776, ibid., 1372-75; McIntosh to Washington, 8 March 1776, *Collections* 12:4.

[63]Great Britain, PRO, Audit Office, Georgia Loyalist Claims, AO 12/1-4 on microfilm at Georgia Department of Archives and History, 162; Joseph Habersham to William Henry Drayton, February 1776, Gibbes, *Documentary History* 1:258; enclosure to Wright to Germain, 26 April 1776, CRG, TS 38, pt. 2:110-11; *RRG* 1:167.

ceasefire as long as "they will withdraw their vessels and troops from annoying us, to Cockspur again."[64] Although some firing did actually occur, when the Georgians realized that the British were taking the merchant ships with them as well, the Whigs, for the most part, honored the agreement, because they felt that they had successfully foiled the British scheme to capture Savannah; they also wanted to secure the release of the hostages and the ships, if possible. For the Whigs, the cost had been only two white men and one Indian wounded; the British may have had only six sailors wounded. By their respective standards, both sides could thus claim some measure of victory.[65]

Uncertainty as to the British intentions still plagued the Whigs, and they continued to take precautions against any future attack against Savannah. As of 7 March slaves were still improving the entrenchments started during the Battle of the Riceboats.[66] The arrival of 289 militiamen from South Carolina, under the command of Colonel Bull, bolstered the overall strength of the forces in Georgia (now including a total of 442 South Carolinians) and allowed the Council of Safety to send many of the local troops home, who had "been greatly fatigued with marching, keeping outguards, ambuscades, and watching."[67] In addition, Colonel McIntosh and Colonel Bull took precautions to secure the ships left behind in the harbor. After tying the *Georgia Planter* and the *Unity* to the wharves, apparently on Hutchinson Island, a party of forty men commanded by Lieutenant Colonel John Stirk, stripped them of their rigging and rudders.[68] Captain Screven and a detachment of his rangers

---

[64]Letter from Demeré and Roberts, 4 March 1776, Force, *American Archives* 5:600; Demeré and Roberts to McIntosh, 4 March 1776, ibid., 601; McIntosh to Demeré and Roberts, 4 March 1776, ibid., 600-601; letter to Barkley and Grant, 5 March 1776, ibid., 601; Demeré to McIntosh, 6 March 1776, ibid. letter, 6 March 1776, ibid.; Barkley and Grant to McIntosh, 6 March 1776, Lachlan McIntosh Papers, Manuscript Collection, William R. Perkins Library, Duke University.

[65]Council of Safety to Barkley and Grant 7 March 1776, Force, *American Archives* 5:602, McIntosh to Washington, 8 March 1776, *Collections* 12:3.

[66]Demeré to McIntosh, 6 March 1776, Force, *American Archives* 5:601.

[67]Colonel Stephen Bull to Henry Laurens, 12 March 1776, Gibbes, *Documentary History* 1:264-65; "General Return. . . ," 10 March 1776, ibid., 261-62; "The Publick of Georgia in a/c with Levi Sheftall," Cuyler MSS; Ewen to South Carolina Provincial Congress, 16 March 1776, *Naval Documents* 4:371.

[68]Bull to Henry Laurens, 15 March 1776, Gibbes, *Documentary History* 1:270; Ewen

arrested the masters of the two ships, Captains Inglis and Wardell. Elsewhere in the province, militiamen confined Chief Justice Anthony Stokes, James Edward Powell, Josiah Tatnall, John Mullryne, Lachlan McGillivray, and William McGillivray to use as hostages to guarantee the return of the Whig prisoners.[69] Finally, the Whigs planned a parting effort directly against Captain Barkley's forces.

Governor Wright, the officers, and other members of the British fleet had been using the houses on Tybee Island as a retreat from the relatively cramped existence aboard ship. The Council of Safety, in order to deny them this refuge and at the same time to keep pressure on the British, organized and directed an expedition to proceed to the island and to burn the houses in question.[70] On 23 March Colonel Archibald Bulloch accordingly assembled a force of about 150 men, including militiamen from Captain Baker's Riflemen, Captain Bryan's Light Infantry Company, Captain Martin's Volunteers, Captain Cuthbert's Fusiliers, and a company of Creeks, and marched them to Tybee.[71] Arriving on 25 March, the militiamen, while in the process of burning all of the houses except one occupied by a sick woman and several children, stumbled upon and attacked a party of marines from the *Symmetry* who were cutting wood.

---

to South Carolina Council of Safety, 4 March 1776, *Naval Documents* 4: 171.

[69]McIntosh to Washington, 8 March 1776, *Collections* 12:3; William Brown to Board of Customs, 23 March 1776, T 1/520, GA, MSS, UGA; of some twenty "Gentlemen" captured, it was rumored that six were to be shot "as an Example to the others" after they failed to join the Whig cause (Wright to Germain, 20 March 1776, *Collections* 3:240); the Whigs seized Anthony Stokes on 3 March 1776 (CRG, TS 39:42); letter from Savannah, 17 March 1776 in the *Morning Chronicle*, 15 May 1776, *Naval Documents* 4:386.

[70]Tybee Island apparently was also a haven for "Rebellious Negroes" (Henry Laurens to Bull, 16 March 1776, "Papers of the Second Council of Safety," *South Carolina Historical and Genealogical Magazine* 4 [1903]: (205); see also Stevens, *History* 2:136-37; Jones, *History* 2:228-29; Council of Safety of Georgia to Council of Safety of South Carolina, 2 April 1776, *Naval Documents* 4:636.

[71]"The Publick of Georgia to Levi Sheftall for Contingent Expences," 23 March 1776, Cuyler MSS; "Memorandum of Stock taken from Sir James Wright farm plantation," 21 March 1776, ibid.; receipt, William McIntosh, 22 April 1776, John Conyers, File II, Incoming Correspondence, Georgia, Executive Department, Georgia Department of Archives and History; Bull to Henry Laurens, 12 March 1776, Gibbes, *Documentary History* 1:266; Council of Safety of Georia to Council of Safety of South Carolina, 2 April 1776, *Naval Documents* 4:636.

A brief skirmish followed, and the Georgians killed at least one man (the Creeks allegedly scalped him), wounded two more, and captured a fourth, who later escaped. They also took as prisoners several Tories and some slaves.

The British responded immediately. Marines and sailors, in ships' boats and flatboats, quickly rowed to Tybee Island to rescue the trapped marines and to chase off the Americans. In the meantime, the *Cherokee* and the *Hinchinbrook* fired several broadsides at the attackers, forcing them to fall back. The rescuers brought off the survivors and returned to the ships. Colonel Bulloch and his troops had fulfilled their mission and, as a bonus, bloodied the British as well without any casualties.[72] This was the last round in the first confrontation between the Georgians and the British. On 31 March, after exchanging the prisoners and after parting company with the merchantmen, the *Scarborough*, the *Tamar*, the *Whitby*, the *Symmetry*—these last two loaded with rice—and their captured prizes (the *Rittenhouse*, the *Georgia Packet*, and the *Violenti*) sailed for Boston. Only the *Raven* and the *Cherokee* remained on station off Tybee Island to show the British flag.[73]

One last act in the drama of the separation of Georgia from the mother country had been played out in the backcountry even as the confrontation at Savannah had taken place. On about 6 March the rangers ceased to exist as the last effective royal military organization, when

---

[72]*Naval Documents* 4:636; a skirmish or skirmishes in which two Whig officers supposedly were killed also apparently took place at Skidaway and Cockspur islands before the incidents at Tybee Island; this is difficult to substantiate. See McCall, *History* 2:68; Jones, *History* 2:228; journal of *Tamar*, 25 March 1776, *Naval Documents* 4:515; Master's log of *Cherokee*, 25 March 1776, ibid., 516; journal of *Hinchinbrook*, 25 March 1776, ibid.; Howe to Germain, 7 May 1776, ibid., 1437-78. James Nichols, a carpenter, died of his wounds on 31 March (Master's log of *Cherokee* 31 March 1776, ibid., 600-602), see also letter from Georgia, 24 March 1776, in *Lloyd's Evening Post and British Chronicle*, 20 May to 22 May 1776, ibid., 495; claim of George Barry, Great Britain, PRO, Audit Office, Georgia Loyalist Claims, AO 13/34 on microfilm at Georgia Department of Archives and History.

[73]Journal of *Scarborough*, 30-31 March 1776, *Naval Documents* 4:602-603; journal of *Tamar*, 30-31 March 1776, ibid, 602; Barkley and Grant to Stokes, 14 March 1776, ibid., 345; minutes of Council, *Scarborough*, 14 March 1776, ibid., 344; McIntosh to Washington, 28 April 1776, *Collections* 12:5; the prisoners were liberated on 27 March 1776 (Stevens, *History*) 2:136; Stokes to Lords Commissioners of Treasury, 5 January 1778, CRG, TS 39:43).

according to the acting commander, First Lieutenant Thomas Waters, "the Rebels took possession of the diff^t. Out Posts in the Ceded Lands."[74] In his pension application, Shadrach Nolen, who claimed to be a former ranger, stated that the entire garrison of Fort James, with the exception of only two officers, enlisted for service with the Whigs after being approached by two recruiters.[75] The last tie had been cut.

The winter of 1775–1776 also proved a decisive time in the other southern colonies. Whigs in South and North Carolina put down military threats posed by the Loyalists. In December 1775 Colonel Richard Richardson at the head of 2,500 militiamen from those two colonies crushed a force of 130 Loyalists ("Scovillites") at Reedy River during the "Snow Campaign." In North Carolina, Whig militiamen from both colonies defeated 700 Loyalists at the Battle of Moore's Creek Bridge on 27 February 1776. The Loyalists of Georgia, South Carolina, and North Carolina were very much in disarray.[76]

After forty-three years as a British colony, Georgia had, as of March 1776, effectively cut her colonial bonds with England. The battle between the British soldiers, sailors, and marines and the local militiamen was merely the conclusion, for the time being at least, of a process that had begun even before the Stamp Act crisis. The political and social tensions had finally boiled over into armed conflict, and blood had been spilled in the thirteenth colony just as it had been in New England months before.

The Whig Council of Safety, after gaining almost complete control of the colony in mid-1775, finished off the matter in a series of dramatic steps in early 1776. In each case, the militia companies, in the absence

---

[74]Sworn statement, 3 June 1783, "Pay Bill," Waters's Claim AO 13/38; ibid., AO 13/37.

[75]Although Nolen does not appear on the pay bills of the rangers, he related a plausible story; see Shadrach Nolen, Pension Claim #S4622, Military Service Records, National Archives, Washington DC; *Collections* 5, pt. 1:55.

[76]Weir, *Colonial South Carolina*, 323-25; Cunningham, "Southern Royal Governors," 305; Earl Milton Wheeler, "The Role of the North Carolina Militia in the Beginning of the American Revolution" (Ph.D. diss., Tulane University, 1969) 143, 150, 162-63.

of other alternatives, had provided the military force to back up the political decisions and had, in fact, been the decisive instrument of military power. Militiamen seized Governor Wright, the members of his council, and other royal officials and thus eliminated the last vestige of Crown rule in January 1776.

Having settled the political problem, the militiamen, led by Colonel Lachlan McIntosh, with equal resolution resisted the incursion of a British expedition commanded by Commodore Andrew Barkley. Thinking that the British were attacking Savannah in order to quell the rebellion, Colonel McIntosh took measures to defend the town and unwittingly allowed the British to seize the rice for which they had actually come. Through errors of inexperience and caution, the Whig leadership and Georgians whom the Council represented could claim only a partial victory, when perhaps a complete victory had been within their grasp. Of greatest importance, most of the militia companies had responded to the call to march to the aid of Savannah, and in the first true tests of combat since the Battle of Bloody Marsh in 1742, they had stood up to an attack by regulars and had even seen some of them run. Although they had lost the rice to the British, they had refuted Governor Wright's prediction that they "would make off to the Neighboring Provinces on the first appearance of danger or trouble."

Chapter 7

Conclusion

Although comprising different forces at different times, the military establishment of Georgia played an important role both in colonial society and in the coming of the American Revolution. Throughout the history of the colony as the British government formed and disbanded units of regulars and provincial rangers, the militia remained the military force that, by its very existence, provided continuity as the final defensive bulwark upon which the survival of Georgia ultimately depended. As John Shy indicated in 1963 and other historians have since confirmed, this organization of citizen-soldiers common to all of the colonies changed throughout the colonial era to conform to varying challenges and in the process performed a wide variety of important tasks. Ultimately, in Georgia the challenges coalesced and produced a shift in the allegiance of the militia as an institution from the royal government to the Whigs' Council of Safety. This reorientation occurred at the same time that the colonists' perception of themselves changed from being English citizens to considering themselves Americans. From the beginning of the royal period to the time of the Revolution, the militia of Georgia, stiffened by the needs of an often hostile frontier, had generally been (with the exception of the Stamp Act crisis) the dominant military arm of the colony.[1] Even when rangers and regulars were present, Georgia continued to rely on the local militia companies and their officers to meet the threats posed by the Indians and the European powers, contrary to the general practice in other colonies.

During the thirty years from 1733 to 1763, the colony of Georgia had been a buffer of sorts, occupying the disputed zone between South Carolina and the Spanish Floridas, the French territory to the west, and

---

[1]Theodore Ropp stated that the quality of eighteenth-century militia was uneven because it was "less stiffened by need and military adventurers." Georgia was one of the exceptions; see Theodore Ropp, "War: From Colonies to Viet Nam," in *The Reinterpretation of American History and Culture*, ed. William H. Cartwright and Richard L. Watson, Jr. (Washington: National Council of Social Studies, 1973) 210.

the Indian tribal lands of the Creeks, Cherokees, and Choctaws, among others. Because of its location, the inhabitants of the province participated in two major wars against the French and Spanish and became the object of several attacks by the Indians, all of which combined to make mere survival seem a tenuous proposition at one time or another. As a result, a strong military tradition, drawn from the English heritage of the bulk of the colonists and nurtured by General James Oglethorpe, grew during the proprietary period, when the military had, to a large extent, been the "principal industry" because of external threats and British financial support.[2]

Three distinctive military forces took root and began to grow side by side, shaped by the demands of the frontier colony and the changing priorities, as Georgia became a royal colony in 1754 and, after 1763, entered a period of relative peace. Although the militia had emerged during the early years as the dominant military alternative, peace shifted the burden from these part-time soldiers to the regulars, first the Independents and then the Royal Americans, and the rangers, who garrisoned forts along the frontier and the coast. These forces were never large but were adequate for the routine duties of patrolling and law enforcement. Always in the background was a growing militia force capable of responding to crises requiring greater manpower.

The events in the five years from 1763 to 1768 fundamentally and perhaps irreversibly altered the relationship between the colonists and the mother country. Peace and prosperity, following years of war and benign neglect by the British government, allowed opposition from an increasing number of colonists as Parliament and the ministry tried to reassert control over an empire that for decades had been adrift. The crises caused by the Stamp and Quartering acts during the period from 1765 to 1768 were indicators of the degree to which American and British interests were now out of synchronization. Although the antagonists reached short-term resolutions of both of these issues and others, wounds had been opened that never completely healed.

The three military organizations—the regulars, the rangers, and the militia—found themselves either involved in, or affected by, the crises themselves and the changing pattern of colonial-British relations. The

---

[2]Ivers, *British Drums*, 214.

rangers proved to be the decisive military force in the Stamp Act crisis, standing alongside Governor James Wright as he faced down the relatively disorganized Sons of Liberty, who opposed the use of stamped papers. Since the rangers were available and loyal as soldiers of the Crown, in this internal disorder involving a popular issue, the governor wisely did not call out the militia, fearing that he would have "armed more against me than for me."[3] Despite the able support of the rangers, a distant government in March 1767 disbanded this loyal, provincial organization. The Royal Americans marched out of their forts a year later. By default, in 1768 as in 1749, the militia remained the only force of any consequence within the colony to face challenges of internal security, expansion into the backcountry, and the Indians during the critical years to follow.

After 1768, growth of an undercurrent of political tension characterized life in Georgia. In this period, despite the presence after 1773 of a small and geographically isolated troop of rangers, garrisoned in, and oriented toward the protection of, the newly acquired Ceded Lands, the militia gradually assumed the dominant military role in the community at large. Although Governor Wright obviously harbored disdain for militiamen as soldiers, he supported and even encouraged institutional expansion. Burdened by additional responsibilities, such as patrolling and enforcement of the laws of the colony, the militia apparently never failed to respond when called upon by the governor to act. In 1774 elements of the rangers and the backcountry militia suffered a defeat in an isolated ambush by a party of Creeks. Of greater importance, the Creek crisis of 1774 confirmed the obvious: despite its shortcomings, the militia, alive and well as an institution, as yet constituted the only military force of any consequence in the colony.

By early 1775 political differences in Georgia had come to a head. The governor increasingly found his power challenged by the growing body of Liberty Boys. Although the colonists were divided in their political loyalties and the Crown party was by no means lacking in loyal adherents, the Whig Council of Safety gradually usurped the powers of the legal government. Continually pleading with the British government for outside military forces, Governor Wright could never quite bring

---

[3]Wright to Conway, 31 January 1766, CRG, TS 37:110-11.

himself to recognize that the militiamen were soldiers upon whom he might be able to rely. He failed to exploit the political divisions that existed within the ranks of the militia companies at least as late as January 1776, and he chose not to capitalize on the support, evident in June 1775, of some of his militia officers in Savannah. Because of the nature of the political struggle and his own mistrust and low esteem for the milita as compared with British regulars, Governor Wright may never have given the idea more than a fleeting thought. As a result, he passed up his only military resource. The Whigs, realizing the importance of an available military force, insofar as possible purged the militia companies of Loyalists by September 1775 and actively used them to solidify their political position, to eliminate dissent, and to enforce their policies. The Council of safety even sent several detachments of militiamen to support similar Whig efforts in South Carolina. In short, by December 1775 the militia emerged for the Whigs as a decisive instrument of political power.

In January 1776 the Whig Council of Safety completed the process of consolidating political power by arresting Governor Wright, the members of his council, and other Crown officials. Moreover, the Council also countered a military challenge as well. Reacting to the threat of a British expedition commanded by Captain Andrew Barkley, sent to Georgia to procure rice for the garrison in Boston, the Council called out the militia and prepared defenses from which to repel the aggressors. Thinking that the British had come to Georgia to punish the rebellious colony and perhaps even to take Savannah, militiamen from outlying parishes and South Carolina, aided by a handful of raw Continetals and some Creeks, bravely fought against Barkley's marines and light infantrymen when they sailed up the river to Hutchinson Island to take the rice for which they had actually come. Although the British obtained the rice that they sought, in the so-called Battle of the Riceboats, the militiamen defended Georgia against regulars of a "foreign" power for the first time since the Battle of Bloody Marsh in 1742. Events since August 1775 had obviously disproven James Wright's deprecating remark that, during the latter part of his tenure as governor, he had had "not a single Soldier in the Province."[4] The soldiers—the militiamen—had been

---

[4]Wright to Dartmouth, 31 January 1774, ibid. 38, pt. 1:170-71.

there all along. They would continue to serve, alongside state and Continental units, throughout the War of American Independence.

By the end of March 1776, as the British fleet had sailed toward Boston and the militiamen in shifts had returned to their homes, Georgians had for all practical purposes achieved their independence. The formal act on 4 July 1776, the Declaration of Independence, would in a sense legitimize the military and political actions of 1775 and early 1776. Many problems still remained to be worked out, but steps would be taken almost immediately to remedy some of them. The so-called Rules and Regulations, adopted on 15 April 1776, established the first temporary state constitution. Militarily, Georgians would attempt an expedition against the British and Loyalists of St. Augustine and East Florida in September, an enterprise reminiscent of the forays against the Spanish there in the 1740s.[5]

In the more distant future, Savannah would fall to another British expedition on 29 December 1778—the drama would bring back memories of the Battle of the Riceboats—and large parts of the state would remain under British control, with Governor Wright once again the Crown's emissary, until July 1782. As before, Wright ironically would discover that, since he never had enough British regulars, he would in large measure have to depend on loyal militiamen to back British authority. Likewise, during these years, the American militia, operating from Wilkes County, which had been carved out of the Ceded Lands, would be the mainstay of the Whig military establishment of Georgia.

---

[5]Coleman, *Revolution*, 101-108.

Fig. 20: Georgia Militiamen.
Drawing by by Jean Schucker.

Annotated List of Sources

Special Aids to Research

No single bibliography deals exclusively with the colonial militia or military of Georgia. The following sources provide useful starting places for students interested in military affairs in early Georgia:

Coleman, Kenneth. *The American Revolution in Georgia, 1763–1789.* Athens: University of Georgia Press, 1958. Remains the definitive work on the American Revolution in Georgia from 1763 to 1789. An objective secondary source, it includes an extenslve bibliography that covers manuscript and printed sources. Used primarily for chronology and for political developments.

_____. *Colonial Georgia: A History.* New York: Charles Scribner's Sons, 1976. A comprehensive treatment of the entire colonial period through the end of the war. It fills in from 1732 to 1763 and then ties together the material of his earlier work. Bibliographic essay. Although not oriented toward military subjects as such, it covers all other phases of colonial and Revolutionary life in Georgia and is extremely helpful for background.

Davis, Harold E. *The Fledgling Province: Social and Cultural Life in Colonial Georgia, 1733–1776.* Chapel Hill: University of North Carolina Press, 1976. Focuses on the cultural and social aspects of colonial Georgia. An objective secondary source with a bibliographic essay that supplements those of Coleman's works, particularly with German sources. Davis places military institutions into a social context, although he does not concentrate on them in any detail. Primarily a background source.

Davis, Robert S., Jr. "New Research Materials on the American Revolution in Georgia." *Georgia Historical Quarterly* 65 (Winter 1981): 31-22. Bibliographic essay of sources relating to the American Revolution, with emphasis on those resulting from the Bicentennial.

Higham, Robin, ed. *A Guide to the Sources of United States Military History.* Hamden CT: Archon Books, 1975.

Higham, Robin, and Donald J. Mrozek, eds. *A Guide to the Sources of United States Military History: Supplement I.* Hamden CT: Archon Books, 1981.

_____. *A Guide to the Sources of United States Military History: Supplement II.* Hamden CT: Archon Books, 1986. American Military sources. A section is devoted to militia sources, in general and by colony.

Rowland, Arthur Ray, and Dorsey, James E., eds. *A Bibliography of the Writings on Georgia History, 1900–1970.* Hamden CT: Archon Books, 1966. Reprint, Spartanburg SC: Reprint Company, 1978. General annotated bibliography of all phases of Georgia history. It includes articles, books, graduate studies, and unpublished research. The only one of its kind. Arranged by author, with a subject index.

For primary sources, four repositories should be visited for documents and other materials relating to colonial and Revolutionary Georgia in general and to military affairs in particular: Manuscript Collection, University of Georgia Libraries, Athens; Georgia Historical Society, Savannah; Georgia Department of Archives and History, Atlanta; and Special Collections, William R. Perkins Library, Duke University, Durham NC. The most useful individual collections are listed by repository in the following section.

Primary Sources

Manuscript Collections

Ann Arbor Ml. University of Michigan. William L. Clements Library.

Gage, Thomas. Papers. Gage Warrants. Contains pay bills for the rangers in Georgia for the period before and after the Stamp Act crisis.

Athens GA. University of Georgia Libraries. Special Collections.

Cuyler, Telamon. Collection. Single most important collection for military affairs in the Revolutionary period. It contains numerous receipts and accounts that were pieced together to develop the militia responses to the directives of the Council of Safety. Untapped before for this type of study.

DeRenne, Wymberley Jones. Collection. Contains the *Acts Passed by the General Assembly of Georgia, 1755–1770*. Used for legal issues in this period.

DeRenne Family Papers.

Georgia. Department of Archives and History. Colonial Records of Georgia. Inventories of Estates. Ordinary's Office Books, F (1754– 1770) and FF (1776–1778). On microfilm. Used to determine the slaves and other property of note held by military leaders.

Great Britain. Public Record Office. Papers relating to Georgia.

Hargrett, Felix. Collection. Contains numerous vouchers, receipts, and account records that substantiate the activities of the Whig militia companies during 1775–1776.

Jones, Charles Colcock, Jr. Collection. Contains some map tracings and documents bound within the pages of his printed works.

Read, Keith. Collection. Similar to Cuyler and Hargrett collections.

Atlanta GA. Georgia Department of Archives and History.

Candler, Allen D., ed. "The Colonial Records of the State of Georgia. 13 vols., typescript, 1937. Supplements the printed *Colonial Records* (Vols. 27-39), edited by Candler et al. (see below under "Books"). Contains the correspondence of the royal governors and other items that cannot generally be found in the United States. They are essential for obtaining Governor Wright's views.

Georgia. Executive Department. Incoming Correspondence (File II, Names), 1754–1800. MSS and on microfilm. Individual items by name. Used file of

John Conyers to verify the participation of militia companies in the defense of Savannah in January–February 1776.

Georgia. "Governors' Commissions." Vol. B-l [1754–1778]. Contains all of the militia and civil commissions issued by the royal governors. Used to reconstruct the organization of the militia, rangers, and volunteer units. One of the major original sources used in this study; it is essential for a study of the military establishment of Georgia.

Great Britain. Public Record Office. Georgia Loyalist Claims. AO 12, vols. 1-4, 5-10, 54-62; AO 13, bundles 34-38, 134, 136. On microfilm. Claims made to the British government for property lost by the Loyalists in Georgia during the Revolution. The claim of Thomas Waters contains items relating to the rangers in the Ceded Lands such as instructions and pay bills from 1773 to 1776.

Atlanta GA. Office of the Secretary of State.
Surveyor General Department.

Campbell, Lieutenant Colonel Archibald. Sketch of the Northern Frontiers of Georgia, extending from the Mouth of the River Savannah to the Town of Augusta. 1780. Used for settlements and key terrain features along the Savannah River and for the Battle of the Riceboats.

Cary, John. A New Map of Part of the United States of North America. 1806. Used to locate Fort James.

DeBrahm, William. A Map of South Carolina and a Part of Georgia. 1757.

_____. Plan of the City of Savannah and Fortifications. 1757.

DeBrahm, William, and Yonge, Henry. A Map of the Sea Coast of Georgia . . . 1763.

McKinnon, John. Chart of the Savannah River. 1825. Used to locate key terrain features for the Battle of the Riceboats.

_____. Map of Savannah. 1798.

Romans, B. A General Map of the Southern British Colonies in America. 1776.

Shruder, Thomas. Georgia. General Plan and Resurvey of the Town of Savannah. 1770.

Stuart, John. A Map of South Carolina and a Part of Georgia. 1780.

Wright, Thomas. A Map of Georgia and Florida. 1763.

Yonge, Philip. A Map of the Lands Ceded to His Majesty by the Creek and Cherokee Indians at a Congress Held in Augusta the 1st June 1773. 1773.

Columbia SC. University of South Carolina. South Caroliniana Library.

Laurens, Henry. Collection. Contains letters of Archibald Bulloch.

Durham NC. Duke University. William R. Perkins Library.

Georgia. Miscellaneous Papers, 1727–1905. Papers relating to colonial Georgia, some of which are military in nature.

Great Britain. Public Record Office. Colonial Office. America and West Indies. Military Correspondence, December 1773–April 1776, CO 5/91, 92, 93 (1). On microfilm. Used for correspondence relating to Indian affairs in Georgia, particularly those of the Creek crisis in 1774.

Habersham Family. Papers. Assessments taken from a journal of James Habersham.

Jones, Noble Wimberly. Collection. Used for a letter from Jones to Benjamin Franklin describing Whig political strength in Georgia.

McIntosh, Lachlan. Papers. Used for materials relating to the British expedition to Savannah.

Oglethorpe, James Edward. Papers.

Savannah GA. Georgia Historical Society.

Berrien-Burroughs. Papers, 1761-1823. Continental commission of John Berrien.

Bevan, Joseph Vallence. Papers. Contains several documents relating to the situation in Savannah in early 1776.

Bulloch, Archibald. Papers, 1769–1777.

Cate, Margaret Davis. Collection. Numerous documents and maps pertaining to the proprietary period in Georgia, including rosters of Oglethorpe's Regiment and the Independent Company and a map of British garrisons. Inventory in Mary Linda Leslie, comp. and ed., *Margaret Davis Cate Collection: Descriptive Inventory*. Brunswick GA: Georgia Department of Archives and History, 1976.

Ettwein, John. Papers, 1765. Map of Savannah in 1765 locates Fort Halifax.

Great Britain. Public Record Office. Audit Office. T 64/20. On microfilm. Contains the pay bills, or muster rolls, for two troops of Georgia rangers, from 1757 to 1763.

Houstoun, John. Papers. Letter from Peter Taarling gives assessment of Whig strength in 1775.

Parsons, Edwin. Collection. Contains a pay bill for the scout boat *Prince George* and letters relating to affairs in early 1776.

Preston, Henry. Paper, 1776. Account of the takeover of the courthouse in Savannah by the Whigs.

Sheftall, Mordecai. Papers, 1780–1796. Reference made to the paying of militia companies in late December 1775, in Savannah. Used to help substantiate militia response.

Taarling, Peter. Paper, 1776.

Washington D.C. Library of Congress.

Bevan, Joseph V. Collection, 1733–1825. Force Transcripts. 1 box.

Washington D.C. National Archives.

Military Service Records. Service records of Revolutionary soldiers. Used the records of John Conyers, #S31617, and Evan Haines, #W8897.

Revolutionary War Pension and Bounty-Land-Warrant Application Files. Records of the Veterans Administration. Record Group 15. (National Archives

Microfilm Publication M804.) Contains the pension claims of Revolutionary War veterans. Claims contain information presented by veterans trying to establish their service. Must be used carefully, since the claims were made largely from memory. Used the claims of Shadrach Nolen, #S4622, and George Thrasker, #W2373.

U.S. Government Documents

Clark, William Bell, and Morgan, William James, eds. *Naval Documents of the American Revolution.* 9 vols. to date. Washington: U.S. Government Printing Office, 1964–. Collection of British and American naval documents of the American Revolution. Ships' logs, journals, and letters give valuable accounts of naval and political activities in the colonies in general and Georgia in particular from January through March 1776. Invaluable for the reconstruction of the Battle of the Riceboats.

Ford, Worthington Chauncey, ed. *Journals of the Continental Congress, 1774–1789.* 34 vols. Washington: U.S. Government Printing Office, 1904–1937. Minutes of the Continental Congress. Used for the text of the association limiting economic intercourse with England.

U.S. Department of Commerce. Bureau of the Census. *Historical Statistics of the United States, Colonial Times to 1957.* Washington: U.S. Government Printing Office, 1960. Used for population and trade statistics.

U.S. War Department. *The Pension Roll of 1835.* 4 vols. Baltimore: Genealogical Publication, 1968. Used to identify the Revolutionary War soldiers who served in the Georgia militia and Continentals. Cross-referenced with Knight, *Georgia's Roster* (see "Books" below).

Vollmer, Arthur. *Military Obligation: The American Tradition: A Compilation of the Enactments of Compulsion From the Earliest Settlements of the Original Thirteen Colonies in 1607 Through the Articles of Confederation 1789.* Monograph No. 1, vol. 2, *Background of Selected Service.* Washington DC: U.S. Government Printing Office, 1947. Laws of the colonies relating to the militia. Part 4, *Georgia Enactments*; Part 10, *North Carolina Enactments*; Part 13, *South Carolina Enactments*; Part 14, *Virginia Enactments.*

Contemporary Newspapers and Magazines

Gentleman's Magazine (London). Contains news items relating to Georgia.

Georgia Gazette (Savannah). The only newspaper printed in Georgia in the colonial period. It reveals day-to-day activities of the colonial era and is particularly useful for personalities, military units, and notices. On microfilm at Duke University, 1763–1770; at University of North Carolina, Chapel Hill, 1764–1770 and 1774–1775.

Pennsylvania Gazette (Philadelphia). Used for one issue (13 February 1766), containing a letter written by a Son of Liberty relating to the Stamp Act crisis.

South-Carolina Gazette (Charleston).

South Carolina and American Gazette (Charleston). Used to supplement and to fill in gaps when the *Georgia Gazette* was not being published or when issues are missing.

Virginia Gazette (Williamsburg). John Dixon and William Hunter; John Pinkney; Rind; and Alexander Purdie—publishers. Used to supplement the *Georgia Gazette*, particularly during the summer of 1775.

Books

Atlanta Town Committee. *Abstracts of Colonial Wills of the State of Georgia, 1733–1777*. Hapeville GA: Atlanta Town Committee for the Department of Archives and History, 1962 Used for information about the property owned by officers.

Boone, Nicholas. *Military Discipline: The Newest Way and Method of Exercising Horse and Foot*. Boston: n.p., 1718. An example of the type of manual perhaps used by the militia officers of Georgia to train their units.

Bryant, Pat., ed. *English Crown Grants for Islands in Georgia, 1755–1775*. Atlanta: State Printing Office, 1972. Contains the royal land grants for the period indicated. Used to cross-reference personalities and to compile acreage data for militia and ranger officers.

_____. *English Crown Grants in St. Andrew Parish in Georgia, 1755–1775.* Atlanta: State Printing Office, 1972.

_____. *English Crown Grants in St. George Parish in Georgia,* 1755–1775. Atlanta: State Printing Office. 1974.

Candler, Allen D., et al., *The Colonial Records of the State of Georgia.* 32 vols. to date. Atlanta and Athens: Printers and publishers vary, 1904–1916, 1975, 1978–1979, 1985, 1986, 1989. Primary materials for the entire colonial period, including statutes, proceedings, and minutes of the governor and council, journals of both houses of the assembly, documents of the trustee period, and miscellaneous items. Each volume has an index.

_____. *The Revolutionary Records of the State of Georgia.* 3 vols. Atlanta: Franklin-Turner,1908. Miscellaneous papers and minutes of the Council of Safety and the Provincial Congress.

Carter, Clarence Edwin, ed. *The Correspondence of General Thomas Gage with the Secretaries of State, 1763–1775.* 2 vols. New Haven: Yale University Press, 1931–1933. Published letters of General Gage, the commander in chief of British forces in North America. A number relate to the affairs of the British regulars and rangers in Georgia.

Clark, Walter, ed. *The State Records of North Carolina.* 25 vols. Winston NC: M. I. & J. C. Stewart, 1886–1907. Companion of The Colonial Records of the State of Georgia. Used specifically for the affairs at Ninety-Six in South Carolina.

Coulter, E. Merton, ed. *The Journal of Peter Gordon, 1732–1735.* Athens: University of Georgia Press, 1963. Recorded entries of Peter Gordon, one of the original settlers, in the first years of the colony. Firsthand accounts of the militia in its infancy.

_____. *The Journal of William Stephens, 1741–1745.* 2 vols. Athens: University of Georgia Press, 1958–1959. Journal entries give a key leader's in sights into the proprietary era and describe militia activities in detail.

Davies, K. G., ed. *Documents of the American Revolution, 1770–1783.* 21 vols. Shannon, Ireland: Irish University Press, 1972–1981. Divided into calendars of documents and then the text of selected documents.

Davis, Robert S., Jr., ed. *Encounters on a March through Georgia in 1779: The Maps and Memorandums of John Wilson, Engineer, 71st Highland Regiment.* Sylvania GA: Partridge Pond Press, 1986. Maps and text describe route of march of Lieutenant Colonel Archibald Campbell's expedition to Augusta in 1779. Used to verify places along the road between Augusta and Savannah.

_____. *Georgia Citizens and Soldiers of the American Revolution.* Easley SC: Southern Historical Press, 1979. Documentary history of the American Revolution in Georgia. Developed to help researchers gain genealogical information, it also has a helpful guide to sources and their locations. It is a useful starting place for the military forces of Georgia in the Revolution.

DeBrahm, John Gerar William. *History of the Province of Georgia.* Wormsloe GA: n.p., 1849. A "participant's history." DeBrahm was the Crown surveyor and spent a great deal of time in Georgia. Maps and drawings.

DeVorsey, Louis, Jr., ed. *DeBrahm's Report of the General Survey in the Southern District of North America.* Columbia: University of South Carolina Press, 1971. Maps and evaluation of the geography of early Georgia. The observer described water, road nets, and militia.

Early History of Georgia Documents. N.p., n.d. Miscellaneous documents relating to Georgia in the Revolution.

Force, Peter, ed. *American Archives.* 4th ser. 6 vols. Washington: M. St. Clair and Peter Force, 1837–1846. Volumes 4 and 6 contain documents about Georgia.

Ford, Worthington Chauncey. *British Officers Serving in America, 1754–1783,* 2 vols. Boston: David Clapp & Sons,, 1894 (vol. 1); Brooklyn. Historical Printing Club, 1897 (vol. 2). Contains a listing of the British officer who served in North America. Used specifically for the officers of the Sixtieth Regiment, serving Georgia.)

Georgia Historical Society. *Collections of the Georgia Historical Society.* 21 vols. to date. Published by the Society. Each of these volumes provides in sight into the respective periods of Georgia history.

  Vol. 3. "Letters from General Oglethorpe to the Trustees of the Colony and Others, from October 1735 to August 1744," 1-157; "Letters from

Governor Sir James Wright to the Earl of Dartmouth and Lord George Germain, Secretaries of State for America, from August 24, 1774, to February 16, 1782," 180-372; "Report of Governor Sir James Wright to Lord Dartmouth on the Condition of the Colony, September 20, 1773," 158-79. Savannah, 1873. These letters are indispensable to a study of this kind.

Vol. 5, Part 1. "Proceedings of the First Provincial Congress of Georgia, 1775," 1-13; "Proceedings of the Georgia Council of Safety, 1775 to 1777," 15-139. Savannah, 1901. These proceedings fill the gap in the *Colonial Records*.

Vol. 6. *The Letters of the Hon. James Habersham, 1756–1775*. Savannah, 1904.

Vol. 10. *The Proceedings and Minutes of the Governor and Council of Georgia, October 4, 1774, through November 7, 1775, and September 6, 1779, through September 20, 1780*. Edited by Lilla Mills Hawes. Savannah, 1952.

Vol. 12. *The Papers of Lachlan McIntosh, 1774–1779*. Edited by Lilla Mills Hawes. Savannah, 1957.

Vol. 13. *The Letter Book of Thomas Rasberry, 1758–1761*. Edited by Lilla Mills Hawes. Savannah, 1959.

Vol. 17. *The Jones Family Papers*. Edited by John Eddins Simpson. Savannah, 1976.

Vol. 18. *The Search for Georgia's Colonial Records*. Edited by Lilla Mills Hawes and Albert S. Britt, Jr. Savannah, 1976. Describes the fate of the surviving colonial documents.

Vol. 19. *Checklist of Eighteenth-Century Manuscripts in the Georgia Historical Society*. Edited by Lilla Mills Hawes and Karen Elizabeth Osvald. Savannah, 1976.

Vol. 21. *The Journal of the Reverend John Joachim Zubly, A.M., D.D., March 5, 1770, through June 22, 1781*. Edited by Lilla Mills Hawes. Savannah, 1989. Journals and letters by a minister, with observations about life in the colonies of Georgia and South Carolina.

Gibbes, R. W., ed. *Documentary History of the American Revolution.* 2 vols. New York: D. Appleton, 1855, 1857. Contains correspondence, diaries, and other miscellaneous items relating to the American Revolution, primarily South Carolina. The Georgia items relate to the expedition to Ninety Six, the defense of Savannah (in which South Carolina militiamen were involved), and the capture of Governor Wright.

Giller, Sayde; Dumont, William H.; and Dumont, Louise M., comps. *Index of Revolutionary War Pension Applications.* Washington: National Genealogical Society, 1966. Listing of Revolutionary soldiers who applied for pensions after the war. Because it has a name index only and no cross-reference by state, it is of limited usefulness.

Greene, Evarts B., and Harrington, Virginia D. *American Population before the Federal Census of 1790.* New York: Columbia University Press, 1932. General population and militia figures; used as a primary source.

Greene, Jack P., ed. *Colonies to Nation, 1763–1789.* New York: W. W. Norton, 1975. Documentary history of the American Revolution. It has copies of tax measures and other primary items and includes helpful annotations.

Hemperley, Marion R., ed. *English Crown Grants for Parishes of St. David, St. Patrick, St. Thomas, St. Mary in Georgia, 1755–1775.* Atlanta: State Printing Office, 1973. This and the following Hemperley volumes are similar to the three Bryant volumes above.

_____. *English Crown Grants in St. John Parish in Georgia, 1755–1775.* Atlanta: State Printing Office, 1972.

_____. *English Crown Grants in St. Matthew Parish in Georgia, 1755–1775.* Atlanta: State Printing Office, 1974.

_____. *English Crown Grants in St. Paul Parish in Georgia, 1755– 1775.* Atlanta: State Printing Office, 1974.

_____. *English Crown Grants in St. Philip Parish in Georgia, 1755– 1775.* Atlanta: State Printing Office, 1972.

Hemphill, William Edwin, and Wates, Wylma Anne, eds. *Extracts from the Journals of the Provincial Congresses of South Carolina, 1775– 1776.* Columbia: South Carolina Archives Department, 1960. Minutes of the Provincial Congress of South Carolina. Used for information about the participation of South Carolinians in the defense of Savannah and for the affairs at Ninety-Six.

Hemphill, William Edwin; Wates, Wylma Arme; and Olsberg, R. Nicholas, comps. *Journal of the General Assembly and the House of Representatives, 1776–1780.* Columbia: University of South Carolina Press, 1970. Records of the state of South Carolina. These provide a view of events in Georgia through the eyes of leaders in South Carolina. Situations in both colonies (states) were similar.

Kimball, Gertrude Selwyn, ed. *Correspondence of William Pitt.* 2 vols. New York: Macmillan, 1906. Letters of Prime Minister William Pitt. Used primarily for those between Governor Ellis and others relating to the rangers during the early royal period.

Knight, Lucian Lamar, ed. *Georgia's Roster of the Revolution.* Atlanta: 1920. Reprint. Baltimore: Genealogical Publishing Company, 1967. Listing of the soldiers who fought the Revolution in Georgia, including Continentals, state soldiers, and militiamen. Names are listed by the source of the data: applications for land, certificates of service, bounty surveys, head rights, land lottery grants, and others. Used to cross-check military officers.

Labaree, Leonard Woods, ed. *Royal Instructions to British Colonial Governors, 1670–1776.* 2 vols. New York: D. Appleton-Century, 1935. Gives legal basis upon which the royal governors operated and has a collection of royal instructions for each colony.

Lucas, Silas Emmett, Jr., comp. *Index to the Headright and Bounty Grants of Georgia, 1756–1909.* Vidalia GA: Georgia Genealogical Reprints, 1970. Contains all colonial land grants and can be used as an index to the series English Crown Grants. Used specifically to compile land acreages for Governor Wright, military officers, and rangers in Georgia.

McDowell, William L., Jr., ed. *Documents Relating to Indian Affairs, 1754–1765.* Vol 2. of *Colonial Records of South Carolina.* Columbia: University of South Carolina Press, 1970. Comparable to the *Colonial Records.* Several documents cite militia activities in response to threats from the Indians in the early royal period.

McPherson, Robert G., ed. *The Journal of the Earl of Egmont: Abstract of the Trustees Proceedings for Establishing the Colony of Georgia, 1732–1738.*

Athens: University of Georgia Press, 1962. One of the trustees. This work
provides insights into proprietary Georgia, the trustees, and Oglethorpe.

Martin, Colonel. *A Plan for Establishing and Disciplining a National Militia in
Great Britain, Ireland and in all the British Dominions of America*. London:
for A. Millan, 1745. An example of the type of manuals possibly used by
militia officers to train their soldiers.

Mereness, Newton D., ed. *Travels in the American Colonies*. New York:
Macmillan, 1916. Used the chapter that records the journal of David Taitt,
an Indian commissioner, which includes most helpful observations of the
militia of the Second Regiment.

Prince, Oliver H. *A Digest of the Laws of the State of Georgia*. Milledgeville
GA: Grantland & Orme, 1822. Compilation of the laws in force in Georgia
as of 1822. Used for militia and patrolling laws.

Reese, Trevor R., ed. *The Glamorous Malcontents: Criticisms and Defenses of
the Colony of Georgia 1741–1743*. Savannah: Beehive Press, 1973. Reprint
of the original. Contains the complaints of a group of the early settlers
against trustee policies. Used only for the introductory comments of the
editor.

Saye, Albert B., ed. *Georgia's Charter of 1732*. Athens: University of Georgia
Press, 1942.

Smith; Capt. George. *An Universal Military Dictionary*. London: J. Millan, 1779.
Reprint. Ottawa: Museum Restoration Service, 1969. Defines the military
terms of the period.

Stacy, James. *History of the Midway Congregational Church, Liberty County,
Georgia*. Newnan GA: S. W. Murray, 1899, 1903. Reprint. 1951. Contains
the minutes of the church meetings, which establishes the involvement of
militiamen from the parish of St. Matthew in the defense of Savannah.

Stokes, Anthony. *A View of the Constitution of the British Colonies, in North
America and the West Indies, At the Time the Civil War Broke out on the
Continent of America*. London: B. White, 1783. A history of early America.
Used for background from the perspective of the former chief justice of the
colony of Georgia.

Sutherland, Stella H. *Population Distribution in Colonial America*. New York: Columbia University Press, 1936. Population figures, particularly 1775; used as a primary source.

Van Doren, Mark, ed. *The Travels of William Bartram*. New York: Facsimile Library, 1940. Used for the physical description of Georgia by Bartram, an American naturalist. It is useful for determining travel times and routes; it provides the only known firsthand description of Fort James.

Warren, Mary Bonurant, comp. *Marriages and Deaths, 1763–1820*. Danielsville GA: Heritage Papers, 1968. Based upon the notices in the *Georgia Gazette*, so it is not definitive. Used to obtain vital statistics of the military officers.

White, George. *Historical Collections of Georgia*. New York: Pudney & Russell, 1855. Collection of Revolutionary documents. Used primarily for political documents and to supplement Collections and the Colonial Records. Sketchy annotations.

Wilson, Caroline Price, comp. *Annals of Georgia: Important Early Records of the State*. 2 vols. Savannah: Braid & Hutton, 1933. Compilation of mortuary records (cemetery) from 1802 to 1832.

Articles

Bain, James, Jr., ed. "The Siege of Charleston: Journal of Captain Peter Russell, December 25, 1779, to May 2, 1780." *American Historical Review* 4 (1899): 478-501. Used for the description of Savannah.

Harper, Francis, ed. "Diary of a Journey through the Carolinas, Georgia, and Florida from July 1, 1765, to April 10, 1766." *Transactions of the American Philosophical Society* 33, pt. 1 (December 1942): 1-120. See Van Doren above under "Books." This item is a report of William's father, John Bartram. The description of Wright's popularity and of his home were useful.

_____. "Travels in Georgia and Florida, 1773–1774: A Report of Dr. John Fothergill." *Transactions of the American Philosophical Society* 33, pt. 2 (November 1943): 1-242. See above. This item includes William Bartram's observations.

Hawes, Lilla Mills., ed. "Letters to the Georgia Colonial Agent, July, 1762 to January, 1771." *Georgia Historical Quarterly* 36 (September 1952): 250-85. Affairs of Georgia were reported in these letters during this crucial period. Used specifically for the evaluations of colonial defenses in the early period.

_____. "Proceedings of the President and Assistants in Council of Georgia, 1749–1751." *Georgia Historical Quarterly* 34 (December 1951): 323-50; 36 (March 1952): 46-70. Provides items not originally included in the *Colonial Records* for the last years of the proprietary period.

Howland, Henry R., ed. "A British Privateer in the American Revolution." *American Historical Review* 7 (1902): 286-303. Used for the description of Savannah in 1779.

"Papers of the First Council of Safety." *South Carolina Historical and Genealogical Magazine* 1 (1900): 41-75, 119-35, 183-205, 279-310; 2 (1901): 167-93. Similar to the "Proceedings" of the Council of Safety of Georgia. Provides the perspective of South Carolina in such crucial matters as the expedition to Ninety-Six, the expedition to Savannah, and the association.

"Papers of the Second Council of Safety." *South Carolina Historical and Genealogical Magazine* 4 (1903): 195-214. See above.

Saye, Albert B., ed. "Commission and Instructions of Governor John Reynolds, August 6, 1754." *Georgia Historical Quarterly* 30 (June 1946): 125-62. Provides the definition and limits of the governor's authority as given by the king.

Maps

Individual maps are listed in the respective manuscript collection, where appropriate.

Blake, Janice Gayle, comp. *Pre-Nineteenth-Century Maps in the Collection of the Georgia Surveyor General Department.* Atlanta: State Printing Office, 1975. Comprehensive index to the originals, photostats, and other types of copies on file in the Surveyor General Department.

Cappon, Lester J., ed. *Atlas of Early American History: The Revolutionary Era, 1760–1790*. Princeton: Princeton University Press,1976. Series of descriptive maps of the period, useful for population, religion, economic data, and cultural and other activities during the American Revolution. Explanatory notes with references.

Cumming, William P. *The Southeast in Early Maps*. 2d ed. Chapel Hill: University of North Carolina Press, 1962. Index to available maps of the southeastern colonies during the colonial period, including some maps. Annotated, with footnotes and bibliography.

Friis, Herman R. *A Series of Population Maps of the Colonies and the United States, 1625–1790*. American Geographical Society Mimeographed Publications, no. 13. New York: American Geographical Society, 1940. Revised ed., 1968. Two maps show the population distribution of the United States, including Georgia in 1760 and 1770.

Georgia. *Georgia State Highway System and Connections*. 1975. Road map used to determine distances today by way of comparison with the contemporary maps.

Secondary Sources

Books

Abbot, William W. *The Royal Governors of Georgia, 1754–1775*. Chapel Hill: University of North Carolina Press, 1959. The definitive work on the royal governors. Used for background material for the royal period and for the political events. Bibliographic essay.

Alden, John R. *A History of the American Revolution*. New York: Alfred A. Knopf, 1972. Provides useful overview of the development of the American Revolution in general and ties Georgia into the Revolutionary picture. It is a helpful guide to understanding the major British ministerial figures. Essay on sources.

_____. *John Stuart and the Southern Colonial Frontier*. Ann Arbor: University of Michigan Press, 1944. Places Indian affairs of Georgia into the southern and British perspectives and provides background for Indian white relations, particularly the Congress of 1763 at Augusta and the Creek crisis of 1774.

_____. *The South in the Revolution, 1763–1789*. Vol. 3 of A History of the South. Baton Rouge: Louisiana State University Press, 1957. Places the political events in Georgia into southern perspective.

Anderson, Fred. *A People's Army: Massachusetts Soldiers and Society in the Seven Years' War*. Chapel Hill: University of North Carolina Press, 1984. Examines the New England provincial armies of volunteers who fought with the British in the Seven Years' War. It provides a basis for comparison with the Georgia militia.

Barnett, Correlli. *Britain and Her Army, 1509–1970: A Military, Political, and Social Survey*. New York: William Morrow, 1970. Survey of the British Army. It provides background for the British military heritage transplanted to America and discusses colonial and Revolutionary military affairs from the perspective of the British. It emphasizes the traditional role of the militia in stamping out dissent at home. The book is a survey and thus does not include a great deal of detail.

Boorstin, Daniel J. *The Americans: The Colonial Experience*. New York: Random House, 1958. Part 3 discusses the altruistic and philanthropic failure of the colony of Georgia. It provides good background for the proprietary era and discusses the colonial militia in a general context. The treatment is perhaps dated but fair. Bibliographic notes by chapter.

Bowler, R. Arthur. *Logistics and the Failure of the British Army in America, 1775–1783*. Princeton: Princeton University Press, 1975. Primary focus is the inadequate logistic organization and the logistic problems that Bowler feels contributed to the failure of the British Army against the Americans. The book also highlights the role of the American militia in keeping the British confined to port enclaves.

Cashin, Edward J. *Colonial Augusta: "Key of the Indian Country."* Macon GA: Mercer University Press, 1986. The book's essays are devoted to colonial Augusta and the Georgia frontier. Chapters 3 and 4 spotlight Fort Augusta and its soldiers.

_____. *The King's Ranger: Thomas Brown and the American Revolution on the Southern Frontier*. Athens: University of Georgia Press, 1989. Definitive biography of Thomas Brown, a loyalist leader and ranger in Georgia and South Carolina who was involved in early disturbances in the backcountry.

Coleman, Kenneth, gen. ed. *A History of Georgia*. Athens: University of Georgia Press, 1977. Textbook of Georgia history. Parts 1 and 2 (respectively by Phinizy Spalding and by Coleman) are devoted to the colonial and Revolutionary periods. Bibliographic notes.

Corkran, David H. *The Creek Frontier, 1540–1783*. Norman: University of Oklahoma Press, 1967. Treats the relations between the whites and the Creeks from the Indian viewpoint as much as possible. Used primarily as background for the crisis of 1774.

Cress, Lawrence Delbert. *Citizens in Arms: The Army and the Militia in American Society to the War of 1812*. Chapel Hill: University of North Carolina Press, 1982. A study about attitudes toward the military in the Revolutionary era, showing the views of the military in the context of Republican ideology. It does not explore the experience in Georgia.

Dederer, John Morgan. *Making Bricks without Straw: Nathanael Greene's Southern Campaign and Mao Tse-Tung's Mobile War*. Manhattan KS: Sunflower University Press, 1983. Places the contributions of the southern militia into context. Washington and Greene never fully appreciated the valuable role of the militia: namely, to keep Revolutionary spirit alive in the backcountry and to prevent counterrevolution.

_____. *War in America to 1775: Before Yankee Doodle*. New York: New York University Press, 1990. Explores the issue of American attitudes toward a regular, professional standing army. Georgia is not considered substantively.

DeVorsey, Louis, Jr. *The Indian Boundary in the Southern Colonies, 1763–1775*. Chapel Hill: University of North Carolina Press, 1966. Excellent coverage of the problems associated with land cessions and the surveying of the Indian Boundary Line in all of the southern colonies. Very useful maps.

_____. *Dictionary of National Biography*. 1921–1922 ed. S.v. "Wright, Sir James." Standard British biographical reference. Used to obtain data on Sir James Wright, whose place of birth is documented as England.

Duncan, A. McC. *Roll of Officers and Members of the Georgia Hussars and of the Cavalry Companies, of Which the Hussars are a Continuation, with Historical Relating Facts Showing the Origin and Necessity of Rangers or Mounted Men in the Colony of Georgia from Date of Its Founding.* Savannah: Morning News, 1906 (?). Early military history of Georgia; argues that Georgia was a military colony. Of particular interest were the lineal predecessors to the Hussars. It treats the militia, Troop of Horse, and the rangers.

Fuller, Colonel J. F. C. *British Light Infantry in the Eighteenth Century.* London: Hutchinson, 1925. Focus on the British light infantry units. Used primarily for background on the formation of the Royal Americans (Sixtieth Regiment). This study is dated, yet is the only one of its kind.

Ganoe, William Addleman. *The History of the United States Army.* New York: D. Appleton-Century, 1942. Reprint. Ashton MD: Eric Lundberg, 1964. Dated history of the U.S. Army. Used to illustrate the long-term impact of the Uptonian school. It has a negative view of the militia in combat in the Revolution and gives a partisan treatment of regulars.

Gipson, Lawrence Henry. *The Triumphant Empire: Britain Sails into the Storm, 1770–1776.* Vol. 12 of *The British Empire before the American Revolution.* New York: Alfred A. Knopf, 1965. Treats the coming of the American Revolution from the British perspective. It is useful for background for the developing crisis, particularly the tensions in 1774 and 1775. Bibliography is in vol. 14, not in this volume.

Greene, Jack P. *The Quest for Power: The Lower Houses of Assembly in the Southern Royal Colonies, 1689–1776.* Chapel Hill: University of North Carolina Press, 1963. Deals with the lower houses of assembly (elected members) of the southern colonies and their attempts to gain an increasing share of political power from the royal governors. It treats issues individually and is very useful for insight into the political process and problems in Georgia. Bibliographic essay.

Greene, Jerome A. *Historic Resource Study and Historic Structure Report. Ninety-Six: A Historical Narrative.* Denver: National Park Service, 1979. Background of activities in South Carolina relating to Ninety-Six.

Hagan, Kenneth J., and Roberts, William R., eds. *Against All Enemies: Interpretations of American Military History from Colonial Times to the*

Present. New York. Greenwood Press, 1986. Essays of American military history. Disappointing coverage of the colonial and Revolutionary militia.

Higginbotham, Don. *The War of American Independence: Military Attitudes, Policies, and Practice, 1763–1789.* New York: Macmillan, 1971. Best military study of the American Revolution and a good starting point for the militia. Chap. 1, "The Colonial Tradition," provides an overview of the militia, and the others develop military aspects of the Revolution. It conveys a real sense of the British and American military heritage. Bibliographic essay.

Hoffman, Ronald, and Albert, Peter J., eds. *Arms and Independence: The Military Character of the American Revolution.* Charlottesville: University Press of Virginia, 1984. A series of essays. Those by Don Higginbotham and Piers Mackesy discuss the militia's contributions during the American Revolution.

Hoffman, Ronald; Tate, Thad W.; and Albert, Peter J., eds. *An Uncivil War: The Southern Backcountry during the American Revolution.* Charlottesville: University Press of Virginia, 1985. Essays relating to southern backcountry.

Hogg, Ian V., and Batchelor, John H. *Armies of the American Revolution.* Englewood Cliffs NJ: Prentice Hall, 1975. Descriptive picture book of the soldiers and weapons of the American Revolution.

Holley, I. B., Jr. *General John M. Palmer, Citizen Soldiers, and the Army of a Democracy.* Westport CT: Greenwood Press, 1982. Biography of one of the proponents of the citizen-soldier. Palmer helped to turn around the Uptonian school.

Ivers, Larry E. *British Drums on the Southern Frontier: The Military Colonization of Georgia, 1733–1749.* Chapel Hill: University of North Carolina Press, 1974. The definitive work on the military forces of the proprietary period through 1749. It is strong on coverage of the wars against Spain and Oglethorpe and is the best starting point for any military study of Georgia.

Jackson, Harvey H. *Lachlan McIntosh and the Politics of Revolutionary Georgia.* Athens: University of Georgia Press, 1979. Biography of Lachlan McIntosh, one of the prominent military leaders of Georgia. It analyzes the role of political factions.

Jenkins, Charles Francis. *Button Gwinnett, Signer of the Declaration of Independence.* Garden City NY: Doubleday, Page, 1926. Biography of Gwinnett, with his letters. This work is dated, but is the only one available.

Jones, Charles C., Jr. *The History of Georgia.* 2 vols. Boston: Houghton, Mifflin, 1883. Dated but still a useful history of Georgia.

Kemp, Alan. *The British Army in the American Revolution.* London: Almark Publishing, 1973. Uniforms, regiments, colors, and other details of the British Army in the Revolution; useful for light infantry and marines.

Lane, Mills, ed. *Savannah Revisited: A Pictorial History.* Savannah: Beehive Press, 1973. Pictures and maps of early Georgia and Savannah. Used primarily for one quotation with a description of Savannah in 1762 not found elsewhere. A coffee-table book.

Langer, William L., ed. *An Encyclopedia of World History.* 5th ed. Boston:Houghton Mifflin, 1968. Used for description of Guy Fawkes Day.

Leach, Douglas Edward. *Arms for Empire: A Military History of the British Colonies in North America, 1607–1763.* New York. Macmillan, 1973. The best book dealing with colonial militias. Focusing on New England, Leach found that the crisis of the American Revolution was a result in large measure of the colonial wars. Impressions of the colonial wars were the "living seeds of revolution and separation." Used primarily for insights into musters, weapons, and equipment. Excellent bibliography.

_____. *Roots of Conflict: British Armed Forces and Colonial Americans, 1677–1763.* Chapel Hill: University of North Carolina Press, 1986. Examines the effect of British regulars on Anglo- American relations and briefly discusses the Forty-second Regiment and Oglethorpe's invasion of Florida.

Lumpkin, Henry. *From Savannah to Yorktown: The American Revolution in the South.* New York: Paragon House Publishers, 1987. Introduction summarizes early military actions in the South; does not mention the Battle of the Riceboats.

McCain, James Ross. *Georgia as a Proprietary Province.* Boston: Richard D. Badger, 1917. Dated standard. Used for general background for the proprietary era. Few references to military affairs.

McCall, Captain Hugh. *The History of Georgia. Savannah GA, 1811– 1816.* Reprint. Atlanta: A. B. Caldwell, 1909. Dated (and sometimes erroneous) history of early Georgia. Fills in gaps because McCall had access to documents no longer available.

McMaster, Fitzhugh. *Soldiers and Uniforms: South Carolina Military Affairs, 1670–1775.* Tricentennial booklet, no. 10. Columbia: University of South Carolina Press, 1971. Descriptions of the Independent companies and the Royal Americans, including their activities and uniforms.

Mahon, John K. *History of the Militia and the National Guard.* New York: Macmillan, 1983. Comprehensive treatment of the colonial and Revolutionary militia, although little emphasis is given to militia in Georgia.

Maier, Pauline. *From Resistance to Revolution: Colonial Radicals and the Development of American Opposition to Britain, 1765–1776.* New York: Vintage Books, 1972. Member of the Bailyn school, which finds the origins of the American Revolution in ideology. Maier traces the development of the resistance against England from the Stamp Act crisis to 1776, concentrating on the role of the radicals within the perspective of the English revolutionary tradition.

Martin, Harold H. *Georgia: A Bicentennial History.* New York: W. W. Norton, 1977. Basic History of Georgia. Three chapters give a succinct overview of colonial and Revolutionary history. "Suggestions for Further Reading."

Martin, James Kirby. and Lender, Mark Edward. *A Respectable Army: The Military Origins of the Republic, 1763–1789.* Arlington Heights IL: Harlan Davidson, 1982. The Continental Army was the "lifeblood of freedom and republican virtue." One section is "The Provincial Militia Tradition." Historiographic essay.

Millett, Allan Reed, and Maslowski, Peter. *For the Common Defense: A Military History of the United States of America.* New York: Free Press, 1984. General military history of the United States. Used for recent interpretation of the militia. Vitality of the militia was tied to military necessity: the Indian threat. Positive role in the Revolution.

Millis, Walter. *Arms and Men: A Study in American Military History.* New York: Capricorn Books, 1956. Best treatment still of American military policy.

This work was part of the early trend toward the reassessment of the militia as both militarily and politically significant.

Morgan, Edmund S., and Morgan, Helen M. *The Stamp Act Crisis: Prologue to Revolution.* Chapel Hill: University of North Carolina Press, 1953. Remains the standard work on the Stamp Act crisis. In dealing with Georgia, it includes military involvement.

Neumann, George C. *The History of Weapons of the American Revolution.* New York: Bonanza Books, 1967. Description and pictures of firearms, swords, and polearms (halberds, spontoons, and pikes) of the American Revolution.

O'Donnell, James H. *Southern Indians in the American Revolution.* Knoxville: University of Tennessee Press, 1973. Indian affairs before and during the Revolution. Describes British and American efforts to use the Indians as allies.

Palmer, John McAuley. *America in Arms: The Experience of the United States with Military Organization.* New Haven: Yale University Press, 1941. Highlights the place of the citizen-soldier in the American military tradition and in the present and future organization of the U.S. Army. Palmer gives favorable treatment to the militia in the American Revolution and is partisan to the cause of the citizen-soldier.

_____. *Washington, Lincoln, Wilson: Three War Statesmen.* Garden City NY: Doubleday, Doran,1930. See above item. This work includes George Washington's "Sentiments on a Peace Establishment" and bases its evaluation upon it. Palmer emphasizes the school of the citizen-soldier rather than the Uptonian school of the regular. He assesses positively the role of the militia in the American Revolution in that it limited British occupation to the major ports.

Preston, Antony; Lyon, David; and Batchelor, John H. *Navies of the American Revolution.* Englewood, NJ: Prentice-Hall, 1975. Pictures with descriptive commentary on the ships, weapons, sailors, and opposing navies of the Revolution. Used for basic information about British ships. A coffee-table book.

Reese, Trevor Richard. *Colonial Georgia: A Study in British Imperial Policy in the Eighteenth Century.* Athens: University of Georgia Press, 1963. Treats

Georgia as a colony in the mercantilistic empire system of Great Britain. Used for background for the early royal period. Extensive bibliography.

Robinson, W. Stitt. *The Southern Colonial Frontier, 1607–1763*. Albuquerque: University of New Mexico Press, 1979. Focuses on the southern colonial frontier from Maryland to Georgia, finding that the frontier was one of the strongest forces shaping the growth of the southern colonies.

Saye, Albert Berry. *A Constitutional History of Georgia, 1732–1968*. Athens: University of Georgia Press, 1948. Rev. ed., 1970. Legal and constitutional study of the development of the political and legal institutions in Georgia. Used for the discussion of the institutions in the colony and early state, including the militia.

Shea, William L. *The Virginia Militia in the Seventeenth Century*. Baton Rouge: Louisiana State University Press, 1983. Looks at early militia and rangers in Virginia, where they first appeared. Used as basis for comparison with the later organizations in Georgia.

Shy, John. *A People Numerous and Armed: Reflections on the Military Struggle for American Independence*. New York: Oxford University Press, 1976. Series of essays on various aspects of the American Revolution, most from the military perspective. Shy's treatment of the militia as the ultimate sanction of the political authorities is particularly useful.

_____. *Toward Lexington: The Role of the British Army in the Coming of the American Revolution*. Princeton: Princeton University Press, 1965. Primarily a study of the British regular army in America, although it deals with the militia as well. An objective, authoritative study.

Sosin, Jack M. *The Revolutionary Frontier, 1763–1783*. New York: Holt, Rinehart & Winston, 1967. A look at the American backcountry before and during the American Revolution, including the activities of Whigs, Tories, Indians, and regulars. Essay on bibliography.

Spalding, Phinizy. *Oglethorpe in America*. Chicago: University of Chicago Press, 1977. Biography of Oglethorpe in his role in the colony of Georgia. Spalding evaluates his efforts as an administrator and military leader and attempts to come to grips with him as a man.

Stevens, William Bacon. *A History of Georgia.* 2 vols. New York: D. Appleton, 1847; Philadelphia: E. H. Butler, 1859. Dated but useful history of Georgia.

Temple, Sarah B. Gober, and Coleman, Kenneth. *Georgia Journeys: Being an Account of the Lives of Georgia's Original Settlers and Many Other Early Settlers from the Founding of the Colony in 1732 until the Institution of Royal Government in 1754.* Athens: University of Georgia Press, 1961. Used for the background material for the proprietary period, primarily for the first settlers.

Upton, Emory. *The Military Policy of the United States.* Washington: U.S. Government Printing Office, 1904. Upton singled out the short enlistments of the militia as one of the weaknesses in military policy in the Revolution. In his own proposed system, the regulars would be the major element, with the militia as a last resort. Used to show the traditional position in support of regulars. Upton's study ends with the Civil War, in which he was a participant.

Utley, Francis Lee, and Hemperley, Marion R., eds. *Place Names of Georgia: Essays of John H. Goff.* Athens: University of Georgia Press, 1975. Sketches of place-names in Georgia. Used for background on rivers, streams, roads, and other critical features.

Ver Steeg, Clarence L. *Origins of a Southern Mosaic: Studies of Early Carolina and Georgia.* Mercer University Lamar Memorial Lectures, no. 17. Athens: University of Georgia Press, 1975. Chapter 3 provides a concise reassessment of the reasons for the founding of Georgia; stresses the military motives, as the colony was a buffer.

Weigley, Russell F. *History of the United States Army.* New York: Macmillan, 1967. The best institutional study of the U.S. Army. Weigley traces the Regular Army and the militia strands of American tradition (a "dual military tradition") and sees need for both. A positive assessment of the role of the militia.

_____. *Towards an American Army: Military Thought from Washington to Marshall.* New York: Columbia University Press, 1962. Develops the dual military tradition that exists in the American military heritage and examines the key American contributors to the developments of citizen and professional soldiers. Used for Washington, Logan, Wood, and Palmer. Predecessor of above.

_____, ed. *The American Military: Readings in the History of the Military in American Society.* Reading MA: Addison-Wesley, 1969. Anthology of readings from key civilian and military leaders and social scientists. The work attempts to show the place of the military in American society. Used for the excerpts from Washington, Upton, Wood, and Palmer.

Weir, Robert M. *Colonial South Carolina: A History.* Millwood NY: KTO Press, 1983. Used for comparative analysis of the militia.

Western, J. R. *The English Militia in the Eighteenth Century: The Story of a Political Issue, 1660–1802.* London: Routledge & Kegan Paul, 1965. Covers in detail the English militia as an institution in the eighteenth century. Used for background to establish the ties of English traditions to the early American settlers.

White, George. *Statistics of the State of Georgia.* Savannah: W. Thorne Williams, 1849. General statistics and those of each county. Used for the estimates of the militia strengths for 1775–1776.

Williams, T. Harry. *The History of American Wars from 1745 to 1918.* New York: Alfred A. Knopf, 1981. Survey of American military history.

Wood, Peter H. *Black Majority: Negroes in Colonial South Carolina from 1670 through the Stono Rebellion.* New York: W. W. Norton, 1974. Useful insights because the colonies of Georgia and South Carolina shared similar backgrounds. Used for the discussion of the Watch Company in Charles Town. Savannah's company seems to have been tailored after it.

Wright, J. Leitch, Jr. *Florida in the American Revolution.* Gainesville: University Presses of Florida, 1975. Used for background relating to the militia of Florida.

Published Articles

Blassingame, John w. "American Nationalism and Other Loyalties in the Southern Colonies, 1763–1775." *Journal of Southern History* 34 (February 1968): 50-75. Provides a capsule analysis of the hesitancy displayed by Georgia in adopting the Revolutionary course; written with a strong pro-British sentiment.

Cohen, Sheldon S. "The *Philippa* Affair." *Georgia Historical Quarterly* 69 (Fall 1985): 338-54. Describes the capture and effects of the merchantman *Philippa* by the Whig schooner .

Davis, Robert S., Jr. "The Battle of the Riceboats: British Views of Georgia's First Battle of the American Revolution." In *Proceedings and Papers of the Georgia Association of Historians*. Marietta GA: Georgia Association of Historians, 1983. Another account of the Battle of the Riceboats.

_____. "Georgia Provincial Rangers." *Georgia Genealogical Society Quarterly* 18 (Fall 1982): 139-52. Briefly describes the colonial rangers; reprints rosters of the two troops from 1759 to 11764 and from 1766 to 1767.

_____. "The Invisible Soldiers: The Georgia Militia and the Siege of Savannah." *Atlanta Journal* 25 (Winter 1981): 23-66.

Ferguson, Clyde R. "Carolina and Georgia Patriot and Loyalist on Action, 1778–1783." In *The Southern Experience in the American Revolution*, ed. Jeffrey J. Crow and Larry E. Tise. Chapel Hill: University of North Carolina Press, 1978. One of a series of essays relating to the southern colonies in the American Revolution. Ferguson gives a positive assessment of the role of the militia, finding that the militia performed functions of political importance, such as stamping out dissent and maintaining law and order.

Flippin, Percy Scott. "The Royal Government in Georgia, 1752–1776." *Georgia Historical Quarterly* 88-13 (1924–1929). Used for the general background of the royal institutions of colonial government in Georgia, including the militia. The series is still a good institutional study, although it is dated.

Green, E. R. R. "Queensborough Township: Scotch-Irish Emigration and the Expansion of Georgia, 1763–1776." *William and Mary Quarterly* 17 (April 1960): 183-99. Used for the description of the backcountry in general and the settlement of Queensborough in particular.

Hamer, Philip M. "John Stuart's Indian Policy during the Early Months of the American Revolution." *Mississippi Valley Historical Review* 17 (June 1930–March 1931): 351-66. Assesses Stuart's role with the Indians in 1775 and early 1776, finding that Stuart exercised restraint and did not advocate turning the Indians against the settlers.

Harrold, Francis. "Colonial Siblings: Georgia's Relationship with South Carolina during the Pre-Revolutionary Period." *Georgia Historical Quarterly* 73 (Winter 1989): 707-44. Examines the colonial and early revolutionary relationship between Georgia and South Carolina.

Hitz, Alex M. "The Earliest Settlements in Wilkes County." *Georgia Historical Quarterly* 40 (September 1956): 260-80. Insights for the backcountry in general and the Ceded Lands in particular; contains instructions to the land commissioners for the sale of these new lands. A list of the warrants of survey is appended.

Jackson, Harvey H. "The Battle of the Riceboats: Georgia Joins the Revolution." *Georgia Historical Quarterly* 58 (Summer 1974): 229-43. Definitive account of the Battle of the Riceboats.

Owens, Loulie Latimer. "A Nail in Time." *Sandlapper* 9 (January 1976): 16-22. Provides details of the South Carolinian delegation to the backcountry in that province to bolster the Whig cause. Outlines the details of the Ninety-Six expedition against Colonel Fletchall, in which militiamen from Georgia participated.

Ropp, Theodore. "War: From Colonies to Vietnam." In *The Reinterpretation of American History and Culture*, ed. William H. Cartwright and Richard L. Watson, Jr. Washington: National Council of Social Studies, 1973. Excellent essay on sources for American warfare. Used for insight into the quality of the militia organizations of the eighteenth century.

Shy, John W. "A New Look at Colonial Militia." *William and Mary Quarterly* 20 (April 1963): 175-85. Used to shape initial thinking about militia. Shy asked the general question that I thought needed to be answered about the colonial militia of Georgia.

Smith, Gordon. "The Georgia Grenadiers." *Georgia Historical Quarterly* 64 (Winter 1980): 405-15. Traces the history of the Georgia Grenadiers through colonial and Revolutionary Georgia.

Unpublished Articles and Papers

Bowler, R. Arthur. "Logistics and Operations in the American Revolution." Paper delivered to the United States Military Academy Symposium on the

American Revolutionary War, West Point, New York, 1976. See Bowler above, in the section "Books."

Bridges, Edwin C. "The Handbill of July 14, 1774, and the Beginning of the American Revolution in Georgia." Atlanta, 1975. A stimulating paper challenging a long-held belief that the revolutionary fervor in Georgia was strong as early as the first meetings in 1774. Based on a reinterpreted piece of critical evidence, the argument is persuasive.

Flint, Roy K. "The Web of Victory: Revolutionary Warfare in Eighteenth-Century America." Department of History, United States Military Academy, West Point, New York, 1977. Advocates that the dominant military factor leading to the American victory in the Revolution was the militias' control of the countryside.

Higginbotham, Don. "Militia in the War of Independence: A Traditional Institution with Revolutionary Responsibilities." Paper delivered to the United States Military Academy Symposium on the American Revolutionary War, West Point, New York, 1976. Militia made "finest" contributions to the new nation in the Revolution, ensuring maintenance of law and order and creating a hostile environment for the British armies.

Millett, Allan R. "Whatever Became of the Militia in the History of the American Revolution?" Paper delivered to the Society of the Cincinnati, Washington, D.C., 24 October 1986. Militia in the Revolution was "a people's army waging a war of territorial defense and population control."

Smith, Gordon B. "The Georgia Continentals." Savannah, 1976. Traces the history of the Georgia Continentals and related units in the American Revolution.

Theses and Dissertations

Abbot, William W., III. "Georgia under the Royal Governors, 1754–1775." Ph.D. diss., Duke University, 1953. See comments above under book.

Aldridge, Frederick Stokes. "Organization and Administration of the Militia System of Colonial Virginia." Ph.D. diss., American University, 1964. Used for comparative study of militia. Found that militia in Virginia was effective enough in colonial period "to defend the colony against its enemies."

Cohn, Martha C. S. "Thomas Browne: Loyalist." Master's thesis, Louisiana State University, 1972. Biography that treats affair in summer of 1775 in Augusta involving Thomas Brown and the Ninety-Six expedition from the Loyalist perspective.

Cole, David William. "The Organization and Administration of the South Carolina Militia System, 1670–1783." Ph.D. diss., University of South Carolina, 1953. Used for comparative study of militia. Cole found the militia in South Carolina primarily a police force to keep slaves under control.

Cunningham, Carol R. "The Southern Royal Governors and the Coming of the American Revolution, 1763–1776." Ph.D. diss., State University of New York at Buffalo, 1984. Examines the responses of the governors of the southern colonies to the Revolutionary crisis and provides political and military situations in Georgia's sister colonies.

Foote, William Alfred. "The American Independent Companies of the British Armies, 1664–1764." Ph.D. diss., University of California, Los Angeles, 1966. Detailed look at the Independent companies of North America and the associated islands. South Carolina companies (Georgia) in a chapter; "Oglethorpe's Georgia Establishment" is in chap. 14.

Jabbs, Theodore Henry. "The South Carolina Colonial Militia, 1663– 1733." Ph.D. diss., University of North Carolina, 1973. Sees significance of militia as a training base. In the 1720s, the orientation of the militia was to control "resident negroes." Used for comparative purposes.

Jackson, Harvey H., III. "General Lachlan McIntosh, 1727–1806: A Biography." Ph.D. diss., University of Georgia, 1973. Biography of one of the critical military leaders of Georgia. See Jackson book above.

Johnson, James M. " 'Not a Single Soldier in the Province': The Military Establishment of Georgia and the Coming of the American Revolution." Ph.D. diss., Duke University, 1980. The basis for this book.

Lamplugh, George R. "Politics on Periphery: Factions and Parties in Georgia, 1776–1806." Ph.D. diss., Emory University, 1973. A political study of Georgia. Only the first chapter deals with the Revolution.

Spindel, Donna J. "The Stamp Act Riots." Ph.D. diss., Duke University, 1975. Interpretation of Stamp Act crisis and its effects in each colony. For example, the crisis demonstrated the frailty of the police structure and encouraged the use of violence as a legitimate political tool. Spindel considers military forces in Georgia, rangers, and militia.

Wheeler, Earl Milton. "The Role of the North Carolina Militia in the Beginning of the American Revolution." Ph.D. diss., Tulane University, 1969. Illustrates the important role played by militia in the political revolt in North Carolina. Used for comparative study.

Index